Born in Anderson, Indiana, Gary Lee Edward Kreigh graduated with an accounting degree from Ball State University. He also studied at the University of Indianapolis for Computer Technology and the Gonzaga University for Organizational Development.

Gary uses his thirty-five years in the fields of forensic accounting, fraud examination, and internal auditing to write about corporate and social issues, and experiences that affect ordinary people in extraordinary situations. His experience spans the banking, retail, finance, education, and medical industries. He now juggles his time and residence between New Orleans and Gulf Shores, Alabama.

This is Gary's third book. His first, *Why Birds Fall,* is a mystery about corruption in the aviation industry. His second, *Masquerade of Truth* is another Reverend Fountain mystery also set in New Orleans.

Gary L Kreigh

AIA PUBLISHING

Payola
Gary L. Kreigh

Published by AIA Publishing, Australia
ABN: 32736122056
http://www.aiapublishing.com

All characters in this publication are fictitious and any resemblance to real persons, living or dead, is purely coincidental.

ISBN: 978-1-922329-25-7

To Wayne Farrell

Chapter 1

June 1956

"Grandpa, may I come with you?"

I heard my teenage granddaughter's request, but I'd just popped a piece of coffee cake with crumble topping into my mouth. I chewed rapidly, hoping to answer before she did so herself, but some of the crumbles reached the back of my throat before their time, and I couldn't speak.

"Is that a nod?"

I swallowed hard and coughed. "No, I was choking, Donna."

Donna curled into a cushioned chair across from me as I drank my morning coffee and ate my breakfast. There was enough of her cropped hair to freefall in front of her face, covering her pleading brown eyes. She straightened the collar of her white buttoned-down blouse and brushed the leg of her capris as she waited for my answer. I couldn't help but imagine that I was seeing a young, vivacious Audrey Hepburn sitting across from me, waiting for her cue to perform again. She looked up and smiled.

I looked away to prevent melting in my chair.

"Is that a yes?" she asked.

"No," I replied earnestly.

"Why not?"

"For the same reason I won't let you have that dog you asked me about yesterday. You're spending the summer in Ontario with your parents."

She started to object, but I shut down her objection by saying my answer was self-explanatory. Her father, my son, had accepted a short-term academic assignment for the spring semester that had been extended for another twelve months. I had agreed to let Donna stay with me in Indiana so she could finish her schooling in familiar territory, but it was now summer, and I believed strongly she should be with her parents. "They'll miss you," I added.

"But you shouldn't go back to New Orleans alone," she rebutted.

"I'll be staying with my friend Mr. Portier. Miss Genny lives next door. They'll watch me closely."

Donna frowned and sat upright in her chair. "They didn't do a very good job of it the last time."

She was right, but I didn't want to give her the satisfaction of knowing so.

"Getting stabbed was entirely my fault," I said to defend their honor. "I placed myself in undue danger. I don't plan to make the same mistake again."

"How can I be sure?"

"Because I don't plan to find a dead body this time."

Donna didn't look convinced. She sighed and said, "I don't see why you have to go. You say you're going to help at that homeless shelter in one of the wards. That woman should be able to run the shelter on her own."

"She does, but it takes a lot of elbow grease to manage a

homeless community like Labreville. Affirmation and mentoring are all she needs. I'll be back home in a jiffy." I had Miss Cora's letter requesting my assistance on the end table beside me. I picked it up so Donna could see. "If you'd read the letter, you'd see she really does need my help. Besides, you'll be in Canada."

Donna shook her head and said thoughtfully, "I read the letter. It sounded more like a prayer request than an invitation."

I didn't dare leave her interpretation to that. "I did pray," I said.

"And?"

"And God answered my prayer. He said He'd be delighted to help Miss Cora. That's why He's sending *me*."

Donna slumped in her chair, defeated. A cool breeze blew through the screened window of the room. She turned to watch the sheers float by her face.

"Besides, you know me, Donna," I added. "It's wrong for me to sit in my favorite chair, sipping on freshly brewed coffee and praying as if my prayers alone were going to clothe the naked and feed the hungry." I stood, and she looked up. "I hope you'll realize through my example that if you don't like the world in which you live, you can't sit on your derriere and expect the world to change. You have to get up and make a difference."

Her eyes twinkled again. She stood with me, smiling gallantly. "I knew you'd agree with me, Grandpa."

I was sure the dumbfounded look on my face pleased her to no end. "What are you talking about?"

"I'm coming with you. You've inspired me." Donna bolted for the stairs. "No time to waste if we're going to change the world."

I stood alone in the room and debated how my lesson in humanity had taken such a terrible twist. She was a clever one, that granddaughter of mine, learning from the best, apparently.

Her comeback had devoured my reasoning so quickly that I stood fumbling with my thoughts as to how I was going to get out of the situation. I continued to be in such a state of stupor that I didn't hear someone step onto my front stoop. The person had to ring twice before I realized I should answer the door.

"Western Union," the man announced. "Richard Fountain?"

I shook the cobwebs out of my head good enough to answer him.

"Telegram, sir." He handed me the envelope and waited patiently.

I took the message and looked at him blankly for a couple of seconds before realizing he was waiting for a gratuity. I reached into my pocket to extract a couple of coins. He tipped his hat when I dropped them in his hand and was off.

I closed the door and read the message quickly.

Delayed in Atlanta. Make yourself at home. Genny has the dog. Portier.

I set the telegram on the end table with Miss Cora's letter and went into the kitchen to prepare another cup of coffee. I hadn't thought about taking care of good ol' Bentley. I was glad Portier's neighbor, Genny Duval, was available to care for him. She enjoyed caring for his golden Labrador while he was away so that she could watch his television in his absence. She didn't have one of her own, but she was also a nightclub singer whose schedule wasn't always the same as an aging pup's. I thought about what I needed to do to relieve her but decided it was a present waste of time.

"I guess I'll worry about that when I get there," I said to myself out loud while putting cream into my cup.

"Worry about what?" Donna asked, walking quietly behind me in her stocking feet.

"Feeding a dog," I said without thinking.

She bounced to my side. "We're getting a dog?"

I gave her a dirty look. "Are you packed for Ontario?" I asked, ignoring her comment and her brown eyes. "We both leave tomorrow, you know."

~

I sat in my favorite chair the next morning, perusing a magazine, while Donna and I waited for a lift to the bus station. My modest grip of clothes and toiletries paled compared to my granddaughter's.

She primped her hair in a small mirror by the front door. "Do I look like Mary Pickford?" she asked suddenly.

I looked up. "Of the silent screen?"

"Yes, I suppose," she said. "I don't really know who she is."

"She was a silent screen star. No, you look nothing like her."

Donna smiled gleefully. "My friend Carly says I do. She says I look old and worn like Mary Pickford with my hair styled like this."

"Mary Pickford is hardly worn, Donna. She's a very pretty woman. Carly is just jealous of you. You should know that by now. She's constantly berating you. What I don't understand is why you continue to be friends with her."

Donna gave me a side glance before turning back to the mirror. "I could ask the same of you, Grandpa. Your friend, that Mr. Portier, isn't a very nice man to you. He's full of insults and negative comments, yet you call me out on *my* friends. I can't believe you're going down to New Orleans to see him again."

I had to agree with her but countered with, "Mr. Portier's insults bounce from me like water off a duck's back. I hardly take notice."

"As does Carly's off mine," she said pointedly. Almost instantly, she looked at me through the reflection in the mirror and asked, "Do I tire you with my nonsense?"

Her comment surprised and saddened me. "Whatever made you say that?"

"Oh, I don't know," she said as if she didn't know how else to say it. "I mean, well, you being as you are, and me being as I am, and you not being used to being with someone my age and all, well, it has to be very tiring for you. It's probably good I'm going to Ontario for the summer to be with my parents."

"But not for that reason. It's wonderful having you here. You have a joyous zest for life. It keeps me young. Besides, being with you puts me in great practice for dealing with people—like Mr. Portier's neighbor."

"Who's that?"

"Genny Duval. You've heard me talk about her. She's a club singer who has a wild flair for the extravagant. She's a bit outlandish and has a mind of her own. She's independent in a co-dependent sort of way."

Donna laughed. "A bit like me then," she said.

"Yes, a bit like you but more tedious."

"How so?"

"Because she's old enough to know better." I set my magazine on the end table and rose from my chair. "Are you ready?"

She curtsied and smiled. "How do I look?"

I noticed the embroidered pink zinnia on her blouse first. I remembered her mother gave her the blouse at Christmas. Wearing it was a thoughtful way to please her mother. The blouse was tucked neatly into forest-green Jack Winter stirrup stretch pants that were long enough to reach her ankles without covering her red ballet flats.

"Like a million bucks," I said with a smile.

She shook her head as if she didn't believe me. "You're a retired preacher, Grandpa. When have you ever seen a million bucks to know what a million bucks looks like?"

I looked at her lovingly and replied with a soft, sentimental tone, "On the contrary, I see it every day."

A neighbor drove us from Spiceland to the bus station in Knightstown. It was a quiet trip on the motor coach. Donna was engrossed in *Billboard* magazine's articles on Elvis Presley's *Heartbreak Hotel* and theme music from the movie *Picnic.* I had to admit they were more interesting than my articles from the *US News & World Report.* By the time we reached Union Station in Indianapolis, we'd stashed our magazines with our other belongings and entered the Grand Hall with its ornate curved ceiling and large, round stained-glass window looming overhead.

"Do you have your itinerary?" I asked, checking the schedule board in the station. "Your brother will take good care of you on the trip."

"I don't need my brother to take care of me," she said obstinately. "I'm not a child."

"Then tell me what line you'll be taking to reach him."

"*The Tippecanoe.*"

"And from there?"

She smiled onerously. "*The City of New Orleans.*"

"That's why you need your brother along," I said.

"I know where I'm going, Grandpa." She used her fingers to count the stops along the way. "From Lafayette, we'll take the *Wabash Cannonball* through Fort Wayne to Detroit, then the *Canadian-Niagara* to Toronto."

I exhaled a sigh of relief. "Your parents'll pick you up in Brampton, remember."

"I know, I know, Grandpa," she said warily. She climbed onto her tiptoes to kiss me gently on my cheek. "And I also knew all along I wasn't going to be able to go with you to New Orleans. I just wanted you to know I can go wit-to-wit with you." Her expression suddenly turned grave. "I want you to be careful. You're so worried about me traveling to Ontario, but I must say I'm more worried about you."

I promised her I'd behave and be careful.

After she boarded the train for Lafayette, I turned to find the gate for *The City of St. Louis*. Boarding was easy and uneventful.

The swaying ride on the train through the rolling hills and valleys of the west central Indiana countryside didn't last as long as I thought it would. I barely had time to finish the rest of my magazine articles before the train glided to a stop at the Effingham station in Illinois. I departed and looked immediately for signs for *The City of New Orleans*. The station was small and the line was not hard to find. I had plenty of time during my layover. I sat on one of the most uncomfortable station benches I'd ever sat on in my life.

I set my things aside and watched the people as they passed. Men in their smart zoot suits and women in light, airy Jerry Gilden dresses, complete with complementing gloves, purses, hats, and jewelry, reminded me of my wife who'd passed some four years ago. I fondly remembered her hats. Wispy and light, she simply had to have something fashionable over her head. It pleased me to see even young women wearing hats. I hoped their appearance would keep my wife's memory fresh a bit longer.

I noticed, however, that the young women looked quite like my granddaughter. Girls went to extreme lengths, it appeared, to look fashionably the same. They all wanted to be different, but in their quest, the harder they tried, the more they looked the same.

Even the young men looked amazingly similar. Apparently, the summer months called for white crew neck t-shirts with a deck of cigarettes rolled into a stretched-out short sleeve. Rolled cuffs in their denim jeans made fashionable highwaters, exposing white athletic socks and black wing tips.

Of course, when I looked at myself, I appeared as other adult males with our white, short sleeves, dark trousers, and skinny ties. The ties set us apart, I decided. Me? I chose a solid knit one. It wasn't practical as I had a terrible habit of spilling coffee and snacks on it, but it was the closest thing to summer in my closet as I gave up Bermudas long ago—and never in public.

A commercial radio near the ticket counter played contemporary Top 40 tunes. The music was filled with static, however, and often interrupted by the station manager announcing incoming and departing trains. I squirmed often on the hard wood seat and rubbed my ears as a reprieve from the new rock 'n roll sound.

I rose to purchase a *Look* from the newsstand attendant. I returned to my seat and had barely sat down when I heard a familiar voice. It didn't come from inside the train station. It came from the commercial radio near the ticket counter. I strained through the static to listen closely but couldn't determine the singer's voice.

A small boy sat next to me, wearing a blue beret and nibbling on a chipped beef and Velveeta sandwich. He looked at me with wide, curious eyes as I looked down upon him pecking at the bread as if the sandwich had to last for several hours.

"Do you know who sings that song on the radio?" I asked, hoping he was attuned to *Billboard* hits.

The dirty look from his mother, who apparently disapproved of a stranger talking to her young son, caused me to abandon my question. It was then I wished Donna were at my side again.

I was sure her magazine would have the information I wanted about the singer.

"Ah, miss," I said, lifting my index finger to catch the attention of a woman in her early twenties. She wasn't that much older than my granddaughter, I presumed. I hoped she had the same interest in music as Donna.

The woman smiled politely in a patronizing way, as people often do when talking to the elderly. "Do you need help?"

"No, something is bugging me," I said, letting her know that mobility was not one of my issues. "Do you hear that song on the radio?"

She listened closely.

"Can you tell me the singer?"

"No, I'm sorry," she replied thoughtfully but loudly, believing I may be hard of hearing, "but I've heard it often on my trips to Chicago lately. They seem to play it in the stations along the line from New Orleans."

"They?"

"Disc jockeys, of course, from the local radio waves. I don't know the artist, but I believe the song is 'Honey, Be By Me.'"

I thanked her as the song faded into the echoed sounds of passengers scurrying to their trains and porters moving luggage from here to there. I was sure I'd never hear the song again, but it made me wonder just the same. In fact, the song made me wonder all the way to New Orleans.

Chapter 2

I stepped into the New Orleans Union Passenger Terminal and marveled at the building. It was just a few years old. The Conrad Albrizio mural in the waiting hall was a walk past Louisiana's history. It intrigued me each time I entered the station.

The covered platform outside the terminal shielded me from the sun but did little to ward off the blast of heat and humidity from the June air. I felt as if I'd sucked two gallons of water into my lungs in my first five minutes in town. I loosened my tie and removed my sport coat for some relief, but it did little to give me any comfort.

A cab, waiting in queue, pulled in front of me, and I relinquished my bags to the driver and gladly hopped in. I gave him Portier's address on Ursulines Avenue, and he drove through the Central Business District to the French Quarter as if he'd taken driving lessons in a Third World country. We arrived in front of the steps to my friend's home before I realized where we were.

Portier's cottage looked the same as it had when I left it in February—drab and lifeless, painted in an uninviting gray. His neighbor's cottage, on the other hand—the one belonging to singer Genevieve Duval—was a brimming yellow with white shutters and flowerpots full of red geraniums and burgundy coleuses.

My friend had given me a key to his place before I left New Orleans last. I barely had it in the lock before I heard the familiar scratching and whining of my other best friend, Portier's golden Labrador.

"Hey, Bentley, how are you, boy?"

The Lab could hardly contain his excitement when I entered. He didn't jump on me, but I could see in his eyes that he wanted to do so. I scratched his ears and patted his fine golden coat with gusto before his feet scattered underneath to gain traction so he could turn and run into the kitchen. I suspected he ran to the refrigerator, expecting a tasty morsel in the form of a piece of sliced bologna.

"Oh, not right yet, Ben-buddy," I said. "Let me get settled first, then we'll see what we can do for you."

He raced back into the parlor to be with me. His tongue limped out of his mouth to one side as he pranced, appearing to smile at the prospect. Bentley followed me into the guest bedroom close on my heels and watched me unpack my grips, splash water upon my face in the bathroom, and change into a white, button-down, short-sleeved cotton shirt and long, dark trousers. When I was through, I walked into the kitchen and looked down upon the floor to find an empty food bowl and water dish.

"Now what do we have here?" I asked Bentley, who continued to watch my every move. "When was the last time you were fed? Have you not had any water?"

His tail wagged.

"We'll not have any of this," I assured him. I replenished his bowls and asked when he last went out to do his duties.

His tail wagged again, indicating he'd gladly go out once more if I was offering.

We played in Cabrini Playground a while before I decided it would be a good idea to touch base with the young man who cared for Portier's Studebaker at the garage. I knew Portier relied upon Jeffrey for more than just his car. Perhaps Jeffrey knew something about Bentley's arrangements these past few days.

I took Bentley with me to the garage. The walk took twice as long to complete than if I'd walked it myself. Bentley had apparently accumulated more human friends in his short years of life than I had in my forty years of ministry. We stopped to talk with each one as they patted his fine coat and jabbered gibberish that only dogs understood—apparently.

The garage was hot, stuffy, and saturated with an oily stench that used to appeal to me in my younger years. A mix of rock 'n roll and swing tunes resounded from an old Zenith Consoltone set upon a workbench among greasy rags, tools, spark plugs, and carburetor parts. I found Jeffrey hunched over the engine block of a gold 1956 DeSoto Fireflite convertible. Perspiration soaked through the back of his olive overalls. A pack of cigarettes was rolled tightly in the short sleeve of his shirt. He lifted his head from under the hood when he heard us stroll in. One flick of his head replaced strands of freefalling hair back into a jellyroll. He smiled broadly, revealing a youthfulness that I'm sure had melted more than one girl's heart over the years.

He looked quickly at the white Westclox on the wall. "Whoa!" he exclaimed. "It's later than I thought. You should've called, Reverend. I could've picked you up from the station."

I thanked him but said I knew he'd be busy, then added, "Good gracious! What a beauty you've been working on here!"

Jeffrey looked at the DeSoto with pride. "Yeah, wish I could call it mine." He leaned over the fender to tweak a nut into place before standing upright again. "They didn't make many like this one, Rev."

"I'd say not," I replied, looking through the driver's side window to the interior. "They only made about four hundred of these gold-and-white ones."

Jeffrey looked around the hood at me, seemingly impressed by my knowledge of the automobile.

"This model was the pace car at the Indianapolis 500 this year," I explained. "I read all about this model. Tony Hulman, the 500 President, said on the news that it handles superbly."

"It's like driving a cloud," Jeffrey said, returning to work.

I marveled at the white leather and gold cloth bench seats in front and the sleek design of the dash. I stepped back to admire the long, tapered tail fins and the gold-and-white two-toned finish. The chrome sparkled even in the dreariness of the oily garage.

"And I see Portier's Golden Hawk over there," I said. "I always thought his Studebaker was a work of art, but next to this car, I must say my eyes have turned elsewhere."

"Don't let Mr. Charles hear you," Jeffrey said, teasingly. "I have to bite my tongue, talking about other men's cars with him."

"Yes," I said, "it's a bit like talking about their wives. It can get you into trouble."

Jeffrey wiped his hands on a soiled rag and stepped around the front of the car. "Is there something I can do for you? Did you come for something specific?"

"No," I said, looking down at Bentley, who sat patiently by my side panting in the heat. "Just came to say hello and to tell you that I've arrived."

Jeffrey looked down at the dog. "How was he?"

I didn't know what he meant by the question exactly, but I

thought I'd use it to my advantage. "Disappointed."

Jeffrey nodded modestly. "Yeah, no doubt. I went over this morning and fed him, took him over to Cabrini for a romp."

"Thank you, but I thought Genny would be caring for him."

"She is," he said reluctantly.

"But?"

He looked at me and shrugged. "I don't know. She's been . . . she's just . . . well, she's been a little—"

"Preoccupied?"

He grinned. "Yeah, something like that."

I waited for an explanation of what was going on with her, but he didn't elaborate. "Okay, if you don't want to tell me, it's none of my business. That's between her and Portier, except that Bentley shouldn't have to suffer." I looked at the Lab again. His tail wagged as if he knew we were talking about him.

"You won't have to care for him for long. I'll be picking up Mr. Charles this afternoon."

"Then you haven't heard," I said. "Portier isn't returning from Atlanta for another day or so. He telegrammed me before I left Indiana."

A look of alarm spread across Jeffrey's face.

"Something the matter?" I asked.

"He knows I can't pick him up tomorrow. I told him before I left that my boss hired me to drive his wife to Jackson to see her mother for a couple of days. I can't back out now. It's good money."

"Will Portier's Hawk be available while you're gone?"

"Well, sure, but—"

"No buts, just make sure it's ready for me to drive before you leave for Jackson. I'll pick up Portier myself. Does he arrive at the Lakeshore Airport?"

"No, Moisant Field. Are you sure, Reverend? Mr. Charles is

used to me being on time and driving him straight home so he can rest after these trips."

"I'm sure I can drive without raising his blood pressure any higher than it already is."

"That's not what I meant," the young man said. "But thank you. That is, as long as you don't mind."

"Not at all. It'll give Portier and me a head start on our sparring. It's been three months since my last visit. I'm a bit rusty, arguing with him. Tell me something: how have he and Miss Cora gotten along? Before I left, he volunteered to help her with the books for the homeless community at Labreville. Have you heard anything out of him?"

Jeffrey sighed. "No, but you know Mr. Charles. A conversation with him can sometimes be like listening to 'No News, or What Killed the Dog?'"

"Yes," I said, laughing. "The story gets worse the longer he tells it."

"Exactly, but I think all's well," he said. "Miss Cora just needs a shoulder to lean on every so often. That's why she sent the letter requesting you to come. Mr. Charles is good at what he does with the books, and he's good at giving his opinion, but lending an ear isn't one of his strong points. I think you telling Miss Cora that she's doing a good job will go a long way. That's my take on it anyway."

"I appreciate that," I said.

The conversation lulled, and Jeffrey returned to work under the DeSoto's hood. I walked casually around the garage before telling him that I should get back to the cottage so Bentley could rest. I almost reached the open door of the garage when I heard a tune coming from the Consoltone. I couldn't hear it clearly, so I walked closer to the radio to listen better.

Jeffrey watched me out of the corner of his eye. I noticed he twisted the wrench in his hand slower and slower the closer I got to the radio.

I listened intently before asking, "What song is that?"

His head lowered. The twisting of the wrench stopped all together.

"Is it 'Honey, Be By Me'?"

He tried to smile. "Yes, I believe it is. Heard it before?"

"Yes, just today at the train station in Effingham, Illinois."

"Ah, Illinois even," Jeffrey muttered.

I walked away from the radio and took several steps toward him. "I couldn't place the voice when I first heard it. I didn't know who the artist was, and no one at the station could tell me. I don't have to ask anymore, do I?"

"Nope."

"I don't know why I didn't recognize Genny's voice right away. I guess I wasn't expecting to hear her on the radio."

"Not in Illinois anyway," Jeffrey said, avoiding eye contact.

I sensed he wished our conversation would end and that I would go away quietly. I wasn't persuaded so easily, however. "How did she get on the airwaves? Does she have a recording contract?"

Jeffrey shook his head as if he didn't know or didn't want to answer the question.

"I see," I said, trying to hold back judgment. "Most budding musicians would be thrilled with a recording contract, and her fans, including you, would be thrilled to talk about it. Am I to assume this contract is something I wouldn't approve of?"

"Let's just say Genny is fortunate that Mr. Charles doesn't listen to the radio."

I nodded and studied his nervous tics closely. "Do you want to tell me about it?"

He shook his head. "No, it's something Genny should tell

you directly."

"Fair enough," I said. "Besides, you're looking a little pale right now—like, needing a cigarette to calm your nerves pale."

Chapter 3

I dropped Bentley off at Portier's cottage with the promise that I wouldn't be long. He ran straight to a bare spot on the cool hardwood floor, plopped down, and looked at me as if to say, "You can go now."

I walked to the club in the Quarter where Genny sang. Perspiration seeped through my undershirt, and I wondered how my outer cotton shirt remained dry. The afternoon sun penetrated my back, making it the most miserable stroll through the Quarter I could remember.

An elaborate sign with the word *Paradox* hung above the entrance. I hadn't noticed a sign identifying the club where Genny sang before. In fact, I don't think I ever knew the club's name. It was almost as if the name didn't matter before now.

Another sign that stuck out from the entrance on the sidewalk intrigued me even more. It announced the shows and talent of their illustrious evening entertainer—Genevieve Duval. I stopped to read the sign and found it interesting. I remembered when I was in town last, Genny had to curse and scream at the manager for any type of outward recognition on the street. Something other than a good scolding must've changed his mind to have a sign erected in her honor. Did "Honey, Be By Me" have anything to do with it? I also wondered if her song had anything to do with the new *Paradox* sign.

The dimly lit, smoky club had only a few patrons. They occupied tables here and there, and only three people sat at the bar, none of them close enough to carry on a conversation with each other. More noticeable was that no one wore gregarious costume, danced erratically, or behaved poorly. If I hadn't recognized the bartender, Tomas, pulling glasses from a watery solution and setting them on the counter mat to air dry, I would have thought I had entered the wrong club.

Onstage, Genny sang a jovial rendition of Patti Page's "(How Much is) That Doggie in the Window." Very few sang with her. The stifling heat seemed to numb their enthusiasm and evaporate their alcoholic buzz. Genny continued to sing, however, with all the gusto she could muster, burdened by a colorful outfit of sheer clothing, an array of bangles on her wrists, and beads adorning her neck. Her golden hair bounced as if her silver tiara, embellished with costume emeralds, rubies, sapphires, and citrines, couldn't control it.

She winked and fanned her hand at me as I took a seat at a table in a corner. She missed very few things while she sang onstage, I remembered. She pointed at a waitress and gestured for her to take care of me as she barked "ruff ruff" after the appropriate words in the lyrics.

Genny even saw the man in the brown-checkered zoot suit enter and stop just inside Paradox's doorway.

I saw him too. He removed his fedora and sauntered to a table in front of her onstage, looking around as if he couldn't believe he was in such a dump. He caught the attention of several people in the club, not because he shouldn't be there, but because he was the only person in a full suit, tie, and cotton shirt with French cuffs and gold cufflinks that glittered just below the bottom of his sleeve. What's more, not a drop of sweat had formed on his brow or along the temples of his head.

"What'll you have, sweetheart?" a waitress asked me, interrupting my assessment of the man.

"Ginger ale," I replied.

"That's it?"

I nodded. "Lots of ice, please."

"Say, I remember you, don't I? You're Genny's friend, that preacher man from up north."

I nodded once more. "Nice to see you again," I said blandly.

She curled her nose as if seeing me again didn't make any difference to her, then left to put my order in to Tomas.

I returned my attention to Genny. She'd finished her Patti Page song and turned to the band, requesting they change the order of the set. One of the band members gestured as if to ask why.

"Please, just do it," I heard her say faintly through the microphone.

She turned and smiled, singing sweetly and sensuously to Jo Stafford's "You Belong to Me." Her demeanor didn't last long, however. Something was different in the tone of her voice. She was flat, unemotional, and out of rhythm with the band. Her gestures were awkward and stoic, and the applause she received when finished was unenthusiastic. "Thank you, thank you," she said, but I could tell she didn't mean it. Her eyes kept darting to the man in the brown-checkered suit.

"Such a nice crowd we have this hot, steamy afternoon," she said, trying to sound jovial, "but we're here to have a good time, aren't we? Anyone here from out of town? What can I sing for you fine folks this afternoon? Any requests?"

The man in the brown-checkered suit was the only person

to raise his hand.

Genny looked at him nervously.

"'Honey, Be By Me,'" he said sternly.

"Oh, I'm so sorry. I've already sung that song in this set. I sang it earlier. I'm sorry you missed it. May I sing something else for you?"

The man glared at her and shook his head. "'Honey, Be By Me,'" he repeated.

Genny smiled and turned to the band who looked at her with reservation. "I guess we can play it again, can't we, boys? It's not like we don't know it." She laughed to hide her nervousness.

The band hesitated but began the song just as the waitress returned with my ginger ale and set it on the table. "Excuse me," I said, taking advantage of the fact that she recognized me. "Do you happen to know who the gentleman is sitting up by the stage? The one in the brown suit."

She glanced toward him but turned back quickly. "No, and I don't want to know."

"Has he been coming here often?"

She shook her head. "Haven't seen him before until the other day and just now. He's interested in Genny, obviously."

I frowned. "The other day?"

"Yeah, he came in looking for her, but it was her day off. She came in later, though. When I told Genny he was here, asking about her, she picked up her belongings and hightailed out as fast as she came in." The waitress turned her attention to Genny onstage. "God, I hope she's not in trouble." She picked up the coins I set on the table for her and left, leaving me with the same concern.

Before the song ended, the man in the brown-checkered suit stood and placed his hand in front of a waitress to let her know he didn't want anything to drink. He walked to the bar, pulled an envelope from his coat pocket, and handed it to Tomas. The man then tipped his hat and walked cavalierly to the door, exiting the way he came in as if the experience had been a waste of his time.

Genny finished her song and sighed with relief when he left. "Let's take a break, boys," she said. They appeared glad to oblige as she stepped off the stage and walked toward me.

"Genny!" Tomas yelled from the bar, lifting the envelope for her to see.

She shook her head and continued walking my way. Her large frame slumped forward and her focus drifted to the floor.

"Genny!" Tomas yelled louder. He gestured for her to take the envelope anyway, laid it on the countertop, and resumed swishing glasses in the sink.

Genny snatched the envelope from the bar and opened it as she walked to my table. She stopped momentarily after reading the words and gasped slightly before stuffing it in a side pocket of her skirt. She glanced over to see if I was watching.

"What is it?" I asked, pointing to her pocket when she arrived at the table.

Genny sat next to me as if she didn't know to what I referred. "Nothing, just good news, bad news. One of those things."

"About what?"

She tried to smile, but her gregarious makeup did little to hide her concern. "You remember Ronni from your last visit, don't you?"

"No. There was no Ronni as I remember."

"Veronica? Really? Sure, you do, Dickie. She used to sing right before me onstage sometimes."

"If she was there, I don't remember. I only had eyes for you onstage."

She pinched my cheek. "Aw, you sweet talker, you." She

turned to see if a waitress was near, but I felt it was more to avoid my imposing questions.

"Who is she?" I asked. "This Ronni or Veronica woman."

"She's in trouble."

"I sensed that by the way you approached the subject."

"But you're wrong about her," she said.

I tried to let her comment pass, but I couldn't. "I don't even know her. I have no opinion right or wrong of her."

"I know, but I know *you*, Dickie, and let's just say . . ." The waitress stopped by the table and Genny ordered a rum runner. She lowered her voice when she left. "Let's just say you'd have an opinion of her if you knew her."

I shrugged as if I couldn't understand why.

"She's a friend of Moline's." She softened her voice even more.

My eyes widened with alarm. Genny touched my arm to calm me, but I leaned toward her and tapped the table in rapid succession with my index finger. "You mean this Ronni gal is a friend of the psychopath who stabbed me the last time I was in New Orleans, who murdered a homeless man on a city park bench, who helped another woman try to steer a poor down-and-out boy from the streets into stealing narcotics for her, and who is also, not to mention, an out-and-out, bold-faced liar?"

"You have a good memory, Dickie, but look, you have the wrong impression about Ronni."

"I only had to hear three words for that impression, Genevieve—friend of Moline's."

"Yeah, I know. In hindsight, I probably shouldn't have mentioned that." She looked toward the bar for the status of her drink.

I could see by her expression that news of her friend troubled her greatly, and I sat back and sipped my ginger ale, giving her time to explain. She didn't say anything, so I prompted her by asking, "You said there was good news, bad news. Tell me the good news first."

Genny pulled the note Tomas had handed to her out of her pocket and slid it cautiously across the table for me to read.

I unfolded the edges and read a one-line message printed neatly in blue ink:

Ronni Mohr is alive

I looked at Genny skeptically. She returned my look, then blushed and looked away.

"Alive?" I asked. "What does this mean? Was she dead once?"

"We thought so, yes. Apparently, she was just in seclusion."

"From what? I'm assuming the answer means you'll be getting into the bad news portion of this good-news, bad-news story, and forgive me if I didn't shout 'Yippee!' over the good news."

Genny looked toward the stage. "How about later? Will you meet me after my last set this evening? I end early. I'd like someone to walk me home. We can talk then."

Chapter 4

The streetlamps along Bourbon Street cast a golden glow as I walked Genny from Paradox to her cottage. Revelers crowded the sidewalks and darted across the street in front of cars' fenders that inched along the swollen avenue. We bumped through the maze of stumbling and gawking partiers and ignored enticing calls from proprietors to enter their clubs. I dodged colorful beads being thrown haphazardly around us and could barely hear myself think above the loud music, but Genny seemed to be in another world. She ignored the liveliness surrounding her.

"Genny! Genny! Genny!" three men chanted from across the street, recognizing her in her garb of elaborate colors.

She walked on.

"Genny, be by me!" another young man sang with his hands cupped over his heart.

She quickened her steps, stumbling in her heels on the cracked sidewalk.

"Be careful," I said.

"I'm fine. Let's just go," she replied. "Take me home, Dickie."

We passed St. Ann Street and slowed to a reasonable pace

where Bourbon Street turned residential. I looked back and saw the crowds swarming in the street behind us. Ahead of us, void of clubs and eateries, darkness shrouded our way except for the random dots of dimly lit streetlamps lining the sidewalk.

"Did it rain?" she asked quietly.

I looked at the street more closely. "No, it just looks that way. Someone has hosed the sidewalk."

"Ah, I always get confused by that," she said.

I had the feeling she sensed I was going to change the subject to something she didn't want to talk about. "Genny, we do need to talk," I said.

She grabbed my sleeve.

I realized suddenly that her reaction wasn't because she didn't want to talk. A man approached in a dark suit with a fedora covering his eyes, his head bent as if being careful where he stepped. His gait was deliberate and quick, his hands secured within his pants' pockets.

Genny slowed, and I slowed with her, glancing at the alarmed look on her face.

I turned back toward the man. The pronounced clack of his heels on the sidewalk timed perfectly with the sudden pounding within my chest. I put my arm around Genny's waist and pulled her close to me, anticipating the worst from the man who gave no indication he was willing to give us any room on the sidewalk to pass.

To our surprise, however, he did pass. The man in the dark suit passed without incident. In fact, he wasn't the same man in the brown-checkered suit who'd given the note about Ronni Mohr to Tomas in the club. What I could see of this man's facial features wasn't anything at all like the man I'd seen in Paradox. The only similarity was his dark suit.

Genny sighed and took a moment to catch her breath.

I didn't say anything until we reached the corner at Dumaine Street and the Clover Grill on the right. I walked to the door and opened it. "Let's grab a bite to eat," I suggested. "I think we need it."

She hesitated. "I'd rather go on, if you don't mind."

"I do mind. There's an empty table in the corner."

She entered, walked to the table I'd noticed, and sat with her back to the rest of the patrons. I took the opposite chair, which gave me a clear view of the diner's interior and of Bourbon Street on the outside through the windows.

"I'm not very hungry," she said.

"And I'm sure you don't mean that. Indulge me and eat something anyway."

We small-talked over the faint tunes of a Motorola until our plates arrived and our second cups of coffee were filled. Only when I saw the Genny I knew—the one who could down a cheeseburger in three bites—did I believe I could talk to her freely. I didn't have to say anything, though. Genny was the first to speak.

"I've never seen him before," she said as her blond curls dangled around her face. "That's the truth."

"I assume you're talking about the man in the brown-checkered suit who was in the club earlier."

She nodded.

"Is he connected to Ronni?"

"I don't know. If he is, I don't know how."

"But he must," I countered. "He gave you a note saying she was alive."

Genny sighed, then nodded as if she realized it, too, but didn't want to believe it.

"I want to know about this Ronni woman," I said, concerned for her welfare.

"Not much to tell. She's a rather nondescript girl." She looked at me and apparently saw by my expression that I didn't believe her. "Who lives on the edge," she added.

That was more like it. I waited patiently for Genny to continue.

"She and her sister came down from St. Louis about two years ago. They both started out by singing at Paradox."

"Does Ronni's sister still sing there?"

"Oh, no," Genny said. A corner of her lip curled up as if she'd thought of something funny. A lighthearted twinkle appeared. "No, she's definitely not singing at Paradox."

"Why's that?"

"Cindy—that's her sister's name—and our boss, the old candy ass, didn't see eye to eye. She gave him the what-for, if you know what I mean. It was funny how she did it. I'm surprised she got on at the club down the street. Owners talk, and if the talk isn't good, you don't get hired, but Cindy sure did." Genny smiled again. "Oh, yes, she sure did."

"And Ronni?"

Genny picked up her napkin and started to tear it into small pieces. I watched what she was doing but soon realized it was a nervous gesture. She didn't answer at first. I surmised she didn't know how or didn't want to tell me, so I repeated my question.

"I don't know for sure," she finally said.

"Weren't you friends with her and Cindy?"

"Friends, yeah, kinda . . . in a sort of . . . kind of . . . kinda way."

I grinned at her evasiveness. "And in an exact sort of way, were you?"

"Well, who could ever be friends with those two, really?" she said in her defense. "They were quite cliquish as some sisters go, acting like ten-year-old schoolgirls sometimes. Ronni was the better singer. Cindy didn't like that. She made it tough on Ronni. That's why I tended to gravitate toward Ronni more. Ronni, in time, got tired of her sister's dissing and moved on."

"Doing what?"

"Waiting tables, but I don't think she made a living out of it. She didn't work that hard. I don't see how she could've made a decent wage, if you know what I mean. It made me wonder. Then I heard she got caught up finding clients for investors."

"Investors?" I asked, shaking my head. "You mean like . . ."

"Lenders."

"You mean loan sharks, don't you?"

"Well, yeah. I told Ronni to get out of the business."

I stopped to think for a second. "I don't think it works that way. One doesn't just get out of a business like that. It's not like she was selling Tupperware."

"Apparently not. Then call them racketeers, if you to want to call them anything. Call them shysters when they hide behind their fancy lawyers. They were like Chicago gangsters, Dickie, bribing city officials and murdering those who couldn't pay back. I'm serious. They were killing people."

"When did this come out into the open?"

"Shortly after Ronni disappeared."

"So you thought they killed her?"

"Wouldn't you? Who wouldn't? She knew things. She knew things the racketeers didn't want others to know."

"What did Cindy think?"

"She thought Ronni was dead too. Cindy was very upset. She went back to St. Louis for a couple of weeks . . ." Genny's story faded while she reflected. "The police got involved. The FBI did, too. So did the IRS. Heads rolled. You know one of the detectives who investigated the case."

"Are you talking about Guy Robicheaux?"

"Yes, but he's French. He pronounces Guy *Gee* with a hard *g*."

"Good thing I never called him by his first name." I looked down at the table and thought back to the last time I was in the city and dealt with Detective Robicheaux. "Yes, he's a good man. I didn't give him enough credit when I was in town last. He didn't investigate my situation the way I would've."

"I remember. I also remember you almost got killed," she said.

I deserved the snide comment. "Yes, which is why his way would've been better. So Detective Robicheaux was able to get to the bottom of the loan sharks' dealings?"

"Yes, and they all went to prison."

"But Ronni didn't return after the sentencing—when all was safe?"

"No, which is why I thought she was dead. I thought they killed her so she couldn't testify against them." She sipped her coffee, but something else seemed to be on her mind.

"What is it?" I asked.

She shook her head. "Nothing, probably nothing. It's just that when Cindy returned from St. Louis, she came back much happier than when she left."

"Wasn't that why she left—to compose herself?"

"Yes, I suppose so."

I leaned over the table toward her. "You don't believe she finished the grieving process in two weeks and returned to New Orleans, do you?" Genny started to open her mouth as if she wasn't sure how to say what she wanted to say, so I answered for her. "You believe she found Ronni, hiding back in St. Louis."

"I don't know any such thing," she said, sipping her coffee again. "There are many reasons why people go away and return much happier."

"Happy or relieved?" I asked.

Genny set her cup on the saucer so hard her coffee spilled

over the cup's rim. "I don't know how it could be relief. She's dead."

"You don't know that."

"And you don't know what they're like," she replied, looking away.

I paused. "And how do you? May I ask?" I hoped she could hear the compassion I had for her by the tone of my voice. "I want to help, Genny."

She looked at me, but instead of gratitude, sadness reflected from her eyes. "I've told you all that I can tell you, Dickie. There's nothing more to tell. End of story."

"Apparently not . . . or that man in the brown-checkered suit wouldn't have come into the club today and hand you a note letting you know she's alive, now, would he?"

Genny's face paled suddenly. At first I thought an ominous memory haunted her, something she recalled about Ronni that explained the note and the man in the brown suit. The longer I looked at her, however, the more I realized her ashen look wasn't about Ronni or the man at all. She was listening to the old Motorola on the shelf above the grill.

A soft feminine voice resounded sensuously from the radio. Although the volume was low, the voice was unmistakable. The chorus to "Honey, Be By Me" had barely begun when Genny grabbed her purse and stood abruptly by the table.

"I'm ready to go," she said.

Chapter 5

Bentley followed me into the kitchen the next morning and plopped down on the linoleum with a grunt. I must've disrupted his routine because he didn't appear ready to start the day. He didn't care that I'd gotten the skillet from a lower cabinet, pulled out a carton of eggs and a butcher-wrapped package of bacon from the icebox, and filled the air with the aroma of a hearty breakfast. It wasn't until I poured some dry dog food into a bowl and doused it with bacon grease from the pan that he became interested.

"That'll make your coat shiny," I said. "Portier'll clobber me, of course, giving you this grease, but it'll be our little secret."

Bentley ate heartily, lifting his head periodically in what I considered to be a gesture of gratitude.

I also ate well and poured myself another cup of coffee before going to the door to see if the morning *Times-Picayune* had arrived at Portier's doorstep. By the time I returned to the kitchen, Bentley had resumed his recumbent position by my chair, licking the remnants of the grease from his jowls.

I'd no sooner sat down and unfolded the paper across the tabletop to read about the new twenty-four-mile-long

Pontchartrain Causeway when several raps on the cottage door startled me to an upright position.

Bentley looked at me. He didn't bark. He just stared, as if to ask if I was going to answer it.

"You know who it is, don't you?" I asked. "You know every knock on the door and who's behind it. I could use a skill like yours in case the person wasn't worth leaving my paper and coffee for."

I darted for the door anyway and was glad I did. A stunning, large woman in blond curls, dangling bracelets, layered necklaces, and enough rouge to paint Portier's cottage stood grinning from ear to ear at the doorstep.

"Good morning, Dickie-boy. Bright new day, isn't it?" she said, brimming with enthusiasm. "May I come in? I have a wonderful idea!"

"That's more like the Genny I know," I said. "Yes, please do. I daresay I left you in terrible spirits last night. That certainly wasn't my intent."

"Poppycock!" she said, flicking the thought away with her wrist as she entered the parlor. "That was last night. I woke up with a charming idea to change all that. I hope you'll approve."

"Will it matter if I don't?"

"Not in the least," she replied, "but you won't enjoy yourself if you don't."

I sighed. "That means you want me to be a part of your idea. Before my second cup of coffee? Before the morning paper? Before Bentley's been for his walk? You're a cruel human being, Genevieve Duval."

She laughed unabashedly. Her bosoms heaved with every bellow and the jangles around her neck sounded like windchimes against each other. "Men tell me that a lot"—she giggled—"especially when I ignore them, but I'm not ignoring *you*, Dickie-boy. Come, finish your coffee. You can read your paper tomorrow. The news doesn't change that much from day to day. I want to talk."

She walked into the kitchen, grabbed my cup from the table, and brought it into the parlor, setting it carefully on an end table next to Portier's favorite chair. "Mm, was that bacon and eggs I smelled?" She rubbed her vivacious belly with vigor. "Dickie, you'd make someone a wonderful husband, you know. Why aren't you married?"

"She passed away four years ago," I replied.

Genny turned and gave me a sorrowful look. "Oh, that's right. I knew that. I'm so sorry."

"It's all right. I learned everything about good country cooking from her. I fix a good breakfast every morning to be near her."

A genuine smile crossed her face. "I'm hardly a woman like your dear wife, Dickie, but you'll indulge me just the same, won't you?"

"It would be my pleasure to do so. Now what's this idea you have?"

She sat on a nearby settee and clapped her hands jovially, eager to tell all. The black eyeliner and turquoise makeup on her eyelids made her eyeballs protrude much farther than normal. She started to talk but noticed a dusting of white powder on top of her breasts. She dipped her finger into the powder and tasted it then laughed gregariously, fluffing the rest of the confectionery sugar from her dress into the air. "Beignets," she explained. "I love them as much as bacon and eggs. They were lovely this morning."

I tried to grin, but it was weak. "Your idea?"

She clapped again. "I'm going to confront Cindy."

I stared at her without expression.

"You remember me telling you about Cindy. She works at The Marina, a bar just down the street from Paradox. It's a crazy-assed place, Dickie. You won't like it. It's cheap and whimsical, even for my tastes. The drinks are weak and overpriced. Tomas beats them hands down at making cocktails. They make this drink—"

"Genny."

She stopped.

I stared at her again and shook my head. "Why must you meet this Cindy?"

She grimaced. "Well, why not? If Ronni Mohr is alive, Cindy owes me an explanation."

I stared at her blankly—again.

"What?" she asked bluntly after several seconds. "Oh, I see. You don't like my idea."

"First of all, Genny," I said in a tone of voice that I hoped indicated that I was willing to reason with her, "it isn't our place to get to the bottom of whether Ronni is alive or not. Secondly, it sounds as if it could be dangerous to do so. Thirdly, I see no reason for you to get to the bottom of it." I let her ponder my comments before I added, "Unless, of course, you're in trouble thicker than what you're telling me."

Genny took a deep breath but didn't say anything.

"I don't suppose 'Honey, Be By Me' has anything to do with your interest in Ronni or Cindy, does it?"

She looked at me skeptically. "Why do you say that?"

"Because it's a wonderful song. You sing it beautifully. You should be proud of it. Not only that, you should be elated that your voice is on the radio from here to Chicago. Royalty checks will be coming in soon. With another recording deal, you could become a very rich woman, maybe even move to the Upper Garden District. You could hobnob with some very influential musicians in this city and become a national sensation. Portier could be your accountant, and Bentley and I would be your biggest fans."

Genny looked away. There were no stars in her eyes from the prospects I described, only sadness. "It's not all glitter and gold, Dickie," she said solemnly. "I don't understand it completely, and I don't dare ask Chuck about it. He'll hit the roof over what I've done."

"And what did you do?" I asked. "Exactly."

"I signed with an agent who got me this recording contract for the song you hear on the radio."

"But that sounds like a normal course of action."

"Yes, I thought so too. Ronni helped me get it."

"Ronni?" My look of surprise had to have been obvious on my face. "When? While she was in hiding?"

"No, before that. Right before that."

"I don't understand. Why Ronni?"

"Why not, Dickie? Ronni's my friend. She came to me and said she knew this guy who could get me a contract. I said sure. I was elated. So this guy, his name is Kip Harmon, came into the club and heard me sing. He said he had connections with Marrs Records on North Rampart. I was flattered. Kip schmoozed me; Ronni encouraged me. Before I knew it, I was signing paperwork, recording in a studio, and hearing my name on the radio."

"So let me get this straight, Genny," I said, sighing deeply. "Ronni's a singer. She knows you sing. She knows this man in the recording business and gets you a contract through him. If Ronni's a singer and has connections with a recording agent, why doesn't she get her own contract with him?"

Genny peered at me and stuck out her bottom lip as if to pout. "I didn't think about that."

"It begs the question," I said. I must've sounded as if I was judging her because she looked at me timidly.

"All I know is that there must've been something in the fine print of that contract, Dickie. That's why I have to find Ronni now that I know she's alive. She was my friend. She wouldn't do me wrong."

I tried to appear empathetic, but I'm sure my skepticism came through stronger. "I don't know what to say at this point," I replied candidly. "You say it yourself, Genny. All that glitters isn't gold. That goes for friendships too."

"Oh, but I'm in really big trouble. I know I am. This Harmon guy has been harassing me for cash. He says I owe him."

"How much?"

"I don't know."

"For what?"

"I don't know."

I paused. "Do you not know or do you not want to tell me?"

"I don't know, Dickie."

I wanted to ask Genny if she'd read the contract she signed, but I figured I already knew the answer without embarrassing her further. "So tell me this," I said instead. "I assume Kip's real name is Christopher."

She nodded.

"So why not go straight to him instead of finding Ronni or Ronni's sister, Cindy?"

Genny placed her palms to the sides of her face. "Oh, I couldn't do that. I couldn't face him. He scares me, Dickie. He was all nice and friendly before I signed the contract, but he's not like that anymore. I'm sure he sent the man in the brown-checkered suit to intimidate me. That's why I need to talk with Cindy. If Ronni's alive, Cindy can tell me where she is."

I sat back in my chair and started to reach for my coffee

but realized it must now be cold. A bad taste had already taken residence in my mouth from Genny's story without adding lukewarm coffee on top of it.

"I'll tell you what," I said. "I'll help you, but not right now. I came to see Miss Cora and to help her at Labreville, the homeless community. I have an obligation to see her first. Then after that, we'll see about talking with this Cindy woman."

Genny smiled. I could tell she wanted to hug me, which would've only smeared makeup and powdered sugar over me, but she refrained from doing so.

I raised my finger in the air to make a final point. "But I'm not making any promises. I have to say, Genny, that I don't like the idea of talking to Cindy at all. I have many reasons for feeling like this, but for right now, let's just say that it feels like a path to nowhere for you, and there's no guarantee it will get you what you want out of Ronni."

Genny nodded rapidly. "I understand," she said reverently.

I wondered if she really did. I was certain she just said that to appease me.

Chapter 6

When Genny left, I called Miss Cora to see if she'd be at home, and then called Jeffrey at the garage to have Portier's Studebaker rolled around for me to drive to the Ninth Ward.

Jeffrey brought the car promptly and reminded me of his trip to Jackson. He told me a replacement for him was available should I need further transportation. I tipped Jeffrey generously and told him to enjoy his trip. I'd see him when he got back.

I was grateful that the traffic on St. Claude Avenue was light, because I knew roughly where she lived, but I couldn't remember the exact street. I found it by chance, however, and parked along the curb in front of Miss Cora's house. Her smoky blue shotgun looked just as I'd last seen it three months ago.

Miss Cora sat on the porch, swinging lazily in the warm breeze, strands of gray hair wisping about her black face. She hadn't changed. Her hands rested in her lap on top of a white apron that covered her faded plum cotton housedress. She brushed a fingertip across the top of an old gold ring that appeared to be a sentimental memory of someone dear. One thing was different about her this time, however: Miss Cora sang a hymn with endearing spiritual lyrics in a voice that expressed her gratitude for a life richly blessed by divine love.

I waited on the sidewalk while she praised the Lord in song. Time paused while she sang. Upon the final chorus, she sensed my presence and turned her head toward me. Only then did I feel comfortable enough to approach.

"You caught me," she said when I reached the porch. "I misplaced my reading glasses. I can't see a thing without them, so instead of reading from the Bible, I thought I'd sing the verses I've memorized."

"And He enjoyed every minute of it, I'm sure."

"Do you sing, Reverend?"

"Like a wrung goose," I replied.

She smiled and dabbled at her hair. "So what brings you this way? It was a pleasant surprise to receive your call this morning."

"You are why I came to New Orleans in the first place," I said. "You and Labreville."

"Oh, I know, but the tone of your voice had some apprehension to it." She lifted her index finger for patience as she rose from the swing. "Have a seat. I have something to give you before I forget."

I sat on an old wooden chair next to the swing. Miss Cora went into the house and came out with a small handmade cross, fluted on one side. Twine bound the two pieces of primitive basswood together. "This is for you," she said, extending it to me. "Leon whittled it. He wanted you to have it."

"Leon," I said, trying to remember. "Is he the one who stutters?"

"But sings like a lark, he does, yes."

"And a leg that turns in a bit."

"Something for him to remember the war by, he says, but I didn't think men who stuttered could be in the military, so I don't know what to make of that."

"That's an old wives' tale," I said, "or so I've heard. You don't have to speak to fight, and for some it's better that they don't. I do remember Leon. A man who's had a hard life but a keen sense of humor. So he whittled it himself?"

She nodded and smiled, then began to discuss recent events in the Labreville community. Progress was being made, finding work for those who wanted and had the ability to do so. Meals were prepared daily, and transportation was provided to those who went to the free medical clinics sponsored by area churches. Miss Cora talked about individuals in whose well-being she knew I had a continuing interest. It wasn't long before the conversation came back around to Leon and his art of whittling.

"He used to whittle for the patients at the free clinic a long time ago. He'd volunteer every week."

"Doing what? I didn't know Leon had a medical background."

"He doesn't," she said, "but there's a lot of tasks the clinic needs done that volunteers can do. Leon did them willingly for many years."

"But you said a few minutes ago he sings too," I said.

"He does, at least, he did. He sang in many of the clubs years back."

"You did too, didn't you?"

Miss Cora was taken aback by my revelation. "Well, yes, in the church choir."

I'm sure my expression indicated that I knew better. "I venture to say you did more than sing on Sunday, Miss Cora. Your voice is good enough to have sung professionally. Did you sing with Leon?"

"Leon?" she asked as if I'd posed the most ridiculous question she'd ever heard. She chuckled under her breath and gave me a discerning look before leaning back in the swing to drift back to her singing days. "That's right, you're from up north, aren't you?

Otherwise, you wouldn't have asked such a silly question."

"Weren't they good days?" I asked, trying to understand. "Or were they days you'd rather forget?"

"Oh, no, not at all. They were very good days, very hard days, very long days, rich days, meager days, feast or famine days, but overall, very good days. I laughed at you, Reverend, because if you hadn't noticed, Leon's White. He sang in the White clubs."

"And you?"

"I enjoyed wherever I could sing—mostly on North Rampart and other places in Tremé. It wasn't the best atmosphere for a young woman to be in, but I loved the raw emotion of singing with a good band. The drinks flowed, the dancing was exuberant, the laughter was pure joy."

I let Miss Cora reminisce on fond memories a little longer before I asked, "But what went with it?"

She grimaced slightly. "Well, what went with it was frightening. There's a fine line between terrific and terror. It's no wonder the two words sound so closely alike." Miss Cora stared into the distance. "I came out okay, though. I sang on North Rampart with a good band—an R&B band. The club was quite popular with the locals. Tourists didn't know about us so much."

"But if they did, they could come?"

"Oh, yes, everybody was always welcome. You have to remember New Orleans is different from the rest of the country. We're segregated, but music brings us together, especially on the radio. WTPS plays Colored tunes along with the White ones all the time. You don't see that anywhere else very much. Where did you say you're from?"

"Indiana. I live in a small town east of Indianapolis."

Miss Cora smiled broadly. "Ah, Naptown. I remember now," she said, chuckling. "Wes Montgomery, that wonderful jazz guitarist, is from Indianapolis. I adore Wes."

"You know him?"

"Oh, yes, Reverend. I met Wes and his brothers Monk and Buddy. He has an octave range you wouldn't believe, and the way he plucks those guitar strings with his thumb is a sound that makes my heart tick faster every time."

The joy on her face made me smile.

"You know, I used to have my husband drive me to wherever Wes Montgomery was playing in the South," she said. "We drove up to Memphis one night to listen to him play. Got to talkin' to him too. I found out he was afraid of flyin'—Wes, that is—so I asked him where his next gig was. When he told me it was Birmingham, I said, 'Well, what do you know? We're headed straight to Birmingham right now!'"

Miss Cora laughed until tufts of loose hair whisked into the side of her mouth. She continued to chuckle as she scraped the strands from between her lips.

"Oh, my husband was about to have a fit," she added, "but he couldn't say no, and that's exactly what we did. We took Wes from Memphis to Birmingham while his band hopped on a commuter plane no bigger than a grasshopper. He and I talked the whole four hours to Alabama, Reverend. He told me Indiana Avenue in Naptown is a place like heaven. He called it the *Grand Ol' Street* and *The Yellow Brick Road*. I can only imagine what it's like. Is that true?"

"I hear that it is," I said, but added honestly, "I wouldn't know, though, not really. I mean, segregation in Indiana isn't like it is in New Orleans, but still, Indiana Avenue isn't a place where I'd go, sadly."

"Why not?" she asked.

I didn't say anything.

Cora burst into another fit of laughter and nearly fell to one side. "Oh, forgive me, Reverend, I plumb completely forgot."

I laughed with her. "You're thinking that I wouldn't go because I'm White and not welcome. No, it's because the elders of my congregation would boot me out the front door of the sanctuary faster than anybody's business if they saw me walking into a lounge by myself in downtown Indianapolis. But I'd love to hear Wes Montgomery, Miss Cora, I really would."

"Yes, sir, I understand," she said, chuckling some more. "Well, other than preacher men, Whites enjoy Colored music as much as their own here in New Orleans. I did enjoy recording. I recorded with Cosimos Matassa at J&M. His studio was just down the street from where I worked. He asked me to sing one of my originals for him once."

"Oh, I bet that was a thrill."

"Dorothy LaBostrie was in the studio. She gave me a couple of pointers, and Mr. Cosimos signed me on just like that. I was so grateful to him for that. I was grateful to both of them."

"Then I assume that's what you refer to as good days," I said, remembering what she'd said earlier. "What about Leon?"

Miss Cora took a deep breath. "I doubt Leon has as great a memory as I do. Even though he sang in the White clubs, he got caught up in the glitz and fake promises of the business. He wasn't patient for success, and some promoter offered him the moon."

"I assume he took it."

"Took it? Why, Leon Adams slingshotted his way there. Oh, yes, sir, he took it all right and didn't look back until it was too late. He took it for a price too. It ended up costing him everything he had: his savings, his wife, his family, his home, and his self-respect. But it wasn't just Leon. Other singers got taken, too. They gave up their soul to get airtime, to get a favorable review, or to grab a gig that got their name in lights."

"Then it wasn't always about the money," I said, trying to

understand.

"Oh, Reverend, you know as well as I do that greed comes in all forms, but it all leads back to money. Getting a favorable review is enough to be indebted to someone for a long, long time. A few articles in a magazine or a promo on radio or TV by a well-known person is all it takes to get noticed—and that leads to money."

"But that goes for anything in life," I said. "Isn't that called marketing and advertising?"

"Not when you're buying a lie, it isn't."

"What do you mean?"

"It wasn't real. These fancy promoters were paying people to have their songs played, and you know where the money was coming from. It wasn't from the big fancy promoters, that's for sure."

"Is that what happened to Leon?"

Miss Cora nodded. The muscles around her lips tightened. "Yes, sir, Reverend. Leon bought lies. He bought a lot of 'em too, before it was too late. Leon's good, don't get me wrong, but he bought a lot of hype and hope that made him sound even better. Didn't pay off for him." She paused before softening her tone. "Other songs are gonna be in the same boat as Leon's if they're not careful."

I looked at her closely. She gave me a side glance to see if I'd caught what she was talking about. I sighed. "Then you've heard 'Honey, Be By Me,' have you? Do you know Genevieve Duval?"

Miss Cora didn't acknowledge that she did, but she turned to me and requested that I keep a close watch on her. "If what I suspect is true, Miss Genny needs your help more than Labreville does right now. You take all the time you need to help her. I mean it. We're gettin' along just fine at Labreville."

"But I don't know what kind of help she needs, Cora. I hear

what you're saying, but I don't know if Genny's really in trouble or she just made a poor business decision and needs to stick with it."

Cora sat quietly, staring straight ahead, twisting her apron with a finger.

"There's something you know that you're not telling me," I said.

"No, I don't know a thing," she replied, readjusting the apron. "I only know what I hear, and I hear on the news there's been a murder over in Biloxi. Did you hear about it? A young DJ—his last name is Bonner, I believe. He was shot dead in his home."

"I hadn't heard. What do you know?"

"I don't know much, but what the police have pieced together so far was that this Bonner man was about to expose some promoter who paid to have certain songs played on radio programs. This, in turn, would boost the artists' ratings on the record charts."

I frowned. "Why are you telling me this?"

"Because one of the artists they believe was being promoted in this way is from New Orleans. His name is Dale Devoe. I don't remember the name of the song because I've made it a point not to know."

"Why is that?"

"Because Leon knows him, and I no longer want to know who Leon knows. All I want is for Leon to whittle more crosses and to forget the anger in his heart by carving a cross for himself someday."

I sat back in the rickety chair and looked at the row of shanty shotguns along the street. If the answer was as simple as whittling to keep people from menace, we'd have quite a magical world. As it was, even though I couldn't believe there was any connection with Genny to Leon Adams, Dale Devoe, or the DJ who was killed in Biloxi, I couldn't easily dismiss it either.

Miss Cora had wisdom beyond my experience. I stood to go and thanked her for the candid conversation.

"You're a remarkable woman," I said in closing.

She gave me a sorrowful look and picked nervously at her apron strings. "Please don't tell me why I am," she said.

"Why not?"

"Because I know you, Reverend. I know you well enough to know that you follow through on loose ends. I fear I may have mentioned a loose end that'll put you or someone you know in very grave danger."

~

I wasn't far from Labreville. In fact, the community was on the way back to Portier's cottage, just a few blocks lakeside of St. Claude. I drove through the narrow streets pitted with potholes and patched asphalt, lined with pastel shotguns and people sitting on their stoops to catch a rare, swampy breeze.

Several tents were erected on the Labreville grounds, but not as many as there'd been last February when the fog had rolled in, creating a thick, chilling dampness. I spotted Leon's familiar stance as he swapped stories with two other men. He wasn't hard to find. Leon had handsome, rugged features and wore the same olive-khaki pants winter and summer with long-sleeved, button-down shirts that he rolled up past his elbows. He saw me climb out of the Studebaker and took several steps in my direction before he paused to turn back and talk to the men.

"Here he is, gentlemen," Leon announced. "The honorary m-mayor of Labreville."

I forgot that he stuttered and had to think a moment about

what he said. I raised my hand to the men, who laughed and asked me if it was an election year and so the reason for my visit.

"No, no," I called back. "I just came to see one of our fine citizens."

The men chortled and slapped each other on the back or delivered a play-punch to the arm.

"If you've come for Leon's back taxes, Mayor, you can't squeeze blood out of a turnip," they chided. "We've played enough poker with him to know he ain't got nuttin' left for taxes!"

Leon laughed with the men and shook my hand. "So what b-brings you out this way, Reverend?" he said, trying to choose words that would come out.

"Just came by to see how you were doing," I said.

"Fair to m-middlin', Rev."

"I also wanted to thank you for the cross."

He hesitated. "Oh, she gave it to ya, did she? You b-been to see her?"

I sensed by the tone of the question that he wished I hadn't. "I just came from there."

Leon smiled. "She's a m-mighty good woman, that Miss Cora."

"And she says the same about you," I said to see how he'd react.

Leon laughed. "Yeah, well, I'm doin' all right." He turned and limped toward a tent not far away that had a pile of belongings on the ground.

I looked at the items, then looked at Leon. "Do you need anything from town? Can I get you anything?"

Leon shook his head. "Nope, doin' p-purty good, Rev. I get three squares and a couple of laughs out of the b-boys. Don't need much more than that."

I looked at him closer. "Your health good?"

"My health? Yeah, I'd say that's okay too," he said. "My ticker's tickin' anyway."

I stumbled for words, hardly knowing what more to ask. "I'm going to be in town for a couple of weeks, so if you need anything at all, Leon . . ."

"Oh, yeah, yeah, Rev, sure. Thanks a lot. I'll have my secretary give you a b-buzz if I think of anything I need."

I smiled.

Leon leaned closer to me. "You wouldn't happen to have some d-dignity in your back p-pocket there, would you? I mean, the kind you drink until you can see tomorrow?"

I shook my head sadly.

"No, I d-didn't think so. How 'b-bout a smoke, Rev? Have you started smokin' yet? No? Aw, m-man, you're no fun. I might have to find me a new friend if you're not careful." Leon tried to laugh his comments off. "I'm just jokin' with you, Rev. You know that."

"Of course, I do," I said, "but I'd like to help in any other way I can."

"Naw, I'm good, Rev. I actually got a friend who keeps me supplied."

"A friend? Who's that?" I desperately wanted to ask about Dale Devoe, the man Miss Cora talked about.

"Some singin' b-buddy."

I tried to be coy. "Yes," I said. "I think I remember a friend of yours some months ago. You used to sing together. What was his name again?"

Leon hesitated and gave me a sharp look. "I didn't say it was a man. I have girl b-buddies too."

I snapped my fingers. "I just remembered. Dale was his name."

Leon continued to stare at me, looking unconvinced. "Yeah, I still run into him once in a while. What about him?"

"Nothing. That was just the friend I remembered."

Leon grinned, exposing a missing tooth, and shook his head,

speaking perfectly. "No, you don't know him, Rev. You've never met him." He sniffed mucous into the back of his throat and spat it onto the ground. "But Miss Cora knows him. You just came from her place. I don't suppose you heard the name from her, did you? I mean, she don't like him much. She never did."

Perspiration dripped down the side of my face thick as mud.

Leon gave me a quick salute and said, "I thought so. Good day, Mayor. Now, if you'll excuse me, I've got some debt to pay back at poker."

Chapter 7

When I returned from Labreville, Genny met me outside her cottage, ready to speak to Cindy Mohr regarding her sister. She spoke rapidly as she reiterated her belief that Ronni would be able to explain to her what was going on with her contract.

"You don't need this Ronni woman," I said bluntly. "All you need to know should be written in that contract you signed or should be asked of that Kip Harmon fellow, not Ronni Mohr."

"But I don't know where I put the contract, and I don't know where Kip is or how to get a hold of him."

"That should tell you a lot right there. Did he say, 'Don't call me, I'll call you?' Is that what he said? Find your contract, Genny, and you've found your answers regarding what your obligations are besides singing."

"Please, Dickie. I know I've gone about this recording deal the wrong way. I know I should've asked Chuck to review the contract before I signed it, but it is what it is at this point. Right now, at this very moment, all I've got is Cindy who knows where her sister Ronni is. Ronni got me into this jam. Ronni can get me out."

"No," I said firmly. "Let's get something straight. Ronni didn't get you into this mess. You're the one who followed through with Ronni. You're the one who signed a contract. You're the one who sang. From what I understand, Ronni did none of that. All she did was put you in touch with this Harmon guy to make it happen."

"But Ronni will know how to reach Kip. Please, Dickie, now that I know Ronni is alive, there's hope that she can help me negotiate with Kip on what I owe. We have to talk with Cindy first to find her."

I wasn't convinced, but I started walking again. As confused and as angry as I was, I couldn't let Genny down. Besides, Miss Cora had implored me not to. The walk to The Marina didn't take long, and the club was just as I imagined from Genny's description—cheap, dirty, gawdy, and musty. The only thing missing was the whimsy. There was nothing whimsical about the place.

Genny marched up to a hostess and requested a table off to the side. The young woman walked away to clear one off.

"What's that supposed to be?" I asked, pointing to some seats built into a fishing vessel.

"It's supposed to be a yacht," she said. "You're supposed to sit in it and feel as if you're yachting in the Caribbean, but I know for a fact that it's a made-up shrimp boat from Bayou La Batre, Alabama. I wouldn't sit my butt in that dirty old mullet bucket even if Jacques Cousteau sat on my lap and bound me with a net. I'm telling you, Cindy didn't do herself any favors, leaving Paradox for this dump. Oh, and stay clear of the Tiki Tower."

"What's that?"

"Their signature cocktail. They mix cheap Caribbean rum with some hideous liqueurs and hand you a shot of ginger beer as a chaser. Oddest thing you ever drank. They sell a million of them, though. It's what keeps them afloat financially, but you'll spend the night in the john, I swear you will. Nastiest drink in the Quarter."

Our hostess returned and said our table was ready.

"Oh, thank you, dear," Genny replied. She turned to me and, in a voice loud enough for the hostess to hear, said, "This is nice. Isn't this nice, Dickie?"

The hostess set two drink menus on the table and left without saying a word.

"Care for something to drink?" Genny asked.

"I'd rather drink from Bentley's water bowl," I said. "I don't want anything from this place. Please, just find this Cindy Mohr woman, say what you have to say, and let's get out of here."

Genny did as I said. She turned and perused the club in search of Cindy. "There she is." She pointed to a woman dressed as a fuchsia mermaid. She lifted a finger for our hostess's attention, and when she arrived, Genny requested that she call Cindy to our table.

The hostess left, and we watched her do as Genny requested. Cindy looked at us, shook her head, and the hostess returned alone.

"She says she's busy," the woman said.

Genny lifted her bosoms with her hands and stood up. "You tell that stinkin' mermaid to get her scaly ass over here or I'll . . ." She leaned toward the hostess and whispered something in her ear I couldn't hear.

Alarmed, the hostess stepped back, turned, and tried a second time to convince Cindy to join us. Whatever she said, she returned with the fuchsia mermaid in tow.

Cindy emitted a weak smile then turned to the hostess and said, "Tell Marcus I'm taking my break now." She reached behind her back, unsnapped the tail portion of her costume, draped it over a vacant chair, and sat between us.

The lighting wasn't good, but it was enough to see that the young woman looked better from afar. Cheap foundation and rouge did little to hide the hard lines of her face and forehead—presumably from years of smoking, hard liquor, or drugs. She had a natural unpleasantness in her eyes, one of skepticism as if we were here to cheat her.

"This is Reverend Fountain, dear," Genny explained. "He's a friend of Chuck's."

"Charles Portier?" she asked. "You mean, the fraud accountant? What does he want with me?"

"Nothing, dear. Chuck doesn't even know we're here."

"I don't believe you," Cindy said. She turned to me. "What do *you* want?"

"Out of here," I said honestly. "But for the moment, let's just say I'm here as Genny's guest."

Cindy pulled a Chesterfield King pack from a sequin clutch and removed a cigarette, turning to me as if I'd be a gentleman and light it for her.

"I'm sorry, I don't smoke," I said.

"I've never known a man who didn't carry a lighter for such occasions, though," she remarked condescendingly, as if she was used to men lighting her cigarettes.

"You're going to have to light it yourself, sweetheart," Genny remarked.

Cindy reached into her clutch again—this time indignantly—and removed a silver lighter. She lit her cigarette and made sure the first plume of unwelcomed smoke blew my way. "What do you want, dear?" she asked Genny, then before Genny could reply, added, "By the way, I've heard you on the airwaves recently. Who did you have to pay to get that arranged?

I bet that was a pretty penny, huh?"

Genny looked away.

Cindy gave me a side glance, continuing to smile. "Did I say something wrong?" She sat back and enjoyed the silence as she smoked.

As seconds ticked away, I realized we weren't getting very far. "We came to talk about Ronni," I said.

Genny jerked forward as if Cindy's insults suddenly angered her. "Ronni's alive, isn't she?" she asked. "You knew all along your sister was alive. You knew ever since you returned from St. Louis months ago. I need to talk with her, Cindy. She helped me get that recording contract through Kip, but she left. I need to talk to her!"

Smoke blew from Cindy's nostrils as she turned to Genny with an apathetic air. "So why are you talking to *me*?"

Genny glared at her.

"If you must know, Genny, I don't know anything about Ronni," Cindy said. "Where are you hearing this? Do you get your information from Mr. Portier that Ronni is in New Orleans?" When Genny didn't answer, Cindy asked, "Then do you get your information from Detective Robicheaux? It would have to come from one or the other. It sounds like something they would say."

"It doesn't matter what either one of them says. We're not here to talk about what Chuck or Detective Robicheaux have to say. We're here to find out where Ronni is."

Cindy tugged nervously at a seashell earring that dangled daintily from her ear. "I can't tell you."

I was suddenly intrigued. It was the first genuine comment Cindy had made, and I noticed that she didn't say she didn't know; she said she couldn't *tell*.

"Why not?" I asked. "You're troubled by something we don't

understand. Why do you feel you must keep Ronni's location a secret? Certainly, you can tell Genny. There's no harm in that. From what I understand, the danger for your sister is over."

Cindy turned to me abruptly. "No!" she blurted out, then glanced around the bar as if fearful she'd been overheard. "That's what you don't understand. The danger is not over. The danger is still with Ronni. That's where you're wrong."

"How can that be?" Genny asked. "The lenders and government officials Ronni was involved with have either been killed or sent to prison. It's safe for Ronni to come out of hiding."

Cindy laughed. "Did you hear what you just said to me? You implicated Ronni by saying she was involved with the lenders and officials. You have beads for brains, Genny. You told me what you believe, now I'll tell you what I believe. I don't believe you want to see her. I believe you're here on Detective Robicheaux's behalf. He's the one who wants her back."

"Why would the detective be interested in Ronni at this point? The investigation he was working on is over."

"Don't give me that. It's not over for him. His interest can mean only one thing."

"And what's that?"

"To have her arrested for her part in the racket."

"As an accessory?" I asked.

"If that's what the charges will be, yes. They'll claim Ronni helped those criminals commit the crimes, and they'll go after her. That's why I cannot and will not tell you anything you want to know about her."

I stared at Cindy, who continued to smoke with agitation. I hadn't thought of Ronni's past situation in those terms. I had only thought of Ronni's involvement in what Genny was going through. If what Cindy said was true, Genny was going to be hard-pressed to obtain any more information out of her about her sister. Cindy was probably not only concerned about Ronni's past illegal activities but also any possible implications Robicheaux may deduce from her involvement with Kip Harmon.

"It's what they do, isn't it?" Cindy added.

"Who?" Genny asked.

"Mr. Portier and Detective Robicheaux. They're fraud accountants and investigators. If a crime has been committed, they find out why. Their jobs are to look for people who do bad things. They think she's involved. That's why they want her. She's a criminal to them. Weren't they the ones who told you she was alive?" Cindy asked. "And please don't lie to me this time."

"I didn't lie," Genny said in a pleading tone. "It wasn't them. It was some man. I've never seen him before. He came into the club and handed Tomas a note at the bar. It said that Ronni is alive."

Cindy snuffed out her Chesterfield King in an ashtray and sat back in her chair to think. I noticed fear and alarm in her eyes. After a few moments, she shook her head and said, "I can't help you, Genny. I'm sorry your recording contract isn't going as you planned. It's a shame, but finding Ronni to help you with it is out of the question. You'll have to leave now."

Genny and I looked at each other with surprise.

Cindy stood and grabbed her costume tail to snap it into place behind her. Before leaving, she leaned over the table, alternating defiant glances between Genny and me. "My sister is not alive," she said softly but firmly. "Do you hear me? Consider her dead. Leave her alone."

Chapter 8

Genny and I stepped from The Marina into the sunlight and reeled with confusion.

"I don't understand," Genny said, taking my arm to steady her steps. "That whole conversation threw me for a loop."

"I'm sorry if it wasn't what you wanted to hear," I said.

"It's not just that. It's as if Cindy has written Ronni off. Didn't it sound like that to you?"

"No, it sounded as though she was protecting her."

"From what? It's *me*, Dickie. Not Chuck or Detective Robicheaux. I can see Cindy keeping a secret, but . . ." Genny shook her head. "No, it doesn't make sense."

"How so?" I asked, trying to understand.

"Cindy and Ronni were sisters as close as spoons. One would think she'd want to protect Ronni, but like I told you last night at the Clover Grill, Cindy treated Ronni terribly. I don't understand the strange turnaround. We need to go back, Dickie."

"Back where? To The Marina?"

I barely had time to call Genny's name before she turned and rushed toward the lounge. I tried to catch her as best as I could but was only able to do so when I reached the entrance of the bar. The hostess met us again, and Genny asked to speak to Cindy. It was urgent, she said, and wouldn't take long.

The young woman appeared empathetic but had a look of alarm and agitation. She regarded Genny warily, then called to someone to have Marcus come to the front.

The manager soon emerged from the kitchen, waving his finger excitedly. "You two! Get out of here. Now! Get out!"

We stood frozen in place.

"I just need to say one more thing to Cindy, sir," Genny said. "It won't take long."

"It will take less time than you think," Marcus replied. "When you left a few minutes ago, she marched into my office and gave me her resignation, effective immediately. No explanation. All she said was that she had to go. She didn't even finish her shift. I have no one to sing onstage now because of you two."

I was stunned, and Genny placed her hand to the side of her face in shock and disbelief. "Oh my," she said. "We had no idea. I'm so sorry to hear that, sir."

"Sorry? No, you're not sorry. You're trouble, that's what you are. I know you from Paradox. You knew Cindy's sister. Her sister disappeared after mixing up with you, and now Cindy is gone. What is it with you that makes people who talk to you want to disappear? I want you out of here."

Marcus turned and stormed back to the kitchen.

The hostess looked at us, hoping we'd go quietly.

"That can't be true, what the manager said," Genny said to her. "He's lying to cover for her. I bet I'll find her in the back."

"Ma'am, it's not a good idea to go there," the hostess said.

"Why not? Will I find her there? Did he think he could trick me?"

"He was not tricking you. It's no trick that there's no one onstage to sing. Do you see her? You better leave. If Marcus sees that you're still here, he'll make sure you receive the same fate as Cindy and her sister. You'll disappear."

Genny looked at me with sad eyes. "What am I going to do? I need to talk with her. What can I do?"

We stood momentarily in the entrance before the hostess took a step closer and said, "Look, there's no love lost between Cindy and me. I lent her three dollars, thinking she'd pay me back one day, but she hasn't. I could use the money, but I know now I'll never see it. I'll tell you what I'll do for you. Give me a second, and I'll get an address we have on record from a book in the back. You can't stand here, though. Move out of the entrance behind the wall so that Marcus can't see you, okay? I'll be right back."

We did as the hostess requested and moved a few feet from the entrance into the sun along Bourbon Street. Sweat saturated my neck under my collar while we waited. Genny and I didn't talk. There was nothing to say. The hostess returned shortly with a square piece of scrap paper in her hand. She placed it in Genny's palm and closed her fingers around the paper so it couldn't be seen. She turned to go.

"Wait," I said before the hostess got away. I pulled my money clip from my pants pocket and released three crisp one-dollar bills from the clasp. "Please, take it."

She took the money and looked at it as if it meant she could now pay her rent or something equally important. Finally, she nodded and went back inside The Marina.

~

"I have no idea where this address is," Genny said, ready to throw the piece of scrap paper the hostess gave us into a trash bin.

"Give me that," I said. "Good gracious, Genny, you made such a fuss about finding where Ronni ran off to, and now you're willing to throw away the only clue you have."

"It's outside the Quarter," she said as if it wasn't worth the effort.

"There's life outside the Quarter, you know."

"Is there?" she asked demurely. "I wouldn't know. I only know of Mobile where I'm from. I should think about going back to Alabama. I have an aunt who'd pamper me with all the Southern Comforts I could stomach. It's very tempting."

"My impression is that your situation won't go away that simply. And you haven't handed the address to me yet either."

Genny flicked the piece of paper toward me and wiped sweat from her brow. "I've never heard of a street name like that."

"Do you have an idea?"

"Mid-City would be my guess, but I don't have the strength to find it right now. Dickie, it's awfully hot. A woman of my status shouldn't be seen perspiring. People may get the idea I have to work for a living. Can we go later, when it's cooler?"

"Cooler?" I asked. "You mean October? This is summertime in New Orleans, Genny. It's not going to get cooler. I'll tell you what we'll do, however. We'll go back to the cottages and freshen up. I need to tend to Bentley anyway. He's probably bursting at the seams by now."

Genny groaned at hearing Bentley's name. "Oh, I'm so sorry about not taking good care of the pup while Chuck was gone, Richard. I really am. You have to believe me. I love that dog, I really do."

"I know, Genny. Portier doesn't have to know. Bentley is happy, healthy, and will have a shiny fur coat when we pick Portier up from the airport."

Jeffrey was in Jackson which meant a different attendant was at the garage when I called for Portier's Studebaker to be delivered to the front of the cottage. This young fellow, although personable, didn't have the same attention to detail as Jeffrey. The chrome on the Golden Hawk wasn't nearly as shiny. The whitewalls were scuffed, and the rearview mirror was greasy on the edges where he'd adjusted it to his liking. The young man didn't even seem to keep himself as smart and well-groomed as Jeffrey. His red hair curled in tangles and frayed at the ends. The overalls over his lean frame were faded and worn, and his black leather boots contained one white and one brown bootlace woven through the eyelets. He was personable, however, and he did know the location of the street on the piece of scrap paper that the hostess at The Marina had given to us. That alone was worth the generous tip I gave him.

The address was indeed in Mid-City. Although not a wealthy neighborhood, the homes were tidy with bushes trimmed as much as could be expected in the summer. That description applied to every home along the street except for the tan stucco bungalow that matched the address written on the paper.

Neglect was apparent from the cracks in the stucco, the faded brown fascia boards, and the overgrown shrubs hiding the home's facade. Like most homes in Mid-City, the house was raised to allow floodwaters to spare the main living area. A small portico came out from the left-front side of the house with steps that led to a short sidewalk to the street.

Genny opened the car door to exit, but I called her back.

"Let's wait a sec," I said, pointing to a woman in a frumpy floral frock watering plants on her stoop next door. Just as I'd hoped, the woman soon finished watering the plants and went inside her home, taking the watering can with her.

Genny led the way from the car up the steps and onto the porch. She knocked on the door but no one answered. She continued to knock as I moved to the front window, but tightly drawn drapes that appeared to have been hung sometime in the thirties blocked my view inside.

"Does anyone live here, y'think?" Genny asked, turning away from the door.

I looked inside the letterbox. It was empty except for advertisements that had been placed on hooks attached under the box.

"The ads are fairly recent," I said, "maybe even from today. Someone must live here."

"They're not home."

I agreed. "Let's come back later."

We made our way down the steps and were almost to the street when we heard the woman in the frumpy frock come out of her house. I looked and saw her picking dead foliage from one of the pots.

"Thinking about renting?" the woman called.

"Why? Is the place for lease?" I asked.

"I hope so. Lord knows it could use some attention. It's starting to become a blight on the neighborhood."

"Do you know who lives here?"

"No, I've never seen anyone," she said. "I've only seen the girl that comes by to pick up the mail."

"Girl?"

"Well, a woman probably. She might as well be a girl, as young as she looks in those skimpy little halter tops and cut-off shorts she wears."

"Is her name Cindy, by any chance?"

"Oh, honey, I wouldn't know her name. I only talk to her long enough to give her my opinion, but you can ask her yourself. She comes by the same time every day."

"I see there's advertisements in the mailbox but no mail. Has the mail been delivered today?"

"Oh, yes. It came a little while ago."

"Then the girl who normally stops by to get the mail hasn't been here yet."

"What? No, she was just here. I don't know why she didn't take the ads. You probably missed her by forty minutes. If you want to talk with her, I suggest you swing by tomorrow about an hour earlier than you did today."

We thanked the woman and returned to our car.

"What next?" Genny asked, rolling down the Hawk's window so a breeze could blow through. "I was hoping to catch Cindy again."

"We have to pick up Portier. Let's go to the airport and get a bite to eat before meeting him. Are you hungry?"

Genny licked her lips and patted her belly. "Honey, I lost thirty pounds walking up those steps. If I don't get something to eat fast, I'm liable to blow away." She laughed, and I couldn't help but laugh with her.

"We can't have that," I said. "You'll need all the strength you can muster when we return tomorrow."

"Oh, honey, I wouldn't miss that for anything in the world."

Chapter 9

We arrived at Moisant Field in time to grab a bite to eat. The unaesthetic terminal was shaped like a hangar—big, bulky, gray, and out of date. Its floor was badly scuffed and the lighting dull.

Genny, however, walked through the building as if it were a fashion runway. She led me to a diner inside the terminal. Spilled drinks and dropped food had crusted onto the Formica tables, left for the next customers to clean. The gray plastic coverings on the chairs were shredded in the middle, exposing worn foam discolored by constant use.

The hostess, dressed as a drive-in bellhop, pointed to a table near the wall for us to sit.

"Yes, that'll be fine," I said. "Anywhere is fine."

"*Au contraire, mon frére.* You'll not sit me against a wall to blend in with the tiles like a cheap statuette," Genny scoffed and turned to the hostess. "By the corridor, if you please. I like to people-watch."

"Oh, baloney," I said. "The corridor has nothing to do with *your* watching. It has everything to do with your being watched."

She laughed as the hostess led the way. Genny chose a chair

with the greatest vantage and pointed to a chair for me—one that didn't block the view of her.

"Ah, this is better, isn't it, Dickie? Yes, much better, even though you have me wrong." She pointed to the gates across the corridor. "This seat isn't about me being seen. There's where the Atlanta flight will come in. I'll be the first to see ol' Chuck when he arrives."

I shook my head as I took a menu. "You're reading the signs wrong, Genny. The Atlanta gate is over your shoulder. You're facing the St. Louis gate."

"St. Louis? Are you sure? Well, if that don't beat all. Why are they marked to confuse me? Believe it or not, Dickie, I chose the corridor for *your* benefit. I didn't want you to be claustrophobic, sitting by the wall, unable to breathe." She grinned broadly. "I know how you older men are without your nitroglycerine pills."

"I can sit by a wall just fine without chest pain," I said. "Your singing charades, however, are a different matter."

"Oh, I should've known the drive to the airport was too quiet with you. You couldn't wait to get that out of your mouth, could you?" Genny turned to the hostess. "I don't need a menu, darling. Just a shrimp po' boy and a bottle of Ski. Yes, dressed, please."

I returned my menu to the young woman. "I'll have the same but with extra pickles, fries, and lots of ketchup."

Genny turned up her nose. "Pickles?"

"Don't change the subject," I said as our waitress turned and went away. "We were talking about your singing contract."

She frowned, then situated her dress so that it didn't bunch so badly in front. As she did so, one of her bangles got caught on a frayed thread attached to her pocket. Genny worked on the tangle to no avail. "Go ahead, Dickie, I'm listening."

I seriously doubted she was, but I continued anyway. "Do

you have a copy of the recording contract you signed? I assume whoever you signed with gave you a copy."

"You've asked me that before."

"I may have, but I didn't get a sufficient answer."

She continued to work on her bangle.

"Did you hear me?"

"Yes," she replied impatiently. "It's in a desk drawer somewhere. What in the world do you want it for?"

"To read it because I assume you haven't."

"Oh, this damn dress. Now my other arm's stuck on a button."

"Exactly. That's what I thought. You haven't been paying attention. I doubt that you gave the contract to Portier to read either, did you?"

She looked up. "Chuck has nothing to do with my contract."

"Perhaps not, but he would've been a good person for advice before you signed it."

She sat back in her chair. "Oh for crying out loud, look at me. I have so many threads attached to my bangles now, I look like a bloated marionette."

Equally exasperated, I stared at her.

"What were you saying?" she asked after composing herself.

"Why didn't you have Portier look at your recording contract before you signed it?"

"Because he wouldn't have understood how much the deal meant to me. He'd have nitpicked the contract apart so bad I'd be stuck with nothing."

"Nothing would've been far better than the unknown position you're in right now, Genny."

"Oh," she said meekly, going back to untangling her frayed threads. "I have a mess, don't I?"

"Yes, but I don't know in what way exactly. That's why I need to see the contract."

"It's at home in a desk drawer in the front room. I thought I told you that. I'll try to find it when we get home, but you have to promise me you'll not show it to Chuck. I mean it, Dickie. He doesn't know about the contract. Lucky for me, he doesn't listen to the radio. He started using the TV for the news instead of the radio except for listening to WWL once in a while. Fortunately, they only play Dixieland, I think, so I've been pretty safe."

I couldn't help but present a sad expression of empathy for her situation. "It's better to be in the doghouse with Portier than to cower onstage in front of a man handing secret notes to Tomas."

Our waitress came and placed our po' boys in front of us.

"I don't think I'm hungry anymore," Genny said.

I reached my hand across the table to comfort her before realizing her arms were constricted by bangles and threads. Our attention was interrupted, however, by the sound of falling luggage outside the St. Louis gate. We turned toward the commotion. The accidental collision of two women had caused one of the women's belongings to crash to the floor, creating confusion and distraction to those scurrying in the corridor. The woman who was inconvenienced said little, but the scowl on her face told the story of her displeasure. The woman at fault expressed apologies and tried to scurry away as if late for a connecting flight.

Genny saw the escaping woman and gasped. "Oh, my!"

"What's the matter?"

"It's Ronni!" she cried. "That woman is Ronni Mohr!"

I didn't have time to grasp the situation clearly. Of all the ways I envisioned Genny and I intercepting the mysterious Veronica Mohr, I didn't fathom it would be in the airport from a freak collision in front of our eyes.

Genny struggled to get out of her seat and to free her arms

from her dress. Out of desperation and frustration, she yanked both arms into the air, ripping her dress but freeing the bracelets from their entanglement.

"Wait, Genny!" I yelled.

I rose to catch our hostess's attention, but since she wasn't anywhere in sight, I gathered enough money from my pocket to pay for our meals and left it on the table. After knocking my chair aside, I chased after the two women, inhaling several deep breaths in my effort to keep up. We needed an additional mishap on the woman's part to close the gap between us, but the woman seemed to maneuver easily through the crowd toward ground transportation. I watched helplessly as Genny scrambled to reach her, but the woman slipped through an open doorway to the outside.

"Ronni!" I heard Genny yell up ahead, but the woman didn't stop.

When I reached the doorway, I could see the woman walking briskly to a row of taxis in a queue. Genny wasn't far behind, but not close enough. A driver met the woman to take her luggage and escort her to the cab. She appeared to give him some urgent destination instructions before climbing into the back seat.

"No!" Genny shouted. "Ronni! Wait!"

To Genny's good fortune, the driver opened his car door and stopped to talk to the driver of the cab behind him. That gave both of us the chance to reach the woman, who sat in the back seat of the cab. The driver saw us and raised his hand to let us know he wasn't available for hire.

"I don't want to go anywhere," Genny said. "This will only take a second."

She approached the cab window and gestured for the woman to roll it down. The woman did so just as I ran to Genny's side, gasping for air and holding onto a stitch in my side. The woman waited for Genny to say something, but Genny just stood there with her mouth open. She didn't say a word.

"Yes, may I help you?" the woman prompted impatiently.

Genny took a step back, a look of surprise on her face.

"I have to leave. What do you want?"

Genny couldn't speak.

I placed my hand on Genny's back, hoping to ground her enough to speak to the woman, but there seemed to be no words to express what was going through Genny's mind.

The woman turned to the driver and requested him to go as she rolled the window shut. The driver did as he was told and pulled away from the curb, blending in with departing traffic.

I led Genny away from the taxi stand and back into the terminal where we sat in metal seats attached to other seats in a long row.

She shook her head in despair. "Oh, Dickie, you must think me a fool. I was so sure that was Ronni."

"An easy mistake. They say everyone has a look-alike in this world."

"But she was more than a look-alike. It was how she carried herself. I was so sure it was her. I didn't even think; I just got up and ran toward her. I don't know how I could've been mistaken, but that was the biggest mistake I've ever made."

I patted her arm and said, "It's because she was on our minds today when we went to Mid-City. She's still on our minds because we have to go back tomorrow. We're so eager to talk with Ronni that you reacted before rationality could set in. Don't give it another thought. We'll find her. Our lead tomorrow will be the break we need. I'm sure of it."

Genny looked at me with pleading eyes now smudged from the wear and tear of the day. "Really?" she asked.

"I'm positive. Now let's go back and have that bottle of Ski we ordered. Shall we?"

She smiled but shook her head. "No, I think I'm in the mood for something stronger. Will you join me?"

"Not on an empty stomach."

"I have some Lifesavers in my purse." She began digging into side pockets.

"I'm pretty sure Lifesavers aren't going to cut it, Gen. Let's get you a drink and me a bite to eat. We'll feel better about this incident in no time."

Genny and I did just that, and before she'd finished her cocktail, she was giggling again. The light in her eyes radiated from her uplifted spirit. We didn't talk of Ronni Mohr or anything related to her song. I was careful not to do so; I wanted Genny's spirits to remain high. Besides, I concentrated solely on the plate of red beans and rice that I'd ordered to replace the shrimp po' boy I'd left behind earlier.

I ate heartily, but Genny looked at me oddly. "Don't you like cornbread?" she asked.

I looked down at the bread plate to the side. I'd buttered the top but left it untouched.

"Yes, very much. Why? Did I make a face?"

"You crinkled your pious nose a bit, yes," she replied.

"Do you want it? You're welcome to have it, if you like."

"I don't eat other people's cornbread. It's a valuable commodity. It's wonderful with red beans."

I looked at the plate again. "I do love cornbread, just not Southern style. I prefer Midwestern recipes."

"Ah, then you must like it sweet," she said. "Here, give it to me."

She extended her hand, and I passed the plate to her. Genny took it and leaned forward to give the cornbread's crusty top a gentle kiss. "There now," she said, handing it back to me. "Let me know if that's too sweet."

I looked at what she'd done. "What shade of lipstick is that?" I asked as it started to bleed into the melted butter.

She laughed heartily. "Blazing cherries. Don't you love it? It's my new signature look onstage." She winked at me. "It makes people wonder."

I had no idea what Genny meant by that comment, but I knew enough of her not to ask. I was simply pleased that the personality of the Genny I knew was back with me.

She started to ask a question, but I could tell by her hesitation that it was a question that had the potential to cause a great deal of consternation. I lifted my finger for her to stop. "Not if it'll upset you," I said.

"I'm sure it won't . . . especially if you lie."

I shook my finger back and forth. "That won't happen. Far be it for a minister to suggest this, but let's get you another drink before you go down a rabbit track you don't want to go down."

"All I want is for you to tell me something I want to hear, whether it's the truth or not."

I set my fork on the cornbread plate and looked at her with compassion. "I know you do, and I don't know much about what's been going on with you recently, but I have a strong suspicion you're in the mess you're in because that's exactly what you've done. You've only heard what you've wanted to hear. So here you are, receiving menacing notes from a man you don't know, chasing a missing woman through an airport who wasn't her, having a past acquaintance tell you to leave her dead sister alone, and anticipating Portier's return as if he was your father about to ground you for six months."

She sighed deeply. "That was what I was about to ask," she said. "Chuck will be angry with me, won't he?"

"No," I said honestly.

She looked surprised.

"As far as I know from what you and Jeffrey have told me, Portier knows even less about what's going on than I do. He has no reason to be angry with you. I'm fairly certain his only thought is to get home, pour himself a drink, sit in his easy chair, and scratch Bentley behind the ears until the poor dog's skin is raw."

She smiled gently and said, "Speaking of which, he should be arriving soon, shouldn't he?"

I wiped a napkin across my mouth and rose. "Yes, in fact, I see some activity at the Atlanta gate. Stay here, and I'll greet him. He may want something to eat or drink before we head back to the city."

I greeted my friend as soon as he entered the terminal. He carried a light overnight case and a scowl that indicated his flight hadn't been a pleasant one.

"Damn turbulence," he said—the first thing out of his mouth. "And a man sitting next to me who chattered nonstop about how it affected his gout. When have I ever given a rat's ass about someone's gout, Fountain?"

"Welcome home," I responded. "We're at the café across the corridor. Perhaps you'd like a refresher before we head to the Quarter."

I followed his gaze to where Genny sat with her back to us. Her golden curls glistened over her outfit of orange, red, sky blue, and pink. She was easy to pick out in the otherwise mundane hangar-style airport terminal.

"Good gracious, Fountain, Genevieve looks like a sunset over there. What in the world is she wearing?"

I reached out my arm to stop his progress. "Please, Portier," I said. "We've had a rough day. I urge you—no, I beg you—go easy on the poor girl."

"Where's Jeffrey?" he asked as if we were talking about his driver.

"He went to Jackson, remember? Your delay interfered with his schedule. He won't return until tomorrow. Anyway, you're stuck with us, so be kind."

My friend began to walk again. "I'm always kind, Fountain. I don't know why you get truth and kindness mixed up."

Genny still had her back to us as we approached the table. She sipped a pink gin and surveyed her damaged dress and tangled jewelry. Portier put his hand on her back and said hello. She looked up apprehensively, then smiled coyly and lifted her hand toward him.

To my surprise, Portier took her hand and kissed the top of it. He looked up and saw a sparkling gimlet at his place across the table.

"I took the liberty of ordering you one," she said softly. "And thank you for the kiss."

He winked at her. "Our little secret, Genevieve. I don't want word getting out that there's a romantic side to me. I'll never be able to do my job as a crusty old accountant who dabbles in fraud. Besides, it was the only kiss I can remember where I was also able to floss my teeth at the same time. How did I get a string stuck to my upper lip?"

Genny blushed.

"How was your trip?" I asked to change the subject.

"Maddening, Fountain, just the way I like it."

"Good. Are you hungry?"

"No," he replied as he picked up his drink. "This is all I want. I had a horrid lunch on the plane." He took a sip then added, "Apparently, chicken Florentine causes gout."

Genny curled her nose and smirked but said nothing. I presumed she thought silence would be the least aggravating alternative to our homecoming with Portier. I decided to join her. I drank my Ski and listened to the overhead announcements of arriving and departing flights.

Portier remained silent as well—a little too quiet. He sat, looking at us judgmentally as he swirled the ice in his highball glass with his index finger. Like a tomcat in a haunch position in tall grass, awaiting the approach of his prey, Portier seemed to sit patiently and await the right moment to spring upon us. He didn't spring, however. He simply asked in a nonchalant tone, "Anything new while I was away?"

I looked at Genny; Genny looked at me. We shook our heads as if we couldn't think of a thing.

"It's been too hot for anything to happen," I said finally.

"Nothing at all?"

"Nothing, except Jeffrey is working on quite a machine in the garage. It's a beaut, Portier."

"He'd better not be neglecting my Hawk."

"Your Studebaker is fine. We drove it here. You'll find it shiny and intact. You've seen what Jeffrey's been working on, haven't you, Genny?"

Genny had been looking away but turned back to us abruptly at hearing Jeffrey's name. "I don't know what you're talking about."

"A DeSoto."

"Who's DeSoto?"

I chuckled. "Well, I don't know exactly. I have no idea, but I couldn't help but admire it. On another note, Bentley is also fine. You'll be happy to know that he has a shiny, soft coat and is fit as a fiddle."

"I like Chuck's Golden Hawk," Genny blurted suddenly.

The comment took us by surprise. We both looked at her as if she'd just announced she was pregnant.

"Thank you, Genevieve," Portier said politely. "I like it too, and I won't be trading it in; and regarding Bentley, thank you for taking good care of him. What do I owe you?"

Genny looked at me with a tinge of embarrassment. "Consider it a gift to you, Chuck."

Portier started to object, but I took his arm and asked him to accept the gift. "Very well, but I'm not looking for charity. I want to be fair."

Genny smiled shallowly then gulped the rest of her pink gin. "Are we through here? I'm sure Bentley could use another walk in the playground." It was apparent that Genny felt uncomfortable with our topics of discussion and wanted to leave before we moved to another one.

I wondered if Portier caught her evasiveness, but he finished his gimlet quickly, set the glass on the table, and said decisively, "She's right. We should be getting on."

I left my half-full glass of Ski sitting where it was and, after paying the tab, followed the two out of the terminal. The walk to the parking lot was hot and oppressive, but somehow it didn't seem quite as stifling as the conversation we'd just had at the café.

~

Portier settled in quickly at his cottage. He made some lemonade, and we spent a lazy summer afternoon under the cabana fan in his back courtyard.

Our conversation was bland. I did most of the talking; he seemed to be deep in thought. I presumed it was due to the letter from the Department of the Treasury he'd received in the mail while he was away. He'd opened the letter and read it, snarling under his breath. The letter indicated that he hadn't paid his 1955 income taxes, and the fines and penalties were now substantial. That was enough to subdue anyone into quiet contemplation.

"I'm sure the invoice can be easily settled," I said, "but I must say I'm quite surprised at you for neglecting your own taxes. You must've been so busy doing everyone else's returns that you forgot your own—a case of the cobbler's children having no shoes, no doubt."

Portier looked up suddenly. "What?"

"That demand note you received from the IRS," I replied.

"What are you talking about? I sent in my return for last year, and I paid my taxes in full. The IRS's records are flawed. I've cleared hundreds of such cases with the IRS in the past. I'll just be doing it for myself this time."

I nodded. Apparently, I was wrong about what was on his mind.

Portier resumed his deep train of thought, his stare into space intense. He twitched periodically around the corners of his mouth and squinted his eyes as if it helped him think more clearly.

Suddenly, he looked at me and, out of the blue, asked, "When did Genny become a recording artist?" He dropped his hand over the arm of his chair to rub Bentley's side. The pup sprawled lethargically over the cool paving stones.

"Oh, so you know about that," I replied noncommittally.

"How could I not? I don't generally listen to the radio, but when you're traveling, you're at the mercy of people who have to be constantly entertained. There are radios blaring everywhere. 'Honey, Be By Me' appears to be a popular song. I know her voice, Fountain, so don't deny it's her."

"I wasn't going to. Why didn't you ask about it while we

were seated at the airport?"

"Because it was quite apparent to me that Genny wasn't in the mood. I had a snowball's chance of getting an honest answer out of her. You, on the other hand, have taken an oath of honesty, so let's hear it."

I didn't know where to begin. Actually, I didn't know how to begin. I told Portier as much as I knew, including the mysterious note Genny received at Paradox from the man in the brown-checkered suit . . . and, of course, her missing friend. "Have you heard Genny speak of a Ronni Mohr?"

"No. Is she the missing friend you just mentioned?"

"Presumably missing."

"What does she have to do with the song Genny recorded?" he asked.

"She got Genny her recording contract. We hope to find her tomorrow."

Portier sat upright in his chair. "I would advise against it. Let her stay disappeared. Genevieve has bigger fish to fry. She'd better concentrate on resolving the issues surrounding this song of hers without the help of the person who got her into the mess in the first place."

"I didn't realize you believed her situation to be so urgent," I said honestly.

He stopped petting the dog and gave me a cold, hard stare. "Don't you? Don't you get the least bit uneasy, wondering how someone as obscure as this Mohr woman has such a major role in a song that Genevieve must track her down before she does anything else? Don't you get the least bit uneasy, wondering how she got to be so popular so quickly in light of what goes on in the record and television business?"

He had me there. I rarely gave the record or television business a second thought. I left that business to the interests of people like my granddaughter and her generation.

"People pay people to get people interested in their songs, Fountain," Portier said. "People get rich off people wanting their songs played and their voices heard. Surely, you know that."

"What you're talking about sounds unethical, almost criminal."

"It's not a crime yet but give it time."

"I can't believe Genny would get involved in something criminal or unethical unless she did so unknowingly. She's so clueless about the recording contract she signed that it's frustrating."

"Dangerous too, I might add."

I looked at him to see how serious he was about his last comment.

"Don't you think so?" he asked, noticing my reticent expression. "If not, perhaps mysterious men handing her ambiguous notes about missing women doesn't concern you."

He had me again. I didn't know what to say. Yes, of course, the man in the brown-checkered suit and the missing Ronni Mohr woman concerned me, but I was oblivious to how they were connected to Genny.

"Look," Portier said, lowering his voice, "all I'm going to say is that we had bootlegging in the twenties, bank robberies in the thirties, and underground markets of rationed goods during the World War. This is the fifties, Fountain. Today, if you want to play, you pay. That's all I'm saying."

Chapter 10

I woke up the next day with my sheets tied in a knot around my legs and bundled uncomfortably under my back. My chest felt as if Bentley had slept on top of it all night. I brushed my thinning hair back from my forehead and sat upright, almost falling back upon the bed from lightheadedness. If I'd slept a solid wink during the night, I was hard-pressed to remember when it occurred.

The mirror over the dresser revealed what I suspected. Large, dark bags drooped under my eyes. The stubble around my chin looked grayer than usual. Rosacea blotted my nose grotesquely, and the pores around it appeared to be so wide and open that I could stick my finger through them. I wasn't prone to cursing, but I couldn't help but wonder what in the world had happened to me during the night.

I stumbled into the kitchen, took hold of the percolator, and filled it with water, hoping the vibrant aroma of Community Coffee would soon permeate my senses. Portier and Bentley were still in their rooms. I was sure the careless clanging of taking the coffee cups out of the cupboard would awaken them, but I didn't particularly care. I wished secretly Portier had been up and about before me with coffee at hand, and all I had to do was to add the cream. Stirring the cream would've been optional; such a task required too much effort.

While the coffee perked, I opened the pantry and pulled out a box of Quaker Oats I'd purchased at the store. I wanted something hearty but not greasy, and I didn't trust Portier's judgment that he could differentiate the two. My hunch was more accurate than I gave myself credit for. When Portier ambled into the kitchen with the morning newspaper and sat at the table with Bentley following slowly behind, I could see a curl from his upper lip upon seeing the box of oats on the counter.

"Would you eat some porridge if I made it?" I asked anyway. "I'm in the mood for something that doesn't have to be killed first."

"Porridge?" he asked, lifting his head as if I'd just asked if the Martians in his courtyard were supposed to be there. "You mean the stuff bears in fairy tales and English peasants eat?" He looked at me with an air of superiority and added, "Hoosiers, too?"

"Call it oatmeal if that sounds better to you."

"Even worse." He turned the page of his newspaper. "We don't eat horse feed for breakfast in the South. Surely, you realize that. I'm surprised you found a box at the store."

"The shelf was well stocked."

"Case in point. No one buys it here or else the shelf would've been empty."

"Not entirely true," I said. "There was a box taken before me. At least one southerner bought it—although I'm sure it was made without cream and maple syrup and had the consistency of plaster paste after they got done with it. They probably even had to throw the pan away."

Portier looked up as he turned another page. "My, my, Fountain, you seem to be in a foul mood this morning. Did you not sleep well?"

"Not particularly."

"Any reason? Did you hear bumps in the night? Was there a pea under your mattress, princess?"

I didn't appreciate his attempt at humor. "No," I replied, "it was my rambling thoughts about Genny and the mess she's in. I hardly slept a wink. I don't know what to do for her, Portier."

"Then by all means, eat your oatmeal. There's nothing like a big bowl of glop sitting on the bottom of your stomach to help you think straight." Portier folded his paper and set it aside. "You should know by now that Genevieve is hardly a topic to dwell upon for a good night's sleep. What about her situation kept you awake?"

"What didn't?" I asked, sitting in a chair beside him. "Your insinuation that she's dabbling in something that could be almost criminal got me to thinking. I'm having second thoughts about seeing this woman in Mid-City today with her."

"Then don't go."

"I promised Genny I would."

Portier shook his head. "She shouldn't be going as well."

"I understand, but she'll do so anyway. You know that. I have to go with her to make sure she doesn't make matters worse."

"Oh, yes, good idea," he replied sarcastically, "because your history for staying out of trouble is impeccable."

~

Genny and I returned to the stucco house in Mid-City just as the mailman delivered the afternoon post. The woman who was on the porch next door sat in a lawn chair on her stoop, wearing the same floral frock. We didn't wave, and the woman gave us no indication that she cared.

The afternoon sun shone brightly on the mailman as he walked up the steps to the bungalow. He deposited a half-dozen envelopes into the letter box that hung next to the front door, then walked to the house next door where the woman in the frock waited patiently.

A small blue '51 Nash Rambler hardtop pulled to the curb in front of the bungalow. The driver emerged from the car and made her way up the steps to the letter box. I could see immediately why the woman in the frock described the woman as a girl. She resembled a teenager—lean, petite, and underdeveloped. Her gait was quick but not purposeful. She tilted her head to one side as if retrieving the mail was one more tedious task of her day.

"I was hoping it would be Ronni," Genny said.

"Have you seen this girl before?"

Genny shook her head.

We got out of Portier's Studebaker and stepped onto the sidewalk, waiting until the young woman finished collecting what the mailman had delivered. She didn't go into the house but turned and came back down the steps the way she'd come, sifting through the envelopes with indifference.

"I'm sorry, Miss," Genny said. "Can you tell me if this is the address for Veronica Mohr?"

The young woman stopped but didn't answer. She returned her focus to the envelopes and shuffled them nervously. In so doing, one fell from the pack to the sidewalk. I bent down to pick it up, but the woman stepped on it first, covering the return address.

"I'll get it," she said. She retrieved the envelope from under her foot, then said, "No."

"No what?" Genny asked. "No, this isn't her address? No,

you don't know Ronni Mohr? What does *no* mean?"

"It means I said no."

I detected more of a Midwestern accent than the slightly New Yorker accent common for New Orleans. There was sadness in her eyes and a weariness on her face. Although not dirty, her clothes were faded and lacked vibrancy. Her eyes were wide and colorless, and the tone in her voice indicated that she wasn't interested in anything Genny or I had to say. I was half-tempted to let her go, but she was the closest, most tangible connection Genny had to Ronni.

"Look," I said, "my name is Reverend Fountain, and this is Genevieve Duval. Genny here is a friend of Ronni's. The reason for our questions is to find Ronni. Can you help us?"

The woman's eyes appeared to soften, but she hesitated in opening a conversation.

"You do know Ronni, is that correct?"

She acknowledged that she did.

"Is she okay?"

The young woman nodded.

"Where can we find her?"

"Please, I have to go."

Genny extended her hand to keep the woman from passing. "Don't go. Please help us find her."

The woman hesitated before asking, "What do you want of her?"

"We don't want anything," Genny said. "We just want to find her. We want to make sure she's okay."

"I just told you she was." The woman sounded unconvinced.

"Yes, I know, but I also know Ronni, and she puts herself in dangerous situations." Genny leaned toward her to get better eye contact. "But she helped me at one time to get a recording contract. I'd like to see her." Genny paused upon noticing the young woman's lack of expression. "Are you from St. Louis?"

"Yes, we all are."

Genny squinted as if she didn't understand. "All?"

"We're roommates: Ronni, Cindy, Julie, and me. It's difficult making it alone."

"So I take it you and the others don't live at this address," I said, trying to understand the importance of the bungalow.

"We used to. We rented this house, but Ronni said we had to move, so we moved to Broadmoor. We live there now, and I pick up the mail that still arrives here."

I smiled to indicate that I understood, but her answer didn't really make sense to me. "May I ask your name?"

She hesitated. "Gwen."

"Gwen, our only motive for talking with you is to find Ronni and to make sense out of a contract Genny signed. Where can we find Ronni? Will you tell us that?"

"I don't know where she is."

"I'm sorry, but I thought you just said you—"

"I think you do," Genny blurted out.

"No," Gwen said defiantly. "Ronni says we have to move again. We may not be where I tell you we are. It'd do you no good." Her voice faded and she looked at Genny with apprehension.

"Please," I pleaded.

Gwen sighed but said, "Julie says she's not going anywhere anymore. She's tired of moving—of being a nomad. Ronni says we can't stay."

"Did she give a reason?"

"No, she just said it wasn't good where we're at. I don't know what she meant by that. It seems fine to me, but there isn't any place that's any good for Ronni. Something's always wrong."

"Does she work?" I asked. "Please, Gwen, it's important that we talk with Ronni about Genny's contract."

Gwen appeared as if she didn't want to tell us, but a reassuring puppy-dog look on my face must've softened her. "Yes, she works for this man. I can give you his address, but please promise you won't tell anyone that I gave it to you." She extended her hand and asked for a pen and a piece of paper.

I pulled both out of my overcoat's inner pocket and handed it to her.

Gwen scribbled an address quickly and shoved the pen and paper into my chest. I barely had time to grasp them before she bolted around me and hurried to her blue Nash.

Chapter 11

"I know what you're going to say," Genny muttered with apprehension when we returned to the car.

"Let's not talk about it," I said.

My statement threw her off guard. "But aren't you—"

"Not in the least."

She cupped her hands and placed them reverently in her lap. "All I'm saying is that if you want to return to the Quarter, I can find my own way to this place Gwen referred us to. The address looks like it's around Claiborne and Carrollton."

Her comment angered me. "That's the dilemma, Genny. That's why I don't want to talk about it. We both know I can't do that. I can't go back to the Quarter to allow you to traipse through this ordeal on your own. By Gwen's own apprehension, this is a potentially dangerous business you're mixed up in. In fact, I've forgotten why it's so important we find her, and if you sit there and try to tell me it's because you're concerned for her safety, I will stop you right there. I'm fairly certain this Ronni woman is alive today because she's capable of taking care of herself."

Genny fidgeted while I started the car and drove toward the

Mississippi River. "No," she said softly. "I've said all along it's to help me make heads or tails out of my recording contract."

I turned to her, trying not to appear angry. I started to give her two cents worth of my opinion but changed my mind.

"What is it?" she asked.

"Forget I started to say anything. I know you, Genny. You're going to do what you're going to do despite what anyone says."

The address wasn't difficult to find although it was on a side street, mostly nonresidential with dusty redbrick buildings lacking visible signage. We came to a halt in front an old block building and eyed it skeptically. It appeared to be nothing more than a warehouse. I pulled into a parking space reserved for freight deliveries and stepped out of the car. Nothing identifying the business was visible except for a sign in the window shaped like a clock, announcing that the occupants would return at eight-thirty the next morning.

Genny stepped out of the car and frowned. "This doesn't look promising." She walked to the building and peered through the front window. "Do you suppose this is Harmon's business?"

"I was about to ask you the same," I said.

"Oh, I wouldn't know," she replied. "I never came to him; he always came to me."

The windows were tinted enough to mellow the sun's rays but also to obscure our view of the reception lobby. Two chairs along a wall near the door, a small receiving counter, and a plastic Ficus tree were all I could see. A banner on the opposite wall hung over some corrugated boxes stacked on a table.

"There's some lettering on the wall, Dickie. Can you make them out?"

I couldn't. I thought I read what appeared to be an A, R, and M and below them an O, C, and I, but that was it. There were letters on both sides of the letters I could see, but they were indistinguishable. "Of what I can see, the letters may spell Har—"

"May I help you?"

We swung around.

Genny placed her hand over her pounding heart. "Oh, you scared me, sir," she said.

The security guard wasn't apologetic. "May I help you?"

"No—Well, yes," she stammered. "You see, I was given this address as the place where a friend of mine works, but I can't tell what business it is, and it appears to be closed."

The guard was unmoved by the explanation. "May I ask what you want?"

"As I said, I'm looking for an address."

"Of a business, yes, I heard. I'm afraid I'm going to have to ask you to leave."

"No, wait. Please, tell me. What is this place? What business is it?"

"Ma'am, if you don't know, then you don't need to know. Let's move. Your car's in a freight zone."

"Do you know the Mohr sisters?" she asked abruptly.

The guard's expression didn't change. If he knew them, he was trained well enough not to show.

"I see," Genny said, turning toward the car. "Thank you. You've been very helpful."

We walked to the car with the guard's watchful eye on our every move.

I started the Hawk immediately, noticing that the guard didn't take his eyes off the car until I'd turned the corner and was out of sight.

Genny sighed. "That put us at a dead end. We might as well head back to the Quarter."

"I want to see where this recording studio is where you

received your contract," I said firmly.

"It's just a studio, Dickie, nothing more."

"But I want to see it for myself. I want to make sure it's real. We have time."

"It's out of the way," she replied.

"You told me once it was on North Rampart Street. Rampart's along the edge of the Quarter. It's not out of the way at all."

I didn't take no for an answer. I drove toward North Rampart and had to find the recording studio on my own. Genny had a lapse in memory of where it was located, or so she claimed. I pulled into a small parking lot in front and saw no sign above the entrance, but I noticed the words *Marrs Recording* stenciled in large gold lettering on the glass surface of the door. I placed the car in park and turned off the engine.

"You don't want to go in, do you?" she asked.

"No, but I'd like to observe who goes in and out of the office."

Several minutes passed before the entrance door opened, but no one came out. It closed slowly on its own, then opened again. A man in a blue suit stood in the doorway, keeping the door open, deep in conversation with someone within.

"That's him," Genny said with alarm, recognizing the man at Paradox who'd handed Tomas the mysterious note at the bar.

The man shook his head repeatedly as if in an argument he intended to win with the person inside. He turned eventually and walked toward a row of cars parked along a wood fence. The door shut tightly behind him.

Another man, similar in stature but younger, emerged and followed the man in the blue suit to an aged Buick Roadmaster. He raised his voice as he approached the car, pointing decisively to the building. The passing traffic made it difficult for me to hear their exact words.

"Can you make out anything they're saying?" I asked Genny.

I turned to face her and realized immediately something was terribly wrong. Even through her heavy rouge and foundation, all color had drained from her face, leaving a pasty dull complexion of fear and dread. "What is it?" I asked.

"That man," she said timidly.

"Yes, I know. We saw him at the club."

She shook her head in a way that made her curls flop wildly about her face. "No, the other one."

I looked more closely at the younger man. "Who is he? Why are you so afraid?"

"He's Kip."

I took a deep breath and exhaled slowly, giving myself time to think as I also tried to listen to the words the two men were spouting back and forth to each other. As I did so, I almost missed a young woman exiting the building. It was the woman's tight, alluring walking suit and long, flowing hair trailing behind her that caught my attention eventually. I nudged Genny. We watched Cindy Mohr position her sunglasses as if it would aid in an escape from the men's watchful eyes.

It didn't work.

The man in the blue suit called her name.

The woman continued to walk.

The man called her name again. This time, Cindy stopped. "Come here!" the man yelled.

She turned toward him and blurted an expletive. When he blurted one back, she yelled something I couldn't hear.

Genny started to ask what they were saying, but I lifted my hand for silence so that I could catch as much of the conversation as I could.

"Cindy's saying something about having risked it all for nothing or something like that," I said.

The two yelled across the parking lot some more before

Cindy finally ended the argument with, "Otherwise, you can screw yourself and leave me alone!"

"Okay, I heard that," Genny said.

"Thanks for not making me repeat it," I replied.

The man's face reddened with anger. Harmon held him back when it appeared the angered man wanted to sprint toward Cindy. The man relaxed when Harmon wouldn't loosen his grip.

When the men began to argue again, Cindy smiled and walked away.

Genny leaned out of her car window and called her name.

Cindy stopped, recognizing the voice. The angry look that was once prevalent on the young woman's face dissipated into bewilderment upon seeing us.

"I'm going to ask you to come here," Genny said firmly, "and I suggest you not tell me to go screw myself."

It looked for a moment that Cindy contemplated fleeing, but Genny's piercing glare and the anger of the men behind her compelled her toward the Golden Hawk.

"So what's going on?" Genny asked when she approached.

"Them? Oh, they're just men. You know men. They're Lotharios—always wanting something from women." When it appeared to Cindy that Genny was unconvinced, she added, "It's true."

"Okay, but I was also talking about what happened back at The Marina and why you left. I'm not interested in those men and what they want from you."

Cindy glanced over her shoulder at the men who were still arguing by the Roadmaster.

"Or should I be?"

"No," Cindy scoffed. "They're nothing."

"Then get in the car. We have to talk."

"I can't."

Genny looked at me with a coy expression. "What's the name of that handsome detective we know at the police department, Dickie?"

"Robicheaux," I said.

"You know Detective Robicheaux, don't you, sweetheart?" she asked Cindy. "He interviewed you when Ronni first disappeared."

Cindy glared at Genny defiantly.

"Now get in," Genny commanded. She leaned forward to let Cindy crawl into the cramped back seat of Portier's Hawk. "Let's get one thing straight," she said. "I'm through playing games. You give us answers, the correct answers this time, and we can all go home. I have plenty of gas money to follow your sorry ass wherever you go. It's up to you."

Cindy folded her arms across her midsection, closed her eyes, and leaned her head against the back of the seat.

I put the Hawk in motion and drove past the two men who looked at us with leering eyes. I came to a small café on the thoroughfare and pulled into its parking lot.

"What's this?" Cindy asked, sitting up with alarm.

"Getting some coffee," I said. "We're going to talk."

"I need something stronger."

"Then order espresso."

"Not here," she said. "Somewhere away from here. Somewhere in Metairie. They don't go to Metairie."

"Neither does anyone else," Genny said. "We're not crossing the parish line."

"Then go to Dryades or Lakeview. We can get lost in the crowds on Dryades."

I started to pull away, but Genny stopped me. "We didn't come this way to hang out with the shopping crowd on Dryades," Genny said. "We're not falling for that."

Cindy shrugged as if it didn't make any difference to her. "Fine, but if you want me to talk, you'll make the drive. Not here. There's a lounge in Uptown. We can go there. It's just a short walk once we park."

The short walk turned out to be longer than Genny and I expected, but I suspected Cindy was hoping it would wear us out. The young woman walked ahead of us, parading pretentiously without an awareness of life outside of her own. She walked as if she wished never to arrive, only to be seen.

Young, handsome men seemed to be the only people who received the benefit of her attention. She brushed strands of dark-brown hair from her eyes to reveal a synthetic innocence in an effort to attract them. She tugged frequently at different places on her outfit where she wanted them to focus and smiled briefly but gave no indication she wanted anything from them other than their admiration.

Genny noticed Cindy's display. She looked at me once and shook her head when it became apparent that we were on a wild goose chase, and Cindy had no intention of giving Genny the information we wanted about her sister Ronni.

"We may not need Ronni," I whispered to Genny out of Cindy's earshot.

"What do you mean?" Genny whispered back. "Of course, we do."

I shook my head. "No, this doesn't make sense. Why was Cindy at Marrs? Why didn't we see Ronni? If you ask me, Cindy appears to be the one pulling the strings, more so than Ronni."

Genny slowed her gait, eyeing Cindy critically from behind. I sensed she suddenly felt the same way as I did.

Cindy stopped at a small bistro with outdoor seating. "Are you coming?" she asked, noticing the gap between our steps and hers. "This should be fine." Assisted by a young waiter who seemed enamored by her presence, Cindy procured a table with an extraordinary view of the shops along the street. She smiled upon seeing a single red rose with greenery used as a centerpiece.

"Ronni's favorite flower," she said as if the comment was meant to warm our hearts.

We sat comfortably and said little until the summery cocktails the women ordered arrived at our table. A light breeze blew past, offering little relief from the heat that reflected from the pavement.

"How did you find me?" Cindy asked, picking the rose from the table to smell it.

"We went back to The Marina after we talked to you," I said, "but you were nowhere around."

"Yes, I had to leave. I had business to attend to."

"What kind of business is that?"

"Ronni's business, if you must know," she said, replacing the rose. "I take care of my sister, and I take good care of her."

Genny started to say something, but I interrupted her. "I don't believe you, Cindy," I said brazenly. "That was a drastic thing to do when you quit your job at The Marina just to help Ronni. Too drastic in my mind."

"What do you know about being a sister?" Cindy asked. "I don't care what you think, and I don't need to go back to The Marina. I have another job."

"One so soon?" Genny asked. "Who is it with? Kip Harmon?"

"Yes, with Kip," she replied indignantly. "I came to his office to receive an offer."

Genny laughed with a menacing taunt. "From what we saw in the parking lot, the interview didn't go very well."

Cindy licked her top lip. "Yes, well, that was a misunderstanding among business associates. Let me explain."

"No, let me explain it to you. Tell her, Dickie." Genny took her cocktail, sat back, and sipped smugly. When I didn't respond right away, she prompted, "Go on. Tell her what you told me."

I gave Genny a dirty look because what I'd said to her on the sidewalk was meant to be held in confidence.

Cindy raised her eyebrows as she set her drink on the table to listen.

"I was just thinking out loud," I said cautiously. "It appears to me that you already have a working relationship with Mr. Harmon based upon what we saw at Marrs."

"That's not true," Cindy said.

"No?"

Her face softened. "Well, mostly not true. Ronni and I have worked with Kip but only on certain clients. I brought him information on those clients, but he wanted more. That was it."

"I don't understand," Genny said. "What kind of job do you have with him? What do you do?"

"Very little. We work there off and on."

"But doing what?" Genny asked. "I didn't know she worked for him until Gwen . . ." Genny stopped, apparently realizing she revealed the source of our information.

Cindy caught the slip up immediately. "Gwen? How do you know Gwen?"

"We ran into her," I said. "She indicated that Ronni does more than work for Harmon off and on. We didn't know about you."

Cindy snubbed her nose at hearing a connection with Gwen. "What would she know about work? Ronni tried to get Gwen involved in a real job at Harmon's, but all she's content to do is pick up mail and write song lyrics that no one sings. I wouldn't listen to her if I were you. She doesn't know."

"She seemed convinced that you have to move from the house you're living in," Genny said. "It seems Ronni feels the need to move quite often."

"That's true," Cindy said. "That's why you saw me at Harmon's. I was trying to get paid. Ronni needs help. She doesn't pay her bills. They come often to repossess the stuff she buys but doesn't pay for. I tell her she has to get her act together. It's always someone she owes money to that she's running from. I'm telling you she needs help. I'm the only person who can help her."

"There's just one thing that doesn't ring true with your story," Genny said. "It's the look on Gwen's face when she talked to us. There's more to the story, Cindy, because there was fear in Gwen's eyes."

Cindy exaggerated a sigh. "Oh, that Gwen," she said, shaking her head. "You know the type. What do they call them—alarmists? Look, we need to move on. There may not be a resolution to what any of us are seeking, but we can still be friends, you and I, Genny."

Genny thought carefully for a moment before turning to me. "I'm ready to leave," she said.

"So soon?" Cindy asked. "You've barely touched your drink!"

"You've told us nothing, not really. We might as well leave."

Cindy reached across the small table and took Genny's hand that was wrapped around the stem of her martini glass. "What if I tell you what you want to know if your friend, the Reverend here, leaves us in private?"

The question surprised us both, but Genny was so taken aback she took her hand away and said, "What could you possibly tell me that you can't say in front of Dickie? How do I know you'll tell me the truth? You only tell the truth when you're caught in a lie, Cindy. Is that why you want him to go—because you believe it's easier to deceive me than it is to deceive him?"

"I don't lie when I drink, Genny, and you're smart. You'll know when I'm lying."

"My gut tells me I'll regret staying."

"Then we don't have to talk. Let's just drink between friends."

Genny hesitated before conceding. "I'll consider your offer, but I must go to the washroom first. Do they have one here?" Genny rose from the table. She looked confused as to where to go.

I suggested she look inside. "But first . . ." I rose and accompanied Genny to the door. When we were safely out of Cindy's earshot, I said, "I'll leave you two alone, but please don't commit or agree to anything, and don't be taken in by anything she says. Do you hear me? Find out about her and Ronni's role with this Kip Harmon fellow, then you end the conversation and leave the table."

"Where will you be?"

"Just a few shops down the street. I'll make sure I can see your table from wherever I am."

Genny nodded, appearing grateful that I'd be close. We exchanged a few words about what Genny should ask of Cindy. When we were through, I looked toward our table on the sidewalk.

"Never mind, it's all a moot issue now," I said.

"Why's that?"

I pointed to where we sat. Genny's purse lay on her chair as she'd left it. The single rose had been removed from the centerpiece and set strategically in front of Genny's martini. Cindy Mohr, however, was nowhere to be seen.

Chapter 12

The next morning, Bentley greeted me in the kitchen doorway, his panting face appearing to smile. He circled once, golden tail wagging, when I entered, then circled again when he thought I was heading for the refrigerator.

"You should know me by now, boy," I said to him, ignoring his silent pleas for a tasty morsel. "Nothing happens before coffee, definitely not the smell of bologna on my fingers. Where's your master? Beg him for a morsel."

Almost as if he understood every word I said, the Lab clawed at the linoleum in front of the door to the outside courtyard.

"Is he out there?" I poured a cup from the percolator, walked to take a look, and opened the door.

Bentley rushed out. Portier sat contentedly at a small patio table, rubbing his knuckles and flexing his fingers. He looked up as I sat near him. He didn't need to tell me his arthritis was acting up again, but he did anyway, and I received a full report on every nook and cranny in his body that squeaked, ached, throbbed, and popped.

"You should get examined. There's help for that," I said, pulling my cup away from my lips, realizing too late that the coffee was too hot to drink.

He looked at me critically and asked, "Then what would I have to talk to you about in the morning?"

"Point taken." I set my cup on the table. "Listen, I woke up with an idea this morning. There's no reason why I shouldn't go back to Mid-City and talk with this Gwen on my own."

"Without Genevieve?"

"That's what 'on my own' means. Yes, without Genny."

"But you're not the one in the predicament; Genevieve is."

"I know, but Genny can't do it on her own," I said with some finality. "I fear the Mohr sisters may take advantage of her without me."

"She's a grown woman. It's her problem; she should be there with you."

"But I want to ask the questions I want without her pouting expressions holding me back."

Portier chewed on his bottom lip as he thought for a second. "And I suspect you're still planning to help Miss Cora at Labreville."

"Yes, I've spoken with her."

"So if you take on Genny's project and help at Labreville, that means you'll be in New Orleans a while," he said.

"I've decided to extend my stay. That is, if you don't mind."

Portier shook his head but did so as if he had something else on his mind. "What about your granddaughter?"

"Donna's in Ontario with her parents. She's not to return to Indiana until the end of the summer."

Portier knew my granddaughter well enough to ask, "And if she decides not to stay in Ontario the whole summer?"

"Oh, she will. I didn't leave her much choice, and I better not find her at the Union terminal building getting off *The City of New Orleans*, or I'll be, how should I say it?"

"Put off?"

"No, I was thinking of the other P word."

"Pissed?"

"No. Perturbed. Now I must call Genny and cancel our plans for the day together."

I grabbed my cup and went back into the kitchen with Bentley at my heels. I couldn't deny the pup any longer and reached inside the fridge to pull out a slimy piece of bologna from the half-eaten package. I broke the slice into three even pieces, throwing them perfectly into the air for him to catch. He did so and the meat disappeared instantly. When I'd thrown the last piece, I felt rather cheated and unfulfilled. "Did you even enjoy it?" I asked. "Because I have to say, Bentley, I don't believe you have the slightest notion about what you've just eaten."

Bentley followed me to the telephone stand and plopped onto the cooler hardwood floor rather than the softer, but warmer, brocade rug. Genny answered my call immediately, and to my surprise, she requested that I go on to Mid-City without her as she had to rehearse with her band at the club. I didn't argue or give her time to rebut. I hung up the receiver, downed my cup of coffee, and hurried to the courtyard where Portier was no longer rubbing his knuckles but dipping his toes into Bentley's water bowl.

I looked at him curiously.

"I think that man on the plane from Atlanta gave me gout," he said.

"Gout isn't contagious, Portier, but I don't have time to discuss it. Is Jeffrey back from Jackson yet?"

"He left Jackson early this morning. He should be back in the city in a couple of hours. Why?"

"I need a way to Mid-City. May I take your Studebaker? Will you call to have that boy who runs the garage when Jeffrey is gone bring it around? In the meantime, I'll get ready to go."

"Suit yourself," he said.

I started for the door but stopped suddenly. The tone of Portier's voice sounded as if he was displeased that I'd decided to go. I asked him what was on his mind.

"I'm just wondering, Fountain, what you hope to find out from this woman in Mid-City. You know me. I deal with facts and evidence, things that are objective, but your interest in meeting this woman again—this time without Genevieve—isn't objective at all. It's not even subjective. It's opaque at best."

I sat back down at the table. "I'll be frank with you, Portier. I'm struggling with it myself. I have just one question in my mind: Is it fraud with an unethical recording company or a bad business decision on Genny's part? I'm hoping that an additional talk with Gwen without Genny to sway the conversation will help me decide whether we need to talk with Ronni Mohr at all."

Portier frowned, contemplating my decision.

"What's the matter?" I asked. "You still look puzzled. I thought you might agree with that approach."

He hesitated. "I'm afraid it won't be that easy. I can't help but believe Genevieve's situation is a complex mix of both poor judgment *and* deceit."

"Why do you say that?"

"You've forgotten my conversation with you about the pay-to-play culture within the entertainment industry."

I shook my head. "I haven't forgotten," I replied, rising from the table. "I just don't understand it fully."

"Then sit back down and bring me up to date on any facts you haven't told me yet. I'll clue you in."

I had a difficult time remembering what I'd told him and what I hadn't, so I started from the beginning with Genny's predicament. Portier didn't seem to mind the redundancies. The refresher seemed to solidify the facts for him in his mind.

When I finished what I thought were the important details and characters, I said to him honestly, "What I don't understand most of all is why Genny and I are chasing people—so many *different* people—to get a copy of one elusive contract that should be at Genny's fingertips in the first place."

"Don't you see?" Portier asked.

"No, I just told you I didn't."

"But that's how such a scheme works, Fountain."

I sighed and sat back in my seat so exasperated that I stared at my coffee cup and ran my index finger over the rim to expel my frustration.

"Money laundering," Portier said.

I jerked my head up. "Money laundering? Surely, you jest. You mean, such crimes as Al Capone and Meyer Lansky tried to pull off?"

Portier chuckled. "I hardly give your cast of misfits the same astuteness as Capone and Lansky, but yes, you could say it that way."

"You'll have to explain. I don't have firsthand knowledge of how laundering works. I had many issues at the Spiceland church where I ministered but laundering the coins we received in the collection plates wasn't one of them."

Portier tried to conceal a grin that crept across his face, but he failed miserably. "The premise is quite simple, Fountain," he said as he cleared his throat. "It's the concealment of illegal money by passing it through a sequence of unlikely or seemingly legal businesses or transactions to try to hide its true origins. I'll use Genevieve's situation as an example. If your Kip Harmon fellow is obtaining illegal funds from Genevieve and making illegal bribes to DJs and radio stations to have her song played, then he needs a way of concealing what he's doing so that it isn't readily noticeable to the authorities who may be targeting his activities. Does that make sense?"

"Not entirely, but it explains why there are so many layers of people involved."

"Precisely."

"So," I said, trying to get my understanding straight, "what could be happening is that Harmon uses runners like the Mohr sisters to find eager talent like Genny who pays Harmon to be her talent scout, who pays the recording studio, which records her song and receives her money, then pays Harmon a kickback, who pays the Mohr sisters a chunk of money, who pay the DJs and radio stations and keep a portion as a commission."

Portier hum-hawed a bit before admitting, "Yes, something to that effect, although I can't say for sure Harmon's racket is being operated in exactly the same way as you described, but yes, you have the general idea why you're chasing the elusive Ronni Mohr who doesn't want to be found. Until the police are finished with their investigation, we may not know how it's being perpetrated exactly."

"Well, then, I may never know," I said, frustrated. "The only detective I know on the police force is Guy Robicheaux, and he's in homicide."

I saw the grave expression on Portier's face immediately.

"No," I said. "Don't give me that look. Don't even think it could happen. I can deal with money laundering, Portier, but we can't have murder. We just can't. I promised my granddaughter."

Chapter 13

I called for the car, and by the time I opened the front door of the cottage and stepped onto the stoop, the young attendant who'd taken Jeffrey's place had Portier's Golden Hawk gassed and ready to go. The car didn't shine any better than before, but the young man was prompt and courteous, so I tipped him well and meandered through traffic on Esplanade toward Mid-City.

I reached Mid-City in good time and parked the car across the street from the tan stucco bungalow. The woman with the ugly frock wasn't on the porch as she had been the day before.

I waited patiently for Gwen's blue Nash. It wasn't long before it came into view. Gwen slowed as she passed me. She didn't stop, however. I caught a glimpse of her fearful eyes moments before she sped away. Alarmed, I cranked the Hawk's engine and made a U-turn in the street. I was fortunate to pull alongside her at the next intersection as she waited for traffic.

A tearful Gwen cried out through her open window into mine, "Stop! Please! Why are you doing this to me?"

"I need to talk with you one more time!" I yelled.

"No!" she yelled back. "No!"

Gwen accelerated through the intersection when the traffic

cleared, but her anguish must have overcome her. She pulled into the next commercial parking lot and broke into tears.

I got out of the car and approached her. "Gwen, what's going on? What's the matter?"

She couldn't answer through her sobs.

"Talk to me! Please!"

"You don't know?" she asked. Her eyes were blotched and wet, her face flushed.

"What are you talking about?"

"It's horrible! It's too horrible! Julie is dead!" she screamed, angry and afraid. "She was murdered last night, and Ronni is gone. The police are looking for her. I don't know who you are or what you want, but you've brought nothing but fear and danger into my life ever since I met you. Please go away. Please leave me alone!"

"Gwen," I said, reaching through the open window to take hold of her shoulder. "I don't know what you're talking about. I had nothing to do with what happened. I'm as shocked as you are. Let me help."

The young woman shook her shoulder free and pleaded again to be left alone.

"Let's go somewhere," I said. "Let's talk this through. You're troubled and not thinking clearly. You shouldn't be driving like this."

She hesitated but eventually nodded, wiping tears from her cheeks.

Gwen followed me in her car to a small outdoor pastry café. She seemed to calm down as we sat in the shade under a table umbrella. She sipped tea and allowed the soothing flavor to ease the tension that caused her hands to shake.

"I'm sorry," she said, still sniffing from the sobs. "I'm very confused, and I don't know what you want from me."

"I don't want anything but to understand what happened last night."

"I don't understand it myself. I was at the house when Julie was murdered. I told the police everything I knew, but it wasn't much. What I said to them was so broken they surely thought I'd lost my mind."

"Why don't you tell me? Maybe it'll make better sense now."

"No, I don't think anything can make sense of it."

"That's not true," I said. "You mustn't talk like that. Last night was no time to be asking you questions. This morning may be different."

Gwen stopped to think. "Well . . . you may be right. I hope so. You see, I'd gone to the store last evening to pick up some things we needed. When I returned, Julie was in her room, packing her belongings."

"What sort of belongings?"

"Just her clothes. I didn't think much of it at the time. I was tired, so after I put the groceries away, I decided to go to bed early. My room's at the end of the hall. When I walked by her room again, she seemed agitated, anxious about something. I asked her what was wrong, and she said she had to leave."

"I'm sure that alarmed you."

"Yes, very much. Then Ronni came in through the front door. Julie let out a gasp and closed her suitcase even though she had more clothes to pack. Ronni asked what was going on. That's when we started talking about our situation at the house."

"What situation?"

"Ronni said we had to move. Julie replied she couldn't live like this anymore and the rest of us could do as we please, but she was finding her own place. Ronni became very upset. She said Julie was too involved to get out."

"Out of what?"

"I don't know."

I studied Gwen's face. She turned away.

"I think you do know," I said. "I know you're upset, but you were standing right there. What did Ronni mean? Does Julie work at Harmon's?"

"No, Julie has her own job, a good one. She was smart enough not to get involved with Kip Harmon."

"Then I wonder what Ronni meant by being too involved," I said. "Was there something that Julie knew about Harmon that made her leery of him and his company?"

Gwen shook her head. "All I know is that she told me once that I was a fool to do anything with Kip if I wanted to have a future. She didn't even like me picking up his mail. That's all I really did for him. I picked up his mail."

"I'm sorry if you think I'm being impertinent, Gwen, but is picking up Mr. Harmon's mail enough for you to make a living?"

Gwen sniffed. Her eyes livened. "No, but I . . . dabble . . . in song lyrics."

I tried to appear supportive. "Ah, that's great," I said, even though I didn't believe it could be any more lucrative. "Have you been able to get anything published? Has an artist picked up a song you've written?"

She shrugged. "Little stuff, not anything big except for one artist who bought a song. I mean, I haven't done enough to make a go of it, but Mr. Marrs says I have a real talent."

"You mean the owner of Marrs Recording?"

Gwen smiled broadly, the first she'd done so since we sat down. The smile faded quickly, however, and she returned to a look of despair. "It's hard, you know. I mean, to make it. I'm so young, and I don't know anyone in the business. That's why I stick with Mr. Marrs. I have a chance with him."

I tried to smile. "So what happened next?"

"I don't know. That's where I wasn't much help to the police. I went to bed. I didn't want to be a part of Julie and Ronni's conversation. I didn't want to know anything about what they were talking about."

"You must've heard something."

"They were arguing. Ronni raised her voice. She scared me. She kept saying what a fine friend Julie was for leaving. She said Julie wouldn't make it on her own without her. Then I heard Julie say Ronni had it all wrong, that it was Ronni who was dependent on her and . . ." Gwen paused for several seconds. ". . . and that they both knew why."

I sat upright in my chair. "Do you know what Julie meant by that?"

"No, and I don't want to know."

"But you must!" I said. "Knowing why could have been the motive for her murder. Did you tell this to the police?"

"No. I was too scared and confused."

"Scared and confused is the reason you must tell them. Gwen, there are some important gaps in what you're telling me. The police will notice them too."

"They did say they had more questions."

"Good," I replied. "And when they ask, you must tell them everything."

Gwen started to leave.

"Where are you going?" I asked.

She looked at me. Her mouth gaped slightly. "Aren't we through?"

I shook my head. "No. What makes you think we're through? You haven't told me about the murder."

"Oh, I don't think I can go over it again." She took a deep breath. "You see, Julie became as angry as Ronni. There was such horrible screaming, so I put my head under my covers and covered my ears with my pillow."

"And?"

"I fell asleep."

I sat back in my seat. This time, it was my mouth that gaped. "I don't believe you," I said. "You couldn't have fallen asleep."

"But I did."

"With them yelling back and forth and you being upset? Is that what you told the police—that you fell asleep?"

Gwen nodded. "I don't think they believed me. Do you think that's why they want to talk to me again?"

"Based upon what you've just told me, I wouldn't be surprised." I leaned toward her and lowered my voice. "Did you find the body?" When she nodded, I said, "Then they'll probably want to concentrate on how you found Julie and what you did after you found her."

"There's not much to tell," Gwen said. "I heard something that woke me up. I heard more arguing. I thought I heard a man's voice, but that couldn't be. We don't bring men to the house. Cindy says we can't trust them. They are all . . . Oh, I forget the word she uses to describe them."

"Lotharios."

Gwen looked surprised. "Yes, that's it. I don't know what it means."

"It's from Shakespeare," I said, "but that's beside the point. The bottom line is that she doesn't trust men. From what I saw of the men she keeps company with, I'd consider it a fair statement, but by the same token, I'm sure the men she knows feel the same about her. You were saying?"

"At one point, the arguing stopped, and the front door opened and shut. I thought it was Julie leaving, just as she said she would, but then the door opened and slammed shut again a few minutes later. That's when I heard a car start and drive away, but then the front door opened again. I was terrified. I thought something bad was about to happen—something to *me*!"

"Why would you feel that way?"

"I thought someone knew I was still in the house. The man's voice was a voice I'd never heard before. I thought he was still there, so I stayed under the covers until I couldn't hear anything for several minutes."

"Is that when you got out of bed and went to Julie's room?"

"No," Gwen said, her voice quivering, "that's when I knew I was going to die. I heard footsteps coming down the hall. The door creaked open, and she looked in."

I waited for Gwen to tell me who it was, but she just looked over my shoulder to the parking lot with a faraway gaze.

"Who looked in?" I asked impatiently.

"Ronni. It was Ronni. My room was dark, but I could see her through slits in the covers. It was Ronni."

"Did she come into the room?"

"No, thank God," Gwen said, sighing. "I don't know why she didn't. I hoped she thought I was asleep. That's when she turned and went back down the hall. I heard the front door open and close again and a car start and drive off. There was silence. That's when I got out of bed. I walked down the hall to Julie's room, and that's when I found her. She was lying on the bed."

"That had to have been quite a shock."

She nodded. "There must've been a terrible fight because her clothes were crumpled as if they'd been pulled halfway off her in the struggle. I assumed Julie was dead because of the blood, and when I called out her name, she didn't move."

"So what did you do?"

"I went to the phone and called the police, then I waited

outside until they came . . . with an ambulance."

Gwen set her hands on the table. I took hold of them and told her I didn't want to know any more about the scene. "What's Julie's last name?" I asked, realizing I didn't know.

"Moreno. Her real name is Julia, but we call her Julie."

"Does she have any family?"

"A brother somewhere, I think."

"No parents?"

"None that she speaks about. When she does, it's in the past tense. I assumed they're no longer living."

"Do you know where Ronni is now?"

She shook her head.

"I'm asking because I fear for you, Gwen."

She looked at me intently. "I'm scared for me too. I don't know where she is. I haven't seen Cindy either."

"So what are you going to do?" I asked. "Where are you going to stay?"

Gwen shrugged as if she hadn't thought that far in advance.

"Whatever you decide, I wouldn't pick up any more mail." I pulled a paper napkin out of a metal dispenser and scribbled Portier's phone number on the surface. "If you feel in danger or want to talk, call me. If you'd feel better about talking to another woman, you can find Genny at Paradox in the Quarter. That's where she sings."

Gwen took the napkin and smiled. She looked at me and started to express her appreciation before her eyes darted over my shoulder again to the parking lot. She gasped, and the whites of her eyes widened with fright.

"What is it?" I asked.

Her lips quivered. "He knows my car."

I didn't have a chance to turn around to see who she was referring to. Before I knew what was happening, she stood and ran from our table to her Nash a few yards away. There was no use stopping her.

I stood and looked over the sago palms to the cars in the parking lot. I didn't see anyone lurking. The only thing I saw was a lone automobile pulling away from the café—a shimmering gold 1956 DeSoto Fireflite convertible.

Chapter 14

I swung by the garage to park the Hawk. The young attendant met me at the entrance as I pulled in, smiling broadly and wiping his hands on an oily rag.

"You're Mr. Charles's friend now, aren'tcha?" he asked, pointing a finger at me.

"You're good with names," I teased. "I don't think I ever caught yours, however."

"Rusty," he said proudly.

I looked at his head. "Ah, I should've guessed."

"What, sir?"

"Your hair."

"Oh, I see, but no, sir; I was named after my daddy and my granddaddy."

"No doubt. Did they have red hair?"

"Oh, yes, sir; we all have red hair. My sister's name is Robin."

I'd heard enough. "Jeffrey not back yet?"

"No, sir, but he'll be comin' 'round soon. He called and said he's on his way."

I turned to go.

"There's a storm coming, you know."

I turned back around. "No, I hadn't heard," I said. "From the gulf or the plains?"

"Gulf, sir, coming north at a fast clip. Yeah, that's why Jeffrey's hightailing it purty quick-like back from Jackson. You know, they got these planes now that can fly into a storm, right smack-dab into the middle of it, to find out what's going on. This storm's a clipper this time, they say."

I thanked the young man and said I should be heading back to Mr. Portier's cottage.

I walked briskly to Ursulines Avenue, ignoring the sun upon my back and the sweat under my collar. Portier's cottage appeared quiet. I bypassed it to go to Genny's door, and she answered it soon after I knocked. The tiara she wore glistened from the sun and nearly blinded my view of her.

"You look like you could use a cool drink," she said, beckoning me in.

"If it wasn't so hot, I could use a cup of coffee," I replied.

"Nonsense. I made groceries after I went to the club. I bought you some chicory for such occasions. I can ice it for you."

I followed her into the kitchen. "How do you *make* groceries, Genny?"

"What?" she asked, turning around. "At the store, silly, where else?"

"Most people buy them."

She laughed. "Not in Nawlins, sweetheart. We *make* groceries here. You better get used to it."

I plopped into the first chair around the kitchen table I could reach.

"Oh, Dickie, I don't think I've ever seen you so frazzled. What's the matter? What's gotten you so hot and bothered?" She pulled the coffee from her cupboard.

"Julie Moreno is dead," I said bluntly.

Genny stopped what she was doing. Her face paled. "Julie? You mean Gwen's roommate? Dead how?"

"Bludgeoned."

"When?"

"Last night."

Genny gasped. She removed the sparkling tiara from her head and set it on the counter, then looked about the kitchen as if everything was in disarray or appeared new.

"Forget the coffee," I said. "It's a shock, I know."

She shook her head. "No, I'd like some myself under the circumstances . . . with some Southern Comfort."

I told her to start the coffee; I'd get the liqueur. I knew where it was. It took some doing to find the bottle, however. By the time I returned into the kitchen, the coffee was percolating, and Genny had taken a seat at the Formica table, using the surface to support her elbow as she massaged her forehead with her fingertips.

"Was she killed because of us?" she asked solemnly.

I set the bottle on the table and pulled her hand from her forehead to caress it gently. "Why would you ask that?"

"I don't know. It just seems too coincidental that we talked to Gwen one day, and her roommate is dead the next."

"It wasn't because of us," I said reassuringly. "It started as a quarrel between Julie and Ronni."

"Ronni?"

I told her what I knew from Gwen's conversation. I described the conversation in detail, but Genny appeared to hear little of it.

"Ronni murdered her?" she kept asking. "I can't believe Ronni could do such a thing. I mean, she's a bit edgy, mind you, but she's no murderer, Dickie."

I didn't know what to say that would make the news easier. "Let's make sure *you* are okay. Do you have that contract you signed with Marrs Recording?"

She didn't budge. "Do you think we're in danger?" she asked instead.

"I don't know. On the surface, her murder appears simply to be bad timing."

"You mean a coincidence? I told you before—the last time you were in New Orleans—I don't believe in coincidences. Nothing can be explained by bad timing. You're just saying that to make me feel better."

"There's only one way to find out," I replied. "Get your contract. I want to see it."

Genny sighed and rose slowly from the table. "Your coffee's ready. You like cream, don't you?"

"The contract, Genny."

She sauntered into the front room while I got up and pulled the metal ice trays from the freezer. I tried to keep my eye on her through the doorway as I broke the ice free from the trays and into two tall glasses. I then poured the brewed coffee over the rapidly melting cubes. When I finished, I listened for noises from the other room but heard very few papers being shuffled.

"Are you finding it?" I called.

I suspected the answer to be no based upon her lack of response, but she soon entered the kitchen, scooting her slippers across the linoleum as if they'd fall from her feet if she didn't do so. She embraced several pieces of paper in her arms before dropping them onto the table in front of me.

"It should be among these," she said, reaching for the bottle of Southern Comfort. She poured a generous shot into her glass.

I sifted through the papers and pulled one of the most promising looking documents from the stack. "Who signed this?" I asked. There wasn't a printed name under the illegible signature.

She glanced at the paper then returned to her drink. "Mr. Marrs."

"How do you know? Have you seen his signature before?"

"No, but who else's could it be?"

"Exactly," I said. "Who else's?"

Genny looked at me perplexed. "Why wouldn't it be Eldon Marrs? It was his studio."

"Kip Harmon could've signed it for him. Legal documents usually include a printed name under the person's signature. I can't tell if this handwritten glop belongs to Marrs or Harmon."

"Does it make a difference?"

"Probably not," I said, "because this isn't a contract. It's the most official looking document you have here, but it's only instructions on what to expect for first-time recording artists. Weren't you given a contract?"

"Now that I think about it," she said, "I believe what happened is that I signed one, and Kip said he'd make a copy and get it back to me later."

"But then he never came back with it." I sat back in my chair exasperated.

"I'm in trouble, aren't I?" she asked, nearly in tears.

"There's trouble, but I don't know what kind. Tell me something. Who owns a DeSoto Fireflite?"

She looked away from my eyes as if she tried to think. "Fireflite? Oh, I'm not sure, Dickie. You sure that's not a Dodge? I'm not very good with cars."

"Genny, please, it's important. I think you do know. I think you knew back at the airport when I was talking about it with Portier. I think you know now."

She snapped her fingers. "Cream. You didn't get your cream," she said, rising.

"Then tell me this: Do you know a man named Leon

Adams?"

Genny pulled a glass bottle of whole milk from the refrigerator and sat down again, pushing the cold bottle toward me. "Yeah, sure, I know him. He used to sing in the clubs around here."

"What can you tell me about him?"

"That's all I know," she said, taking a long, shallow sip of her spiked iced chicory.

"I heard he used to have a recording contract."

"Yes, I heard that too," she said, looking away. "Just scuttlebutt, though. I can't imagine it was anything big. I'm not even sure if he's still in town or if he's still alive or what."

She wouldn't let me catch her gaze. "That wasn't very convincing."

Genny shrugged.

"Look at me," I said.

She did so sheepishly. "What?"

"That wasn't very convincing."

"Okay, so I've seen him."

"Yeah, he's living in Labreville," I said. "Why the secrecy?"

Genny swallowed hard and nearly choked. The news of Leon living in a homeless community appeared to bother her, but she shifted in her seat so I couldn't fully see her expression. The side of her face appeared to flush, and she stared blankly at the table for several seconds. She composed herself, however, and shifted back toward me.

"I have something for you." She lifted her finger to change the subject, then rose to walk into the front room and returned with a goldenrod envelope. She opened the envelope, bound by a thick ribbon, and pulled out several loose-leaf papers.

I moved her so-called contract papers out of the way.

"Gwen stopped by the club while I was there," she said.

"That can't be," I said, baffled. "I was just with her in Mid-

City, talking about Julie's murder."

"Well, then, she must've hightailed straight to the club after talking with you, Dickie, because I was rehearsing with the boys when she walked in. She was a frazzled mess, I have to say."

"What did she want?"

"Not much of anything. Apparently, she writes song lyrics. She thought I'd be interested."

"Did she want you to put a melody to them?"

"I have no idea. I looked at them, but they're not me. They would've been a stretch. Too folksy. A cross between Lonnie Donegan and Odetta."

I grimaced. "That's quite a cross."

"Take a look for yourself."

I lifted some of the papers and began to read. Many of the lyrics were written on pastel floral paper, some written on bistro napkins, others on college-ruled paper. Genny was right. There was a sense of American folk, blues, jazz, and skiffle with a bit of Donegan and Odetta among the clutter. They included titles such as "Kissed by a Pink Feather," "Our Mother in Yellow," and "White Fawn." I read a few of the lyrics then scooted the stack back toward Genny.

"You know me, Dickie," Genny said. "I'm all for color, but this is a hard sell even for me."

I sighed. "Well, hold onto them for a while. She's in a precarious state right now. I encouraged her to talk to you if she needed to confide in another woman."

"But she didn't talk. She mumbled a few words then shoved this envelope into my belly. She has an odd way of reaching out." Genny reached for a lyric to read from it. "Listen to this: 'Cadence, sang beautifully in tune with a vision of you near the lake, donning a soft yellow bonnet of the sun.' Why would I want to sing something like that onstage?"

I smiled. "I don't know. However, the lyrics would stop mysterious men in brown-checkered suits from making requests onstage."

Genny bellowed a laugh that I hadn't heard in a long time. I was reminded of how much I missed it.

"She's meeting the police again this afternoon," I said.

"Who? Gwen?"

I nodded. "I want to talk to her after their chat. That reminds me: Do you have a piece of scrap paper? I want to write down a few questions I have for her while they're fresh in my mind."

Genny laughed again. "I have plenty of scrap paper. I have recording documents in this pile and song lyrics in the other. Take your pick."

I laughed with her. "Something neutral."

"My pocketbook is on the counter. I'm sure I have plenty of paper in there unless you need something bigger." She got up to grab her purse and scrounged briefly in its side pockets before holding a slim piece of white paper in the air. "Will the back of a grocery receipt do?"

I gave her a doubtful look. "Do you have something bigger? If not, I can wait until I go back next door."

"No, you don't. I'm resourceful, Dickie. I'll find something here. Ah!" She pulled another sheet of paper from her purse, this one letter size, folded into quarters. "This should do it."

She proudly handed me the piece of paper and sat down beside me.

I unfolded the paper and looked at what was on the face of it before I turned it over to write my questions.

"So what more do you want to know from Gwen?" she asked.

"I want to find out what the police asked her and what she told them. I want to see if her story changed from what she told me. Then I'll ask her if she killed Julie Moreno and tried to pin it on Ronni Mohr."

Genny's eyes widened as if she was astonished at what I'd just revealed. "Oh, Dickie, you can't be serious. Why in the world . . .? How could . . .? Oh, that doesn't make sense. You think she could've killed Julie?"

"Why not? What do we know about her except that she picks up the mail at a tan bungalow every day? What does she do with the mail? Does she go through it herself, picking out the pieces that she thinks she can benefit from personally? Gwen could be just another chiseler in this sordid mess."

"Oh, no, I think you have Gwen all wrong," Genny said. "She didn't look at all like someone who could pull off her own racket."

"Okay, then what else do we know about her? That she cries at the drop of a hat? That she can hear the front door open and close and cars come and go outside while she covers her ears with pillows, but she can't hear a brutal murder occurring down the hall?"

Genny sighed. "When you put it like that."

"No doubt the woman has suffered some trauma, but her story doesn't add up," I said.

"Then write away, Dickie." She rose from the table. "You may not have enough paper to write down all the questions you have after all. Do you want any more coffee?"

I didn't answer. I scanned the piece of paper she'd given me, puzzled by the mix of letters and numbers typed in neat rows. "What's this?" I asked.

She peered at the paper over my shoulder. She didn't know.

"It's the paper you handed me from your pocketbook."

She shook her head. "It couldn't have been. I've never put anything like that in it."

I looked at the letters and numbers more closely. "Could be anagrams of something," I said. "Does anything look familiar?"

She plopped down beside me in her chair and sighed. "You know me, Dickie. I'm not very good at deciphering things."

"That's because you don't try, Genny. Think for a second."

Even though she whined a bit and reminded me every ten seconds that she wasn't good at puzzles, she tried to determine whether any of the letters and numbers made sense to her. "No, I'm sorry," she said after a while.

I stood to go.

"You're leaving?"

I showed her the paper. "Do you mind if I take this?"

"Be my guest. It means nothing to me."

"Yes, I've noticed that about a lot of the important papers you have," I said, giving her a disparaging look.

Chapter 15

Sprinkles from a dark, low-lying cloud spat at me as I made my way next door. Bentley was there to greet me, but I warded off his advances with a pat on the back and promises that a tasty morsel would be his after I made an important phone call. I should've waited until evening to make the call—long-distance rates were cheaper then—but I was anxious to learn the answers to my questions.

"Donna, is that you?" I asked through a staticky line. "Can you hear me?"

My granddaughter responded that she could hear me quite clearly.

"Okay, good. You're a little fuzzy on my end. Speak up if you can; that'll help."

"This is a nice surprise, Grandpa," she said. "Do you miss me?"

"I do indeed, sweetheart. I miss your vast array of youthful knowledge."

She giggled. "Why? Do you have another murder that needs to be solved?" she asked jokingly.

I didn't answer.

"Oh, Grandpa," she said, realizing the truth. "You were

supposed to go down there to help that woman with the homeless community. You weren't supposed to find another dead body. Daddy will be furious with you."

"Your father doesn't have to know. Look, I need you to do something for me. Do you have that *Billboard* magazine still with you—the one you took on the train?"

"No, but I bought a new one."

"Even better," I said. "I'd like you to look for something, if you don't mind."

"I don't, but you can buy your own copy just as easily at the dime store, Grandpa."

"Thank you, but you'll forgive me if I refrain from being seen doing so."

She laughed as she set down the receiver. Moments later, she was back on the phone, apparently with the flimsy magazine in hand. I could hear the cheap, newspaper-like pages being flipped between her fingers. "What do you want to know?"

"Does it contain any news?"

She hesitated. "News? *Billboard* is hardly a *U. S. News & World Report*, Grandpa."

"Yes, I figured that, but I was hoping it contained articles of interest to young people."

"Such as?"

"Scandals in the music industry, details of upcoming legislation in the entertainment business, statistical trends, that sort of thing."

"Seriously?"

"Then how about the murder of disc jockeys around the country?"

Silence.

"Apparently not," I replied, answering my own question. "Then turn to the top songs for the week."

"That I can do," she said. The pages ruffled again between her fingers. "Any song in particular?"

"You don't happen to see one by my friend, Genevieve Duval, do you?"

She emitted a "hmm" while she looked. "No, nothing."

"Any newcomers on the list? Any song or artist you don't recognize?"

"No, Grandpa, I'm pretty much in tune to what's played on the radio," she said convincingly. "I'm sure I've heard everyone and everyth—Oh, wait. Here's one I don't know. It's number thirty-six and on the list for the first time."

"What is it?"

"'Sand Tan Catamaran.'"

"Sand tan?"

"It's a color, Grandpa," she replied condescendingly. "The color of sand."

"Who sings it?"

"A group I've never heard before—Dale Devoe and the Dares."

Thoughts raced of Leon's friend Miss Cora had mentioned when I met with her. I couldn't remember the name exactly, but Devoe sounded very familiar.

"Grandpa?" a sweet voice asked on the other end of the line.

"Oh, I'm sorry, dear. Thanks so much, but I must go now. The information was exactly what I needed. Give my regards to your folks. Love you much. Talk to you later. Bye bye."

When I ended the call, I was certain my granddaughter was frustrated with me, given her innate curiosity (inherited from yours truly) about my sudden interest in the top *Billboard* hits. My abruptness couldn't be helped. It was imperative that I didn't divulge anything more to her than was necessary. The less said to anyone, the better.

Besides, I had work to do. The first order of business was to call the garage where Portier stored his automobile. I rang, and the dutiful but unimpressive Rusty answered immediately.

"Is Jeffrey not back yet?" I asked impertinently.

"No, sir. Should be on his way, though." Rusty paused a second before asking, "Anything I can help you with?"

"No," I replied, not wishing to talk to him. On second thought, I asked if Mr. Portier had taken his car.

"Oh, yes, sir. He said he had to go out, something about taxes. He was cursing mostly, but I did happen to catch the word 'taxes.'"

"Thank you. Just so you know, I may want the car brought around when he returns."

"Yes, sir, but it better be sooner than later, sir. That storm's a-comin', you know. It's a fast one. You shouldn't be caught out in it."

"I'll take that into consideration, but I've driven through storms before."

Rusty let out a long, drawn-out moan. "Ooh, gads, not in N'Orleans, you haven't," he said in a scolding tone. "We're below sea level here, sir. No place for water to go. Roads can turn into rivers in no time if you're not careful."

"It's not supposed to arrive this afternoon, is it?"

"No, sir. In a day or two."

"Well, then, there you go." Portier's Studebaker was faster than a Conestoga wagon. I was sure I could get to Labreville and back before the storm hit the city . . . in a day or two.

I ended the phone conversation and waited for Portier's return, reviewing the mysterious piece of paper Genny found in her purse. If the letters and numbers were anagrams, deciphering the entries would take time but wouldn't be impossible. I sat under the cabana fan at the kitchen table with the puzzle, a pad of blank paper, and a pencil.

The phone rang from the parlor. I answered it, and an authoritative voice on the other end of the line said, "Detective Robicheaux here. Is this Reverend Fountain?"

"Speaking."

"I've just had the opportunity to speak with a Gwen Handerson," he said. "I believe you're acquainted with her. I've interviewed Miss Handerson regarding the death of Julie Moreno. I suppose I shouldn't have been surprised that your name came up during the course of my conversation with her. I wonder if I might have a word with you, Reverend."

"Certainly."

"In my office."

"I can be there in fifteen to twenty minutes," I said.

The detective didn't thank me. He hung up abruptly, and I realized his invitation wasn't a social one. I strode out the door and down the street toward the French Quarter, Marigny Triangle District office of the New Orleans Police Department, a short but sticky walk. The light showers had stopped, but low-hanging clouds remained, trapping heat and humidity in the atmosphere, causing my undershirt to cling unmercifully to my back. Nervous anticipation made my heart thump faster, and perspiration rolled down the side of my face.

Inside the police building, I noted the difference in temperature. The block walls kept the air cool, though a stale dampness lingered as I crossed the linoleum floor. The officer at the front counter was expecting me. He opened the door to a long, sterile hallway built from more blocks painted an off-white, presenting a dingy and uninviting welcome.

Detective Robicheaux extended his hand as he greeted me but appeared to be no more welcoming than the hallway. He spoke in one-syllable words meant to be efficient rather than hospitable.

I offered no additional niceties. They would've fallen on deaf ears or worse yet, they would've antagonized him more than what his body language exhibited. I sat in a chair across from his desk, craning my neck around a stack of folders from unsolved cases that obstructed my view of him.

The detective was a solid, handsome man in his early forties. Tips of graying hair on his temples and just above his ears gave him the distinguished, credible look of a man wiser than his years. He had dark, penetrating eyes under naturally manicured brows, giving him an air of refinement atypical of his peers. He bit the corner of his lower lip as he concentrated, a tic I presumed he perfected while conducting interrogations to let those being interviewed know that he didn't care about anything but facts and the truth. The detective released a plume of frustration over the mess on his desk and looked for a specific folder related to our conversation. He took it in hand, opened it, and scanned the information as if to gather his thoughts.

"Busy day?" I asked to break the ice.

Detective Robicheaux looked up as if I'd just asked if he knew what he was doing. "Busy summer," he replied. "The heat does little to quell angry tempers in the city." He waved his left hand over the piles on his desk. "Case in point." He then looked at me critically and said, "And I'm beginning to suspect this murder of Julie Moreno isn't anything more than just that—a summer squabble among roommates that got out of hand."

"Do you think so, Detective?"

"Why not? I've talked to Gwen Handerson and Cynthia Mohr. They both said there was a heated argument between the deceased and Veronica Mohr about having to move again after they've moved so many times before. Veronica Mohr has been known to steal items of value from Miss Moreno. Did you know that?"

"No, Detective, that's news to me."

"Miss Moreno confronted Veronica, and Miss Moreno was murdered while Ronni, as she's called, took off to points unknown. We have bulletins posted throughout the Gulf Coast and up the Mississippi Valley for her whereabouts."

"Well," I said, not sure I should add anything to the mix, "it appears you have the case well in hand."

"Not quite."

"How's that?"

"Miss Handerson mentioned your name in the course of our interview."

I smiled congenially. "She needed consoling."

"But when I heard your name, I had to ask myself how you got involved in the first place."

"I'll not beat around the bush, Detective. I'll be quite honest with you."

"That would be refreshing," Robicheaux said. "If I remember from our last encounter, being forthcoming isn't one of your strong suits."

"I've learned my lesson, thanks to you," I said humbly, although I was doing my best to think of a way not to tell him everything—especially any part about Genny's involvement with Ronni Mohr. "I met Miss Handerson in a roundabout way through her roommate Cindy."

Robicheaux waited for more explanation. When I sat silently without elaboration, he said, "I gathered that, Reverend. It's the information surrounding the roundabout that I want to know."

"You do know of Veronica Mohr's notorious background, I assume. I learned that she was back in town from St. Louis. I wanted to talk with her to see if she had any connection to friends I have here in the city. I met with Ronni's sister, Cindy, who gave me the slip, so I was able to get an address from a waitress who led me to Gwen Handerson so that I could talk with Ronni Mohr. There you go."

Detective Robicheaux sat back in his chair, placed his hands together at the fingertips, and smiled. "You're a piece of work, Reverend. You do realize you are, don't you? You just told me nothing about everything and then topped it off with: 'There you go.'"

"Yes, sir, it's a Hoosier trait I've been able to perfect over the years."

He leaned forward. "So tell me why you were so interested that Veronica Mohr was back in town."

"I'd rather not involve the person," I said.

"That's not an option at this point."

He was right. I couldn't keep Genny's name out of the investigation if I wanted to be helpful and credible. Besides, what I knew so far of Genny's predicament sounded as if it was something for the police anyway, whether I knew enough about the situation to make that determination or not. "It involves Genevieve Duval," I said.

"The singer?"

"Yes, and anything you can do to assist her would be helpful."

I told Detective Robicheaux the complete story of Genevieve's recording contract and her song, "Honey, Be By Me."

Robicheaux listened attentively before picking up a pen to jot a couple of notes. He also mentioned that he was familiar with the song and with Marrs's studio. "But I'm having trouble connecting Miss Duval's story with the murder, Reverend," he added candidly.

"They may not be," I said. "I don't know, but it's how we became acquainted with Gwen Handerson and the murder of Julie Moreno."

Robicheaux sat back in his chair again, more relaxed than

before. It was apparent he was less interested in what I had to say. "In any of your discussions with Miss Handerson, did she ever mention Miss Moreno's next of kin?"

"I believe she said Julie had a brother. Are you having trouble locating him?"

"I'm having trouble locating anyone. Miss Duval's group of acquaintances are an elusive bunch. That's why I'd recommend you not meet anymore with Gwen Handerson, Cynthia Mohr, or anyone connected with this murder. I'd steer clear of them at all costs."

"That may be rather difficult, Detective," I said not wanting to relinquish my assistance to Genny just yet. "Miss Genny is my friend. I believe she's in trouble. I don't know just how yet, but I believe something is terribly wrong with her involvement with Marrs Recording. I can't leave her to fend for herself."

"Perhaps I should speak with Miss Genevieve," he said, setting his pen aside.

"You could, Detective, but I doubt that you'll find her to be very informative."

"Why is that?" he asked.

I shrugged and replied honestly, "Because I haven't."

~

Portier returned to his cottage shortly after I arrived back. His mood was somber at best. Discussions with the Internal Revenue Service about his unpaid tax bill were unsuccessful. As he walked through the door, he eyed Bentley and me as if we were planning to bilk him too. He didn't say much about the experience, just enough for me to realize I shouldn't ask further.

"We should have an early dinner," he said as a diversion. "I suggest we go out. We'll not have a chance to do so for a day or two."

I agreed—storm or no storm. My friend rarely had to talk me into going out to eat in New Orleans.

We chose Leroux because it was close. The weather was cloudy but still hot and sticky. In fact, the closer the storm came to the northern Gulf Coast, the more humid the air seemed. We had a fine meal and spoke infrequently, which gave me the opportunity to enjoy my favorite pastime—watching other people. I saw no one who interested me, but watching them gave me time to reflect on the events of the past couple of days.

"Two St-Rémys, please," Portier announced to the waiter while I was in one of my trances. "You don't mind, do you, Fountain?"

"No," I said, pleased. "I can't think of anything I'd like better."

When the brandies arrived at the table, Portier toasted, sipped, and asked before his snifter touched the table, "What's on your mind, Fountain? You've been deep in thought this evening."

"Not at all," I replied. "Just looking about the dining room and wishing my life was as easygoing as the patrons in this restaurant appear to be."

Portier looked around the room. "Don't fool yourself. There're more sinister secrets and plots being discussed at these tables than you can imagine."

I laughed. Even for Portier, his cynicism was too comical to ignore.

"Don't laugh when I'm being serious," he said. "Just tell me what's on your mind. Living with your granddaughter, perhaps?"

"No, she's a delight."

"Miss Cora?"

"No, she's a delight."

"Genevieve Duval and her band of nibblers?"

Delight wasn't a word that came to mind. "No," I replied, "but I've almost decided I need to step away from Genny's situation."

Portier picked up his snifter again and placed it to his lips. I don't think he took a sip because he was able to talk with it to his mouth. "Did something happen while I was bantering with the IRS agent?"

"Detective Robicheaux called, and I went to the police station to talk with him. I'm not sure he sees a connection between the death of Julie Moreno and Genny's problems. I told him I was unwilling to let her situation go, but perhaps he's right. Perhaps I'm reading too much into the whole set of events, and I should let Genny fight her own battles. She's a grown woman. If she wants to play with the big boys, she needs to stand up on her own."

Portier swirled his brandy within his glass as he looked at me critically. "Do you believe that?"

"I don't know what to believe, Portier. That's the trouble."

"Normally, I'd agree with you," he said candidly, "but from what I know based upon what you've told me, Genevieve is in new territory. Oh, she'll tell you she knows this town like the back of her hand, and she knows the cast of characters as well as her own siblings, but she's naïve, Fountain. She looks only at the good in people and refuses to acknowledge that some people don't care about her or her good nature."

"What's your point?" I asked, hoping to be spared a long dissertation.

"I'm afraid Genny is involved in a crime as deadly as if someone held her at gunpoint."

I took a deep breath and paused to think about my friend's comment. "I've been sensing that too," I said honestly, "but apparently Detective Robicheaux feels differently."

"That's because he doesn't have all of the facts to make an informed decision. Please don't be hasty about giving up on Genevieve. Far be it from me to encourage pursuing something like this, but it isn't in your nature to quit on someone in need, and I implore you not to do so just yet."

I did more than sip my St-Rémy. I gulped it. "That's what I told Detective Robicheaux this afternoon."

"Good." Portier sat back in his chair. "I hope he respected your decision. This murder you've come upon adds a disturbing complexity to Genevieve's situation. What do you know about Julie Moreno?"

"Very little. Only what I've learned from Gwen Handerson."

"Did Cindy escape with her sister, Ronni, after the murder?"

"No, I believe she's still in town. Detective Robicheaux said he talked with Cindy. He couldn't have done that if she left town."

"What does Cindy say about her sister?"

"If she knows where Ronni is, she isn't talking."

"As if you expected a different answer," Portier reminded me.

"A more interesting piece of information is that Julie Moreno's body has yet to be released because a family member has yet to claim the body," I said.

"That is interesting. Yes, they usually like a family member to make a positive identification. You're right. Nothing will happen for a couple of days with Two in the air."

"Too?"

"Two."

"You mean *also*?"

"I mean Two, Fountain. Tropical Storm Two. That's what they've named it."

I shook the cobwebs out of my head to let my friend know that he should've been more specific from the beginning.

"I didn't think an explanation was necessary," he said. "I thought you kept up on the news and weather."

"I do, but I didn't realize the storm had been named. In that case, I'm going to spend tomorrow morning at Labreville to help with preparations."

"Those people are self-sufficient," he said as if there was no need to go.

"That may be true, and I may be exaggerating the intensity of Two, but I'm well aware that a strong tropical storm is as dangerous as a weak hurricane. I'd rather not leave Labreville to self-sufficiency."

"Then be sure to hurry home afterward," he said, finishing the bronzy liqueur from his snifter. "I fear there's a bigger storm brewing in the cottage next door."

Chapter 16

"What did you mean by that" I asked Portier the next morning. "I mean, by a stronger storm brewing next door?"

"I thought it was obvious," he said. "I've told you before. Genevieve is potentially in a lot of trouble. She's in a business where people have to pay to play."

"So? If she has to pay to have her record played, how is that different from a company having to pay to market and distribute their products through retail? What's the harm in that?"

"Because the practice is nothing more than a racket to deceive the public into believing a song is more popular than it really is. It makes the artist believe they are more talented than they really are. People are getting unduly rich over artists' vanity and misconceptions, and the public is being duped into buying things they wouldn't ordinarily touch. It's dishonest. Paying disc jockeys and radio stations to make an artist a star is a dishonest kickback."

I didn't say anything because I didn't know how to respond. I didn't refute Portier's claims. He was inclined to know more about the industry than I was.

"That's the real problem," Portier continued, noticing my reticence. "The public doesn't realize they're being duped any more than you or Genevieve realize it—or Detective Robicheaux, for that matter. Until law enforcement and the public see white-collar crime as bad as robbing Mom and Pop with a handgun, such crimes will never be punished and stopped. People will lose everything from their dignity to their life savings because of our inability to grasp who the victims are and why they became victims."

I thought of Leon Adams in Labreville. "Is that what you think could happen to Genny: she'll lose everything?"

"What else am I to think if Genevieve won't produce a contract for you to review?"

For once, I understood what Portier was saying without having to ponder it first.

~

First things first, however. Tropical Storm Two was rapidly approaching. I had to get to Labreville to help Miss Cora and the community. I promised Portier I'd take good care of the Golden Hawk if he'd let me borrow it for a couple of hours. I also promised to have Jeffrey or Rusty wipe it down thoroughly if it got smudged. He told me he wasn't that shallow about his automobile, but I knew that wasn't the case.

Occasional gusts blew under looming scud clouds as I walked to the garage in the Quarter. Few tourists lingered on the streets. Proprietors boarded their windows with sheets of plywood or shut their shutters if they had any. There was no time for greetings or idle chitchat. Residents and shopkeepers concentrated on the task at hand to protect their property.

I entered the garage where Portier stored his Studebaker to the familiar greasy stench of oil and gasoline. I was relieved to see Jeffrey instead of Rusty at his workbench, cleaning tools with a soiled rag. His back was to me as I entered, but he turned quickly upon hearing my footsteps across the cement floor.

After a brief greeting and asking about his trip to Jackson, I asked, "Have you heard if the tropical storm has strengthened?"

Jeffrey shrugged. "Still comin' at a fast clip, that's all I know. It's more contained than most storms. It doesn't have the usual feeder bands around it."

"What will that mean for us?"

"Who can tell, but I suspect it means it could have a bigger punch when it hits, just won't be as large. Doesn't sound like it'll be a hurricane, though." Jeffrey turned back to his cleaning as if, either way, the storm was going to have little effect on him. "I got my cot right over there to spend the night. This old cement block garage won't budge an inch."

I stood silently behind him, watching him work. It must have unnerved him slightly as he turned to me and asked if he could be of assistance.

"I'd like the Hawk in a bit," I said. "I'm going to help Miss Cora at the community."

He smiled as if that was a nice thing for me to do, but that he didn't care very much.

"More importantly, I want to know who owns that DeSoto Fireflite you were working on the other day."

Jeffrey's smile disappeared. He continued cleaning the same tool over and over. After several seconds, he set the tool down, wiped his hands on the rag and sat on an old stool by the bench. Then he reached for a pack of Kools tucked in the peg of his shirt before assessing my expression. I was sure he was trying to discern how angry I was. "Kip Harmon," he said calmly, lighting his cigarette and taking a long, hard drag.

"How did he find you?"

"Dunno. I guess he found out I liked working on cars, and I'm a sucker for a shiny chrome grill. You've seen his car. Harmon has a beautiful machine. I reckon he knew I'd take good care of it."

I nodded unconvincingly. "He didn't happen to know you were a sucker through Genny, did he?"

Jeffrey took another drag. "Dunno, may have." He shifted to his other thigh on the stool.

"I assume he has more than one car you work on."

"He's a wealthy man."

"And I assume he pays timely on what he owes."

"It's good money, Reverend."

"For whom?" I asked brazenly.

Jeffrey snuffed out his cigarette on the floor and kicked it away. "For Genny. Is that what you want to know?"

"I want to know how much."

"How much what?" he asked indignantly. "How much he pays me?"

"How much she owes him. I assume he doesn't pay *you* a dime."

"What's this about, Reverend? What business is it of yours how much I get from Harmon or if it's nothing at all," he replied. Jeffrey looked at me for several seconds before adding, "Besides, I don't know how much it is, and even if I knew, I doubt Genny would like for me to tell you. I just do the work."

"And as long as you do the work, she stays safe, is that it?"

Jeffrey glared at me.

"Why you?" I asked.

"Why not me? Who else has a skill that can pay her debt? I'm her friend, Rev. I'm the only friend she has that doesn't run away at the sign of trouble or judge her for what she's done. You think any of her lowlife friends are around to help her? Do you think Mr. Charles would help without giving her a stern lecture first?"

I realized he was right. Genny was surrounded by good-timing friends. Portier called them magnets attracted to each other. They were in no position to help her financially even if they wanted to do so. Jeffrey was also right about Portier. He would help her instantly upon request but not before a good scolding.

"She needs money to pay Mr. Kip," Jeffrey added sternly. "Some marketing agent he's turned out to be. The only thing he promotes is himself. Is that what you want to know?"

I didn't say yes, and I didn't want to know more. I asked for the keys to the Hawk, took them without saying a word, then opened the car door and sat behind the wheel.

Jeffrey followed me to the car. "She needs my help, Reverend," he said, peering through the driver's side window at me. "Don't tell her I talked to you, and don't tell her she shouldn't use me. I'm going to help her whether you like it or not."

I gritted my teeth to prevent saying something I'd regret. It wasn't his helping Genny that angered me. It was a combination of Kip Harmon taking advantage of two vulnerable individuals and Jeffrey putting me in my place that irked me. I detested both equally.

~

I drove to an area near St. Roch where the Labreville community had an isolated piece of ground under a canopy of live oak trees covered in Spanish moss. Rain began to fall consistently, and small gusts of wind blew leaves and limbs from the trees in front of my steps. Puddles of murky rainwater soon saturated the ground and those out walking trampled the footpaths into mud.

Labreville was occupied mostly by men who had been banned from local shelters for breaking house rules, including the abuse of drugs or alcohol, fighting, and curfew violations. The not-for-profit organization operated by Cora accepted donations to provide them tents, food, water, and medical supplies despite what the men had done.

Several residents had established a makeshift foundation for an elderly veteran unable to secure his tent on his own. It consisted of four cornerstones and a center block covered by a large piece of plywood, supplied by Labreville, to set his tent above the floodwaters from the storm's deluge. Other men simply laid an extra layer of tarp upon the ground before re-setting their tent upon it.

That's what Leon Adams was doing to his own camp when I saw him. His leg turned inward from an old injury, slowing his progress and making the laying of the tarp more difficult. I didn't ask Leon if he needed help. I started working without his permission, and he let me work, looking periodically out of the corner of his eye as if I had an ulterior motive for being there. I had no motive except to be an extra set of hands, but I noticed his skepticism and kept the observation in the back of my mind.

"Are these your things?" I asked, pointing to two duffle bags on the ground.

He nodded.

I picked one of the bags off the ground to find a place to shelter it from the rain, but Leon said to let it be.

"One p-place is as wet as another," he said.

I let go of the bag and looked at him, hoping he'd look back.

He didn't.

"What happened to your face?" I could see dark splotches on his cheekbone and around his eyes. Dried blood coagulated on the corner of his lip.

He shook his head. "Nothin' you'd understand, Reverend."

"I understand plenty. I know a beating when I see it."

For the first time, Leon stood erect and faced me. I could see the damage inflicted on his face more clearly.

"Just a rumble with some of the b-boys," he explained, barely able to get out the sentence.

I didn't believe him, and I knew Leon well enough from the past that his stuttering got worse when he was tired, bashful, or lying. "Looks like more than fists hit your face."

Leon ignored me and returned to the tarp.

"I need you to look at something," I said.

I pulled out the sheet of paper Genny had found in her purse, the paper with letters and numbers that appeared to be anagrams. Rain pelted the surface, dimpling the paper as I held it out to him. He stood slowly and took the paper. His eyes seemed to widen with interest, but he handed it back to me almost immediately.

"Mean anything to you?"

He shook his head.

"Recognize any of the numbers or letters?"

"Looks like gobbledy-gook to me."

"Yes, I suppose that's what's it's supposed to look like. You handed it back to me quick-like. Why's that?"

Leon smirked. "Well, if you didn't happen to notice, Reverend, it's rainin' cats and dogs right now. I kinda got other things on my mind than that odd little piece of paper of yours."

He spoke without stuttering that time. Sarcasm was an apparent cure for him.

I folded the paper and put it back into my pocket. "It could help a friend, Leon, if you could tell me something about it. She's in trouble, like what you were into once."

Leon stuttered again. "No trouble here. Got all I need and all I want."

"But I may be able to help you too."

Leon glared at me with his bloodshot eyeball. "Not sure what fantasy world you live in, Reverend, but this p-place here at Labreville ain't no Coney Island. I'm b-beyond help, and I don't want it. I feel bad for your friend, Reverend, but I'd just as soon be left alone. Now, I gotta get b-busy here before my ass gets any wetter than it already is."

I stepped back and noticed Leon glancing off to the side. I followed his gaze and saw the silhouette of a small-framed woman in a yellow raincoat and galoshes passing out rations. To my surprise, Leon pointed in a different direction.

"Better help ol' Jimmy over there," he said.

Leon took off toward the men I'd seen setting plywood for the elderly man earlier.

I couldn't see the woman's face underneath her floppy rainhat, but I suspected it was Miss Cora. I wondered why Leon wanted to avoid her, but if he'd been fighting, I'm sure it was to avoid being reprimanded and possibly expelled from the community.

I splashed my way across the common ground to where the woman spoke personably to those accepting what she had to offer. Three other women stood beside her, divvying out nonperishable food and personal toiletry items.

Miss Cora greeted me warmly and thanked me for coming to help.

"No problem," I said. "I was over there, helping Leon set up an extra tarp under his tent."

We both looked to get a glimpse of Leon, but he wasn't near

his site. I looked to where the men were helping old Jimmy, but he wasn't there, either.

"He must've gone off to get more of the supplies that arrived," she remarked.

"I think he's avoiding us," I said. "Have you had any trouble with any of the men lately? I heard there was a small fight among them recently."

Miss Cora looked at me with a concerned expression. "Not at all, Reverend. There's been no fights. In fact, the men have come together quite nicely with this storm coming. It's been all hands on deck. Why? Where have you heard this?"

"Nothing. Never mind. I must've misunderstood. I was led to believe there was an incident on the grounds, but you'd know for sure if that were the case. You keep up on such things very closely."

"Then what do you believe happened?"

"Something off-site. Nothing that affects Labreville."

"I see," she said unconvinced. "Who was involved, may I ask?"

I declined to answer. I thanked her instead and requested she stay safe during the storm. She responded likewise but gave me a critical expression as I turned to leave.

A small portion of Leon's tent had collapsed from the work he'd put into it. There wasn't much I could do, but I decided I could move his exposed duffle bags into the tent's partially erect opening to move them out of the elements. The first bag was quite heavy with clothes and personal effects. The second bag was lighter. I suspected it hadn't reached capacity and could fit some of the loose items strewn about his site.

I opened the bag to put a metal canteen inside when I noticed a note tucked along one side. There was something familiar about the notepaper. I pulled the note from his bag and glanced at what had been written. Four words were typed neatly in the middle: *Ronni Mohr is alive!* The blue ink spread immediately upon being hit by the raindrops and leaked onto my fingers.

"What are you doing?" a voice admonished me from behind.

I twitched from being startled and turned around quickly.

Miss Cora loomed over my shoulders, rainwater dripping from the rim of her hat. Her expression indicated she wasn't pleased to find me looking through Leon's personal items. "I don't know what you're looking for or hoping to find, Reverend, but we have strict codes of behavior at Labreville, and they include respecting the privacy of other people's belongings no matter how meager they may be."

I stood and excused myself. "I understand," I said. "I was only trying to protect his items left loosely on the ground."

"Then I suggest you put that piece of paper back into his bag."

I handed the note out to her, but she didn't take it.

"I recognized the notepaper," I said.

"That still gives you no right."

"Yes, but I'm sure you'll forgive me."

"You're assuming something highly out of line with my character, Reverend," she said without wavering.

"I'm sure that's true," I responded, "but you told me yesterday on the front porch of your home that you were afraid you'd said something to me that would put me or someone I know in great danger. Do you remember that?"

I could tell by her expression that she did even though she made no admission.

"Then consider this note as part of your redemption," I said sternly. "You may have saved one or more lives by allowing me to read it."

~

I helped a few more men batten down their tents and secure their possessions before walking toward Portier's car to leave. Before reaching the edge of the community, I spotted Leon Adams under a water oak with three other men.

He saw me too.

I gestured for him to meet me at the corner of the street out of Miss Cora's eyesight. From there, I recommended a late breakfast. I figured Leon could use a good meal, and he'd be more likely to talk away from Labreville.

We found a small café in the Bywater still serving breakfast. A handwritten sign, poorly printed with misspellings, indicated the restaurant would close at three and be closed for the duration of the storm.

"Better eat while we can," I said halfheartedly in an attempt to break the ice with Leon, who'd become tight-lipped since our last encounter.

"Will you be okay during the storm?" I asked.

He shrugged a shoulder. "I've done it before."

"Each storm is different, though. You have enough food? You okay medically?"

"Yeah, I get checked up. Docs from Charity Hospital come 'round. Miss Cora sees that we get what we need. She takes us to that free clinic in B-Broadmoor when we need it."

I nodded my satisfaction but didn't say anything.

Leon appeared uncomfortable by the silence. "I don't know nothin' about that paper, Reverend," he said, stuttering as hot coffees were place in front of us. "I don't know what those numbers and letters mean if that's what you want to talk about."

"It isn't," I said. "Not about that piece of paper, anyway."

He looked up from adding several teaspoons of sugar into the black sludge in his cup, "Well, you didn't drag me this way to talk about my health," he said candidly as he stirred.

"No, I didn't, you're right. How do you know Ronni Mohr?" I asked.

His expression revealed that I'd caught him off guard. He sipped his coffee, but I suspected it was to give him time to think of a plausible answer.

"If you're considering a cockamamie story about how you don't know her, there's proof in one of your duffle bags that you do," I said. "And if you want to change the subject by scolding me for reading your private correspondence, consider it done, and consider this as my apology. Now please answer the question."

He sighed. "I knew her months ago, b-before she disappeared and went back to St. Louis."

"You mean you knew her before she got mixed up with those individuals who were sent to prison for their loan rackets?"

"Not before, during."

"Are they the ones who ruined you financially?"

"Yeah." The muscles around his lips tightened. "And Ronni was the one who set it up, she sure did."

He must have noticed my look of surprise.

"What?" he asked, grinning. "You don't think a dame can be a chiseler too, Reverend?"

"I'm not naïve. I know full well that someone like Ronni can be a chiseler. Somebody else knew it too, I suspect, someone who knew you might be interested in knowing that she wasn't dead and was back in New Orleans. Who gave you the note?"

Leon shook his head and stirred his coffee some more. "Never seen him before. Some man all decked out like Bugsy Siegel drove up and parked along the street outside of Labreville and asked for me. He handed me the note and was off.

That was it."

"Was he wearing a brown-checkered suit?"

"He coulda been wearin' a clown outfit for all I cared. Brown, blue, hell, I didn't pay attention. Bugsy Siegel is the only description that comes to mind."

"What was he driving?" I asked. "Did you notice his car?"

"Yeah, it was a nice one."

"A Roadmaster?"

Leon looked suddenly perturbed. "Yeah, it was a B-Buick. Hey, if you know the guy already then why b-bug me with all the questions?"

"Because I'm thinking."

"How about thinkin' over somethin' to eat?" He grabbed a laminated menu from a metal stand at the end of the table and motioned for our waitress to come to the table.

She didn't act like she was interested in taking our order, but the more we ordered, the more engaged she became. "Not sure when it'll come out," she said. "Short staffed in the back."

I ignored the excuse and looked at Leon when she left. "Tell me the truth this time about your face."

Leon rubbed his fingers over the bruise around his eye as if he'd forgotten it was there.

"And I noticed there wasn't a penknife in your belongings for you to whittle."

"I lost it."

"Tell me how you lost it," I said. "The truth."

Leon cursed at me without stammering and told me it was none of my business.

"Did you go looking for Ronni?"

I could tell by the way he hesitated and rubbed the corner of his mouth that I was on point. "How did you know where to look?" I asked.

"I just knew."

"What happened?"

He shook his head as if irritated at my questions but had resigned himself to answering. "I went to her place just to scare her. I wanted to let her know I hadn't forgotten how I was cheated and how she ruined my life, getting me a so-called recording contract."

"Through a man named Kip Harmon?" When Leon nodded, I asked, "And Marrs Recording?"

"Yeah, except when I got to where Ronni lived, some thugs hanging around outside attacked me like they'd been watching the place."

"Did you see who they were?"

"Naw, it was dark. They roughed me up and left me on the sidewalk. That's how I lost my knife."

"When was this?"

Leon looked away.

I cleared my throat.

He turned back, eyes narrowed. "You're not going to give up, are you?"

I shook my head. "If my friend's in danger, I want to know about it."

He sighed, and then said quietly, "That night."

I raised my eyebrows to indicate that I needed more information.

"The night that woman was killed."

I sat back and shook my head. If I was prone to cursing, I was sure more than *fiddlesticks* or *pshaw* would have come out of my mouth.

Leon saw my exasperation and said, "What? You don't believe me?"

"No, that's the trouble. I do believe you, and I believe you could also be knee-deep in mud because of it too. What I don't believe is that you expected to scare people associated with Kip Harmon with a penknife you used to whittle crosses. You mustn't have wanted to scare them very badly, or you went there with an entirely different purpose in mind."

I tried to ask him about his contract with Marrs Recording, but like Genny, he was vague on details and didn't have a copy. I asked about his relationship with Dale Devoe, the artist on the *Billboard* charts, but he said Devoe was of no concern and none of my business. I asked if there was anything more that he could tell me. Leon blurted an expletive and said he was keeping his mouth shut.

"Well, then, this is going to be awkward," I said. "You're done talking, and I don't like this place's coffee. To top it off, the waitress said it'd be a while on the food. So I guess we can sit here in silence and wonder what Detective Robicheaux of the NOPD is going to think of your visit to the Mohr house on the night of Julie Moreno's murder because, quite frankly, Leon, I believe your story has more holes than a sidewalk in the Quarter."

He set his jaw and said nothing.

Chapter 17

My meal with Leon was a quiet affair except for a weathered, old man with a cornet who played a soft rendition of "How High the Moon" near our table. I was glad for the man's diversion. Leon, however, couldn't have cared less. He concentrated more on sopping up the roux from his étouffée with a crusty piece of bread that he grabbed off my plate. When he belched, following his last scoop of étouffée, I didn't waste any time paying the tab and walking out. I figured Leon was smart enough to follow if he wanted a ride back to Labreville.

He did, but the ride wasn't any more informative. Leon stuck with the version of his story he'd told at lunch, and I stuck with my opinion that his story was probable but seasoned with malarkey.

When he stepped out of the car, however, he peeked his head through the passenger window and asked, "What does Miss Cora think?"

I shook my head and told him not to worry about Miss Cora. "She believes in you. That's all that matters."

Rain dripped down the side of his face. He looked at me, hoping for one last chance to convince me of his story.

"I have to get going, Leon."

I drove straight to Portier's cottage. Bentley met me at the door, panting and wagging his tail as if he could exert no more in the heat and rain. Portier sat in his chair, reading *Band of Angels* by Robert Penn Warren. He, too, must've felt fatigue. The pages didn't turn very fast, and he seemed to yawn between paragraphs.

"I don't suppose you feel like going somewhere," I said as I sat nearby.

"With my terrible disposition?" he asked.

"Yes, exactly."

"Must be someplace important for you to want to go out. What happened?"

"Nothing. I want to prevent something from happening. I think it's time I meet the owner of Marrs Recording and find out what kind of an operation he's running."

"Eldon Marrs isn't going to talk to you. You're a nobody."

"That may be true, but you're not." Before he could object, I added, "You're very influential in business and accounting matters in this town, Portier. Don't be modest. You've had a successful career, and I know for a fact that Detective Robicheaux thinks very highly of your forensic accounting skills."

"He's involved, is he?"

"Only on the murder side of this sordid affair. He won't touch Genny's predicament. That's why I'm appealing to you. Will you go with me?"

I was right about the book. Portier closed it without placing a bookmark between the pages. That could only mean he didn't plan to open it again. He sighed but agreed to go with me.

"On one condition," he said sternly.

"Anything."

"I do most of the talking. I'll not have you squawking about insignificant matters that won't get us the information you need. You have some of the facts, Fountain, but not enough facts to make a meaningful conversation. We'll want to ask pointed questions but not in a way that closes the door on future conversations. Do you understand?"

"I hear you loud and clear."

"I didn't ask if you heard me. I asked if you understood me. There's a difference. A puppy can hear, but that doesn't stop him from chewing his master's shoes."

His analogy annoyed me, but if I wanted my friend's assistance, I had to acknowledge that I understood. "And I promise not to chew on Eldon Marrs's shoes," I said.

~

Portier and I walked the dozen or so blocks to Marrs Recording Studio. We decided we'd be just as wet and would get there just as quickly if we walked straight from the cottage than if we went to the garage, retrieved the Studebaker, drove to the studio, and tried to find a place to park.

"Of all days you choose to visit him," Portier said as we splashed through rainwater that flowed from the sides of buildings across the sidewalk. "Be careful where you walk."

I was doing my best to do that. Water filled to the brim camouflaged crevices in the sidewalk. We could easily stumble unbeknownst into the depths of what I considered to be caverns. I was also careful not to bend my umbrella downward. The deluge of rainwater dripped unmercifully upon the front of my pants' legs when I did so.

My leather wingtips were completely drenched by the time

we reached Marrs's studio. There weren't many cars outside the building and even fewer people inside.

No one sat at the lobby reception, so we walked down the hall until we came to the first sign of life. A secretary stuffed papers into a beige filing cabinet and slammed the drawer shut, barely looking up when we approached her desk. Her nameplate identified her as Melinda Price. I called her by name.

"Yes?" she asked, as she pulled a gray plastic cover over a ten-key adding machine.

"Is Mr. Marrs in?"

Miss Price looked at me as if I'd lost my mind. "Yes, but he's busy preparing for the storm, as we all are. Is it important?" She brushed a blond curl from her face, looking at me for the first time. Large hazel eyes over rouge-tinted cheeks glared at me.

I suspected that at any other time she would've smiled professionally and politely and addressed me with a softer demeanor.

"Yes, it's very important," I said. "I'm Reverend Richard Fountain, and this is my colleague Charles Portier. We won't take more than fifteen minutes of Mr. Marrs's time if you'd be kind enough to ring him."

She looked at her watch. "Fifteen minutes?"

I smiled warmheartedly.

"All right," she said with a sigh. "Please have a seat. I'll see what I can do."

Miss Price stepped around her desk and knocked upon an unmarked door. When a masculine voice on the other side acknowledged her, she opened the door slightly and announced our arrival. We couldn't hear the man's response. She closed the door and turned to face us.

"Fifteen minutes," she said, then walked to her desk and placed a typewriter cover over her Royal.

I looked at Portier, who shrugged and gestured the way. "Apparently, we're welcome to see ourselves in," he said loud enough for her to hear.

Miss Price ignored us.

Eldon Marrs—portly, midfifties, with dark, Brylcream-laden hair—stood up behind his desk as we entered. He greeted us more warmly and genuinely than I thought he would. His small black eyes, tucked deeply into his overstuffed cheeks, even seemed to gleam with pleasure. I noticed his light blue seersucker pants immediately, because they seemed to clash with a thin red knit tie worn loosely around the collar of a lavender shirt. Marrs lit a cigarette and pointed to a carved wooden box on his desk.

Portier and I refused.

"Have a seat, gentlemen," he said, releasing a plume of toxic smoke in our direction.

I recognized the Picayune aroma—a rancid, bitter cigarette that many men in southeast Louisiana smoked. I turned my head to let the cloud pass.

I also noticed the remarkable clutter and disorganization of his office. His jacket hung misshapenly on the back of his chair. The surface of his desk was scratched badly and in need of varnishing. His other furniture showed an eclectic array of different woods and styles, none of which reflected what I envisioned a recording executive would have.

I tried to re-situate myself in the chair I'd chosen, but my seat cushion sank below the frame of the chair as if the springs or straps holding the seat's bottom had broken loose. Portier had a similar experience with his chair. He gave me a side glance as if fifteen minutes with Eldon Marrs was going to be ten minutes longer than he wanted to stay.

"What can I do for you?" Marrs asked. "My secretary said it was urgent, but I must tell you that we won't be auditioning for new talent until after the storm passes."

"That's quite all right," I said. "We're here regarding the recording contract of a current talent."

"And who might that be?"

"Genevieve Duval."

Marrs leaned forward in his seat and smiled. "Ah, Genny dear," he said. "Quite a doll, she is. Love her to the moon and back. Is she unhappy? If she's unhappy, please tell her to be patient. Her first recording was just released. Tell her to give it some time. She'll see it'll be a tremendous hit someday."

"Thank you, but we were wondering if you'd be kind enough to pull her contract. She's misplaced it somewhere and would like another copy."

Marrs hesitated as he released another plume. "Yes, sir, we can get that for her."

"Today?"

"No, not today. My secretary is about to leave, if she hasn't already. There's a storm coming, you know."

"I understand, but perhaps you'd know where it's filed."

"Not a clue," he said unabashedly. "I expect her to handle the filing of contracts so that I don't have to. Who are you anyway?"

"My apologies," I said and introduced us.

Marrs gave Portier the once-over after hearing his name. "You're an accountant here in town, aren't you? You have some entertainers as clients. Your name has come up a few times around here."

Portier gave no indication by his expression that he was impressed by the executive's recognition.

"He also deals with fraud," I said, realizing Portier wasn't going to say anything on his behalf.

Marrs looked at my friend again. "I assure you that fraud is the last thing you'll find in our studio, especially regarding

Miss Duval."

"I'm not here in an official capacity, Mr. Marrs," Portier said reassuringly.

"Yes, but if you're a hammer, you look for nails."

"You misjudge me, I'm afraid. I don't actively search for fraud as a rule. If you were one of my engagements—which you are not—I'd approach your engagement through the eyes of the authorities who may be interested in what your records have to say." Portier looked at his fingernails as if he had better things to do. "Doing so allows me to determine how to tackle a problem, should a problem with that authoritative body exist. Government officials are no more interested in wasting their time on wild witch hunts than I am. This is not a witch hunt."

"Oh, yes, of course," Marrs said, sitting back to chuckle. "We all know how the government despises a good witch hunt. Then what are you doing here? What's the reason you've come?"

"We'd like to see Miss Duval's contract, just as Mr. Fountain requested," Portier replied.

"Because you suspect fraud?"

"No. We suspect nothing, but the more you ask about it, the more we'll be inclined to consider the possibility."

Marrs looked at Portier skeptically before jotting a note on a piece of scrap paper he picked randomly from his desk. "I'll have Miss Price pull the contract as soon as she returns from the storm. Now, is there anything else?"

"Yes," I said. "What can you tell us about Kip Harmon? I understand he introduced Miss Duval to you as a potential recording artist."

"Yes, he did. Mr. Harmon is a great help in finding quality talent."

"Is he an agent?"

"An independent agent."

"Are his terms documented in Miss Duval's contract?"

Marrs paused to take another puff from his cigarette. "Yes, in the contract."

"What about Veronica Mohr? Is she an agent?"

"Who?"

"Veronica Mohr. I believe she goes by the name Ronni. I understand she works with Mr. Harmon. I thought, perhaps, you'd know her."

"You'll have to ask Mr. Harmon."

"Is it because you don't know her?" Portier asked. "Not knowing who you do business with is a funny way of running a business, Mr. Marrs."

Marrs's plump face turned bright red. "I'm not trying to be adversarial, and I don't find your sarcasm the least bit funny. I run a successful recording studio, Mr. Portier. It's not a one-man show, however. We're successful because each person has a role to perform, and each person does it professionally and to the best of their ability with minimal supervision."

Portier tried to say something, but Marrs cut him off.

"I don't have the time to look over the shoulder of every Tom, Dick, or Harry that walks through the door. Mr. Harmon has his role, Miss Price has her role, I have my role, Miss Duval has hers, as do the dozens of other people affiliated with the studio."

"And Veronica Mohr?"

"If this Miss Mohr has a role, then I assume she also does it to the best of her ability. Seriously, your insinuations are out of line. We run an honest business, helping new talent find a way into this godforsaken industry. I help these people professionally and with integrity."

Portier crossed his legs and put his fingertips together in front of his chest. "But you're not entirely sure about Miss

Duval's contract, are you? You're not sure about the terms of the contract or if there even is a contract for Miss Duval in the filing cabinet out there."

Marrs glared at him. "I will ask Miss Price first thing after the storm."

"But you're not sure."

Marrs exhaled heavily as he snuffed out his Picayune in an ash-laden tray on his desk. "I dare say, Mr. Portier," he retorted, "I've heard about you around town. I've heard about the interrogation tactics you use on people, and I'm astute enough to recognize that you're trying to use those tactics on me. You must be a very unhappy individual to derive such pleasure from a career based upon the distrust of individuals who are only trying to make a decent living for others. It makes you a very small person inside no matter how big you think yourself to be."

Portier smiled. "You may be right," he replied calmly, "but at least I stand for what I believe. At the moment I'm having difficulty determining if you feel the same way. So tell me, Mr. Marrs, what do you and your studio stand for?"

Chapter 18

"Not at all how I thought our conversation with Mr. Marrs would go," I said to Portier as we exited the studio and splashed through the rain once again.

"I believe I struck a nerve," he replied.

"Not of guilt."

"No, something worse. Neglectful ignorance."

"Is that criminal?"

Portier thought for a moment. "It can be, depending on what happens. Civil for sure if Genevieve is being deceived. I'm not sure a case can be made against them, however."

"Don't you believe she's being deceived?"

"Most definitely," he said, "but I'm not sure if it's Eldon Marrs, Kip Harmon, Veronica Mohr, or Genevieve doing the deceiving."

"Genny?" I asked surprised.

"Yes, *Genny*. Have you ever given it thought that those people have been up-front with her about the recording and the expenses involved, and it was Genevieve who deceived herself by ignoring the warning signs?"

Yes, I'd thought briefly of Genny in that way, but Portier

made a more concrete observation. Whether Genny wanted to admit it, she had a strong role in her own situation, and she was either naïve or negligent, getting involved with the characters surrounding her recording.

"Speaking of Genny," I said, "she's singing at the club this evening. It would be a nice gesture for one of us to give her a lift home when she's done."

"That won't be anytime soon."

"I doubt the crowd will stay much longer. It's raining harder; the storm is fast approaching."

"That doesn't mean a thing to the misfits that attend Genevieve's shows, Fountain. They live for any reason to throw a party, and a hurricane or tropical storm is the perfect time for one. You're welcome to use my Studebaker if you're so inclined. Me? I plan to be fast asleep by the time Genevieve steps off the stage, storm or no storm."

That evening, I took Portier up on his offer and squeezed the Golden Hawk into an illegal parking space close to Paradox. I rationalized the fine would be worth the convenience of a handy spot if a ticket had appeared under the wiper blade when we came out.

As soon as I entered the club, I realized Portier was right. Genny's fans really did love a good hurricane party. Costumed revelers danced. Confetti and ribbons littered the floor. Mamie Eisenhower pinched my butt, but the thick, dark stubble on her face threw me for a loop, and I turned the other way.

Genny sang onstage. She wore a muumuu with printed clouds that seemed to float around her as she swayed back and forth to the song. Her white simulated pearls swung like a Hula-Hoop around her neck. They might have strangled her if she hadn't slowed down, running out of breath as she tried to belt out another chorus of "Blow the Man Down." The crowd sang along with her, raising their mugs of brew and rocking back and forth in rhythm to the clouds on her dress. She waved at me, and I waved back, careful not to draw attention to myself that could attract an attack by another bearded woman.

Most of the tables were taken, and I wondered where I was going to wait in comfort until I saw an empty stool at the bar next to a woman wearing a long, blue-and-gray chiffon dress shredded into strips and adorned with silver sequins to make it appear as if she was the wind, blowing ferociously. She'd frayed her blond hair and combed it back, sticking long white pipe cleaners out behind her head as if the wind also controlled her hair. The costume accentuated her lean, young body, but it was the expression of indifference on her face that I noticed the most. I'd seen that expression just a few hours before, on Melinda Price of Marrs Recording.

I surprised her by my presence and surprised her even more when I pulled the stool back to sit next to her.

"Reverend Fountain, is it?" she asked politely.

"Miss Price, nice to see you," I responded.

A spray bottle sat by her purse on the bar. I pointed to it and asked what it was for.

She picked up the bottle and squirted two sprays of water into my face. "I not only blow with the wind, Reverend . . . I can rain too."

"Clever," I said, taking a cocktail napkin from the bar to wipe my face.

"I must apologize to you," she said as she reached for her half-empty glass of beverage.

"For spraying me?"

"No, that was fun. For being rude to you this afternoon at the studio. I wasn't kind, and I'm sorry. It's no excuse, but I was anxious to leave."

I scanned the dance floor and took another look at the patrons in colorful costumes. "To come here?" I asked indignantly.

She smiled, apparently sensing my judgment upon her. "I didn't say my reasoning for leaving the office was honorable. I figure I have a few months yet to make it off Santa's naughty list. You'll forgive me, won't you, if I came here for a little rakishness?"

Tomas, the bartender, approached. I ordered a club soda with lime.

"Do you come here often, Miss Price?" I asked.

"Melinda, please. On occasion, yes."

"Then you know Genny outside of business."

She shrugged. "We're not friends, but I know her well enough."

"Were you the one who referred her to Mr. Harmon?"

"That wasn't me," she said, taking a sip of her cocktail.

"Was it Veronica Mohr?"

Melinda laughed and rubbed her index finger sensuously around the rim of her glass. "Dear Ronni," she said. "Technically, you could say it was her—at least, that's what some people would like you to believe. I know for a fact, however, she's just a puppet. She does what she's told to do."

"By whom? Mr. Harmon?"

"And her sister."

"Cindy?"

Melinda lifted her finger off her glass and raised it in front of her as if I'd earned a point. "Like Mutt and Jeff, they are. Peanut butter and jelly. Mashed potatoes and gravy. Get my drift?" We sat silently for several seconds before she added, "Quite frankly, I'm surprised Cindy works with *her*."

I caught the emphasis. "You say that as if she had a choice."

Melinda appeared taken off guard. "I didn't mean anything by it." She looked at me apprehensively. "So what did Eldon have to say about Genny?"

Tomas set my club soda on the counter. I paid him, including a generous tip.

"I don't remember mentioning at the studio that I was there to talk about Genny. I only mentioned that to Mr. Marrs," I said.

She smiled coyly. "You're right, you didn't. I happened to trip when my heel caught a snag in the carpet. My ear landed against his door quite by accident. It took several seconds for me to compose myself, and I couldn't help but overhear your conversation."

"I see. Then you're probably aware that he was evasive in his answers."

"Not evasive, Reverend, just unknowing. Surely, you saw his office. Eldon Marrs is hopelessly disorganized and completely clueless about the inner workings of the office. For instance, did he offer you a cigarette?" After I nodded, she asked, "Did you take one?" When I said I did not, she responded, "If you had, you would've discovered there were no cigarettes in the case. I hadn't replenished it. The man doesn't even know when he's run out of cigarettes. That's how clueless he is."

"Then I take it his strengths are elsewhere or he wouldn't be in business."

"You're right again. You're absolutely right. His strength is in the studio, providing our clients with the best atmosphere for their voices to sound like stars. That's his forte; it's not recordkeeping. If it weren't for me, Eldon would be reckless with his papers, his finances, his relationships, and the information he has on others—among other things."

"Like contracts?"

Melinda eyed me with suspicion but forced a smile from her lips.

"Is there a contract between Marrs Recording and Genny

Duval?" I asked.

She took a sip of her drink and reached for her purse to pull out a cigarette. She waited patiently for Tomas to notice the cigarette, hanging between her lips.

He approached on cue, gave her a light, and accepted the kiss she blew his way.

"There must be one somewhere," she said, "or else Genny wouldn't be on the airwaves, would she?"

"That's what I'm asking. Mr. Marrs said he'd have you pull it for me as soon as the storm passes."

Melinda laughed. "I could pull contracts until the cows came home, Reverend."

"What does that mean?"

"Her contract's not *with* the studio, and it's not *at* the studio either. I'm afraid you'll have to ask Kip Harmon about it. Maybe you could ask Ronni Mohr."

"I doubt that would be possible."

"Is she still at large from the police?"

"You must know something about that to ask."

She shook her head and took a puff. "Just what I read in the *Times-Picayune*. I don't know why she'd run. Ronni's not the type to hurt a soul. I can't believe she'd do such a thing. Now, that roommate of hers is another story."

"You mean her sister, Cindy?"

"No, the other one," she said with an air of disgust. "Gwennie somebody. Weird-ass little cookie. Belongs somewhere in Haight-Ashbury or Greenwich Village but not in New Orleans. She comes into the studio periodically, trying to sell her song lyrics to Eldon or to some of the new talent. She doesn't get far, but that doesn't stop her from trying."

"Yes," I said, reflecting on what I read in Genny's cottage. "I've seen some of her lyrics. I'd have to agree with you."

"They're not the be-bop, rock 'n roll, jazz, or swing that Marrs Recording is looking for. They're too folksy or whatever genre she wants to call them."

"When was the last time she was in the studio?"

"Oh, it's been a while. Before the murder anyway."

"Do you think she'll be back?"

Melinda finished her cocktail, set the glass firmly on the counter, chuckled, and said confidently, "Not if she knows what's good for her."

I didn't have a chance to ask her what she meant by her last comment. Genny finished her set and told the club's revelers that she was calling it a night and the next singer would be onstage to entertain them. Men heckled her, begging her to be by them during the storm, but she ignored them and approached the two of us at the bar without expression. Even the tiara holding her trademark curls in place glistened listlessly. Melinda acknowledged her but continued to smoke as if Genny's presence didn't make any difference to her.

"I'm ready to go, Dickie," Genny said. "I just need to get my things. Thanks for giving me a ride."

I turned to Melinda who released a cloud of smoke into the air. "May I give you a lift too, Miss Price?"

She smiled but shook her head. "No, I'm content where I am, but thank you." She picked up the spray bottle and exerted a quick, subtle squirt in my direction. "Enjoy the storm," she said before turning back to her cigarette.

Chapter 19

Genny and I ran unprotected from Paradox to Portier's car. Dodging rain pellets was fruitless. The deluge bore down at an angle with the wind. Gusts whipped Genny's muumuu around her large frame and tried to jerk her handbag from her grip. I fumbled with the keys to fit the lock to Portier's car, but rainwater streamed into my eyes and blurred my view of the keyhole.

"Hurry, Dickie!" Genny pleaded.

Once inside the car, we both breathed heavy sighs of relief. Our clothes were so wet they clung to our skin and felt ten times heavier than they normally were.

"Did the weather bureau up the ante on this thing?" Genny asked.

"Not that I've heard. It was still a strong tropical storm when I left Portier's to come get you."

"This is much worse than I thought, or I'd have had Tomas yell for last call an hour ago."

The only consolation for the weather was the lack of a parking violation tucked under the windshield wiper.

"Your lucky day," Genny quipped.

Normally, Genny would've bellowed a couple of crude jokes about how wet she was and how the rain exposed the luscious curves of her full-bodied bosom. She'd even laugh and find humor at tainting the interior of Portier's Studebaker with our soaked, smoke-laden clothes from the club. She didn't do so, however. She seemed unnaturally subdued.

I pulled away from the curb and made my way through the narrow, flooded streets of the French Quarter.

Genny looked sullenly at me as water continued to streak from her limp curls across her plump cheeks. "What did she have to say?" she asked. "I saw you talking to her at the bar."

I glanced at Genny. Her expression was grim. "If you're referring to Melinda Price, she didn't have anything to say. I asked her about your contract."

"How do you know her to even ask that?"

"The question is, Why didn't you tell me about her in the first place?"

"She's just a secretary, Dickie. She's nobody."

"I beg to differ," I said. "Melinda Price is more than just a secretary to Eldon Marrs. She's his life and blood. The place would collapse without her."

"According to her, no doubt."

"You don't like her."

"I didn't say that."

"You don't have to. I could tell in the club there was no love lost between the two of you. Your questioning of her only confirms it."

"I'll tell you why," Genny said, her voice rising. "She should keep her nose out of Eldon's business. She's always buttin' in, gettin' between him and his artists. He's creative, and she's just a paper pusher."

I jerked my head in her direction. "Goodness, Genny, are

you having an affair with him?"

She laughed for the first time. "Not on your life. How dare you think such a thing! I just don't trust her is all. Eldon Marrs has been nothing but kind to me. He gives me pointers to help my voice, but she has a finger in everything he does, and she doesn't let up. I believe she's the reason I'm getting strange notes from strange men at strange hours at the club. I wish Chuck would look into her."

"I think *Chuck* believes the person responsible for your problems is sitting next to me in the car."

She gasped, and sensing her piercing glare through the darkness, I glanced her way. The dashboard lights cast an eerie glow off her cheeks, blushed with anger.

"Pull over," she demanded.

"What?"

"I said pull over. I'll walk the rest of the way."

"No." I pointed up the street. "Your cottage is just ahead."

"It doesn't matter. I'm already soaked to the gills. Pull over."

"Genny, it doesn't make sense to drop you here."

"And it doesn't make sense to take me to the door either. You can turn here at this intersection and go straight to the garage. Whereas, if you drop me off in front of my cottage, you'll have to swing around another block. You could be swept away by the drain water and never heard from again. Pull over. I mean it."

"Genny, no. It would be irresponsible of me. Just because you're angry with me is no reason to put yourself in this wind and rain any longer than necessary."

"I want to be alone, Dickie."

I stopped the car. "You know Portier and how he thinks," I said, trying to quell her anger. "Please, he didn't mean anything by what he said, and I shouldn't have told you. I wish you'd reconsider. Genny, please, do this for me. It's a torrent out there."

Ignoring my comments, she pulled on the door handle, grabbed her handbag, and stepped into ankle-deep water that swirled around a storm drain adjacent to the car.

"Oh, Genny," I said under my breath.

She slammed the door and waved me on. "Go!" she yelled, nearly in tears. "Just go."

A defiant burst of anger swelled inside of me, but I did as she requested. I turned left and careened down the street. Before reaching the next block, however, an incredible sense of remorse overcame me.

I shouldn't have let her out! I have to go back!

I accelerated, creating a wake behind the Golden Hawk that splashed oily rainwater from the pavement onto the sidewalk. No cars, carriages, or pedestrians impeded my way. I made the full circle around the block until I saw her blurry figure ahead of me.

Genny was a cottage away from her home but appeared to have stopped to search the contents of her purse, presumably looking for her house keys. She turned her back to the rain, but the wind caused her to lose her footing. Her free hand grabbed her tiara, nearly letting her handbag slip from her grip.

The gust even rocked my moving car. "Genny," I scolded. "You're as stubborn as Chuck sometimes."

Just then a figure walked out from between two cottages and onto the sidewalk. I tried to focus between the swishing of the wiper blades, but the blades couldn't clear the rainwater from my windshield fast enough to see clearly. The figure seemed to stand momentarily on the walk rather than hurry through the wind and rain to its destination. I realized then that the individual had a different purpose in mind.

The person grabbed Genny's arm and swung her around so that he or she could break the purse from her grip. The motion knocked her off-balance, but she managed to stay on her feet enough to keep hold of the purse's strap as her other hand hit the pavement. The perpetrator jerked on her other arm, lifting her slightly.

I accelerated so quickly that the rear end of the Hawk hydroplaned on the wet surface and fishtailed to the right. Instinctively, as if I were sliding on ice, I let up on the gas and turned the steering wheel into the swerve.

Genny stood and swung at the figure with her free arm, but the strike did little to halt the attack.

I honked my horn and stepped on the floorboard button to turn on the headlights.

The person glanced in my direction, then struck Genny's arm where she clung to her purse strap.

Another blow; this time harder.

Genny let go and fell to the wet sidewalk.

The sudden release nearly propelled the attacker to the ground, but the person broke free and ran swiftly away.

I brought the car to a screeching halt, jumped out, and ran to Genny's side. I helped her stand.

She looked at me, frightened and gasping for breath. "Oh, God, Dickie! Oh my God! Did you see him? The son of a bitch took my purse."

"I know. Are you okay?"

"My driver's license. He took my billfold and my license."

I tried to console her, but the shock of the assault began to consume her. "It's okay, it's okay," I repeated over and over.

"No, it's not okay, Dickie. Don't you see?" she cried. "I don't care about the purse. I want my license. I want my keys. I want to get into my house."

Genny fell against my chest, and I held her tightly. The rain pelted harder, as if the storm were a guilty accomplice to the perpetrator's master plan. She sobbed, unable to hold in her anger and frustration, and spouted hateful words at the man who now forced an inevitable and unwanted trip to the Department of Motor Vehicles to replace her license.

"My keys, too, Dickie," she muttered. "What about my keys?"

"Come," I said, comforting her to no avail. "Forget the keys. You can't go home tonight anyway. You're staying with Portier and me, and I'll call the police from his place. They'll know what to do."

~

I awoke with a start the next morning. Wind and rain continued to patter against the parlor's windows, but I could tell the worst of the storm had passed in the wee hours. My neck ached from sleeping at an awkward angle on Portier's settee so that Genny could have my bed.

Portier clattered in the kitchen. I heard the percolator go *pop, pop* as the delicious brew entered its glass dome and dripped into the pot.

I staggered to my feet and stumbled toward the aroma.

"Here," Portier said, putting Milnot into a creamer. "Genny's still sleeping—rather comfortably, I might add. I gave her a sedative to help her sleep. She was near hysterics last night."

"Where's Bentley?"

"In with her, the good dog. He was as upset as she was at what happened. Dogs can sense such things, you know."

"She was more worried about her license and keys than her life."

Portier glanced my way, seemingly disappointed at my

remark. "I don't blame her. A trip to the DMV is a horrid experience. They must serve muffins and tea in Spiceland, Indiana, because the experience isn't quite so pleasant here in New Orleans. You should be more considerate."

"I'm sorry. I should, you're right. I know from my ministerial experience that people often evade their trauma by focusing on something less significant. Besides, I shouldn't have let her walk alone."

"You should've known better, I agree. No gentleman in his right mind would've done such a thing. Why did you do so?"

"It was her anger."

"Good gracious, Fountain," he said, giving me another stern look. "People have been angry with you before. What did you say to her that would compel her to get out of the car and walk home in a raging storm?"

I had to be honest with him. "It's not what I said, it's what you said to me. I told her that she was as guilty as anyone for the predicament she was in regarding her recording contract. She didn't want to hear it. She didn't like hearing it."

The kitchen window shutters shook from a stray gust of wind. It didn't startle me half as much as Portier's glaring judgment toward me. "Please," I begged, "don't withhold coffee as punishment against me for what I told her."

"It doesn't matter," he said, brushing my comment away. "You know better than anyone that evil will do what evil can. Besides, neither you nor Genevieve were to blame. From what the police told us last night, the perpetrator may have been someone targeting Genevieve personally and specifically. It wasn't a random purse-snatching."

"I thought that myself," I replied. "Last night was a poor night for a mugger to be doing business. There was no one on the street except for Genny. Still, it doesn't make it any easier for her."

"The purse and its contents are nothing more than dust in the scheme of things, Fountain," he said reassuringly. "They can all be replaced. She's lucky she wasn't injured more seriously. Here, go into the other room and relax in my chair. I'll bring your coffee to you."

The phone in the parlor rang.

"Answer it," I said. "I can get my own coffee."

Portier did as I suggested.

I plopped into a chair at the kitchen table and stirred the Milnot Portier had poured into my cup until the coffee was a nice murky brown. I'd taken several sips before Portier returned. He had a pressing look about him. It meant only one thing to me. "The police, I presume?"

"Yes," he replied. "It was Detective Robicheaux. He's looking into the case."

"That's odd. He usually takes cases more complex than muggings. Like homicide."

Portier shrugged. "Apparently, he sees more into Genevieve's incident than what meets the eye."

I set my cup on a saucer to listen.

"Some good news, in a way," he said. "They found her purse a block from here. It was thrown beside some cement steps next to a house. Easy to spot. Genevieve will be happy to learn that most everything was intact inside her purse, although rather water-logged. It appears the robber wasn't interested in money or her identification."

"Thank goodness," I said. "Genny will be pleased that she'll be getting her driver's license back."

"You're premature on your gratitude," he said. "She'll be getting her license back all right, but they didn't seem to find what they were looking for in her purse."

"How do the police know that?"

"Her house keys were missing. The robber took her keys."

I thought carefully for a second. "I don't understand. How do they know from missing keys that the mugger didn't find what he was looking for in her purse?"

"Because," Portier said grimly, "he used the keys to ransack her cottage as we slept."

Chapter 20

Commotion from Genny's bedroom signified that her sedative had worn off.

"Not a word about the break-in," Portier warned me. "She's had quite a shock. She doesn't need another one so soon."

Genny appeared in the doorway to the parlor, looking disheveled and wobbly. She maneuvered herself to the nearest chair by grasping anything that was planted solidly on the floor, then plopped onto the seat cushion and extended a leg across the hardwood floor.

Portier wandered into the kitchen and came back with a cold, damp dishcloth to drape across her forehead.

"Has there been any news?" Genny asked, whimpering as she did so.

"Nothing that can't be discussed later," he said.

Genny sat up. "Then there has been some news. They found my purse?"

"Yes, dear, they've found your purse. You have everything back. You can rest comfortably now."

Genny looked at me to validate what Portier had just told her.

"Almost everything," I said.

Portier shot a quick, dirty look in my direction.

"What does that mean?" she asked.

Portier resituated the dishcloth that had fallen from her forehead. "It means you have everything you need right here in my cottage. You don't need to worry about anything else."

Genny looked at me again, this time with more apprehension.

"Your place was ransacked," I said. "You have your driver's license, but the mugger took the keys from your pocketbook and tore through your place."

"What?"

Portier tried to calm her. "Quiet now," he said, raising his hand to me like a school safety patrolman would command a child to stop at a crossing. "Pay no attention to the nincompoop in the room. You've been given a shock. Fountain should've used better discretion before he allowed his tongue to wag."

"No, I want to know," Genny said. "I want to know everything."

Portier sighed and stood. "Then I'll leave you two to discuss it, and I'll exchange the dishcloth for a washcloth and some coffee."

When he'd left the room and passed out of earshot, I gave Genny a quick synopsis of her situation based upon the report from Detective Robicheaux.

She took the update in her stride, removing the dishcloth and looking intently at me. "If the mugger had my keys and knew what cottage the keys belonged to, that means he knew me and was specifically out to get me."

I agreed with her and said that Detective Robicheaux believed in the same hypothesis.

Genny tried to stand. "I can't stay here any longer."

"You're not going anywhere," I said firmly. "Certainly not back to your place, if that's what you're thinking. You can't. Now put that cloth back on your head before he walks back in."

"But I'm putting you two in danger, staying here."

"Nonsense. No one knows you're here."

"It's not nonsense, Dickie. I started out as the hunter in pursuit of that note about Ronni, and now I've ended up as the hunted."

I tried not to be dramatic, but I couldn't help but speak with emphasis to impress her situation. "I think it's much graver than that, Genny. I don't think you were ever the hunter. You've been the prey ever since that man in the brown-checkered suit gave you that note about Ronni Mohr at Paradox, probably even sooner than that, if you'd be totally honest with yourself."

"Then what are we going to do?"

"*We* are not doing anything," I said. "After Portier comes back into the room, you're going to drink your coffee and put the washcloth over your head. I, on the other hand, plan to have a telephone chat with Detective Robicheaux to determine his next course of action."

~

The wind had died down considerably, and the rain was nothing more than a drizzle by the time I got around to calling Detective Robicheaux. I wanted to wait until Genny fell back asleep with another sedative, so she couldn't overhear my conversation.

Detective Robicheaux accepted my call right away.

"Very kind of you to follow up on Miss Duval's unfortunate incident, Detective," I said.

"I don't believe a commendation is necessary, Reverend. Following up is my job. It's what I do."

"Normally, I'd agree, but we both know people don't always

fulfill duties as effectively as you."

He ignored my buttering. "What can I do for you?"

"I called to tell you that I had the opportunity to speak with Eldon Marrs of Marrs Recording and his secretary, Melinda Price."

"And how did this opportunity come about?" he asked, sounding doubtful.

"I went to his office."

I heard the detective sigh through the line. "That's what I thought. Are we back to our old tricks, Reverend? I should warn you that your investigative tactics have a history of backfiring on you with dreadful consequences."

"Tricks, Detective? Certainly not. I was just making some inquiries about Miss Duval's contract with Mr. Marrs."

"What did you find out?"

"There is no contract. That begs the question of how Marrs earns his revenue and where Genny Duval's expenses are going."

"Isn't Miss Duval transparent with you about her expenses?"

"It's easy to be transparent when you're oblivious, Detective."

"I see. What expenses are we talking about?"

"Could be as onerous as kickbacks to have her song played on the radio. I don't need to tell you that such kickbacks could lead to other crimes that have been committed relative to the case."

There was silence on the other end of the line. I prompted him to respond.

"I'm thinking," he said.

"I hope you're thinking about the murder of Julie Moreno."

He didn't say.

"By the way, Detective, may I ask if a relative has come to claim her body?"

"The storm has delayed positive identification, I'm afraid, but now that it's let up, I'm optimistic someone will come forward. I received a call from a relative just this morning, in fact."

"From St. Louis?"

"No. I wrote down his name someplace. We're looking into it."

"That sounds like you're questioning the validity of this relative's claim."

The detective paused briefly. "I have no reason to question him."

"Then why are you guarding your words, Detective? I detect reticence in the tone of your voice."

"Nothing, just something that struck me funny about him," he said. "The man said he was from Texas, but he sounded more like he was from Chalmette."

"Ah," I said. "You would know. People from that part of New Orleans have an unmistakable dialect that resembles nothing like a Texan accent."

"Then you catch my drift, but as for Eldon Marrs, Reverend, we can take it from here."

This time, it was I who was silent.

"Did you hear me?"

"Yes, Detective, I was just thinking—"

"No thinking, Reverend. We'll take it from here. Miss Duval's attack should come as a wake-up call to you, even if Julie Moreno's murder did not. As I've warned you before, I can have you arrested if you obstruct our investigation in any way."

I told him I understood. Just as I hung up the receiver, Portier stepped into the parlor from the kitchen.

"Did you overhear my conversation?" I asked.

"I heard enough. It sounds like the detective is taking this case more seriously now."

"Yes, he is."

"Then why the glum face?"

I sat down and shook my head. "I told Detective Robicheaux

about Eldon Marrs. I told him he should interview him. He seemed interested in doing so."

"Then *bravo*! We should celebrate."

"Not so fast. He told me to butt out."

"As well you should."

"But there's the matter of Genny's contract," I said thoughtfully.

"Let the detective follow up on that, Fountain."

"I will, but I believe a brief follow-up of my own wouldn't hurt to make sure all bases are covered."

Portier flared his nostrils and said he needed something stronger than coffee to drink.

Chapter 21

The sun tried to break through the low-hanging clouds as I made my way back to Marrs Recording Studio. Traffic had picked up on the streets, and life as I knew it in the French Quarter appeared to be resuming like any other day. Even Melinda Price was back at her desk, pecking away at her Royal, answering the telephone, and transferring calls with efficiency. She looked up when I approached her and gave me a professional greeting, one that was much more pleasant than the last time I'd been to Eldon Marrs's office.

"Good morning or good day, whatever it is, Miss Price," I said.

"It's good afternoon," she replied. "I assume you're here to see Mr. Marrs."

"Unless you have the contract of Miss Genevieve Duval at your fingertips."

Melinda rifled her fingers through some papers next to her typewriter. "I have it right here, Reverend, just as you requested . . . Oops! It's gone." She winked at me. "Care to have a seat? Mr. Marrs will be happy to discuss what he knows nothing about."

"You're serious, aren't you?" I asked.

"Very. I thought I made that clear at Paradox when we spoke."

"But I'm serious about wanting a copy of her contract."

"I have no doubt that you are, but as I said before, we don't handle such contracts. You'll have to speak to Mr. Harmon."

"Is Mr. Harmon here?"

"No, he is not."

"Then I'll speak to Mr. Marrs, please."

Melinda picked up the phone's receiver. "I'll see if he's busy." Before she could dial Marrs's number, a woman's loud voice echoed from the lobby. Melinda replaced the receiver on the hook. Her eyes widened with alarm as her head turned toward the commotion. She stood and excused herself before rushing down the hall to where the woman continued to raise her voice.

Melinda placed her hands on her hips, but I couldn't see the other woman as she was around a corner and out of my line of vision. Whoever the woman was, Melinda wasn't pleased to see her. "You shouldn't be here," she said. "I told you to never come here. What's the matter with you?"

The woman lowered her voice, but it was still loud enough for me to hear. "Scared out of my wits, that's the matter, Melinda. They haven't stopped following me."

Melinda turned to see if I was listening, but I looked away in time to avoid detection. "You have to go," she said. "We'll talk about this later."

"No, we'll talk about this now. I'm not comfortable doing this any longer."

At that, Melinda disappeared around the corner, apparently to lead the frightened woman to the studio's exit.

I made sure Melinda was gone before I scampered around her desk to see what she'd been typing. I wasn't surprised by what I found in the carriage: a half-typed page of a contract with carbon paper used to make a copy. I squinted my eyes. The contract appeared to be between a promising singer and . . . but who? I couldn't find within the typewritten pages who the contract was with. I reviewed the document more closely, careful not to get my fingertips soiled with black carbon. There it was: *Christopher "Kip" Harmon*. I expected to see Eldon Marrs's name or Marrs Recording alongside Harmon's, but it wasn't there.

I scurried around the desk to my seat, pretending to wait dutifully for Mr. Marrs when Melinda came clacking down the hall. She walked past me, glancing down to assess my interest after what had just transpired with the woman.

"Trouble?" I asked.

Melinda smiled reassuringly. "No, she was just . . . lost, apparently in the wrong recording studio."

I contemplated whether I should move before lightning struck through the ceiling.

The door to Marrs's office opened suddenly. Marrs poked his head through, ignoring me. His agitated glare was directed toward Melinda. "What's going on out here?" he asked. "I heard a commotion somewhere."

"Nothing we couldn't resolve, Mr. Marrs. A woman was lost."

Marrs didn't look convinced. "I thought I heard that woman's voice again."

Melinda smiled and shook her head.

"Yes, I did," he reiterated. "In fact, I looked out of my window and saw her coming up the walk. I told you before I can't have her in this office. It's utter chaos when she's here. She disrupts our clients and ties me in knots. Just hearing her voice—even behind closed doors—is enough to boil my blood. Did you call the police?"

"It was nothing, Mr. Marrs. Please, Reverend Fountain is here to see you."

He turned his head and saw me for the first time. "Oh," he

replied, embarrassed. He opened the door to his office wider and welcomed me in. "I haven't long, mind you, but what can I do for you?"

"I won't take much of your time. I can see that you have some unsettling business in the office."

"It's nothing, apparently." Marrs closed his door, then appeared to have an afterthought. "Just a second, please." He opened the door and said sternly through the opening. "Call the police, Miss Price. Tell them she was here." Marrs then reclosed the door and returned to his desk, rubbing his left temple as he did so.

"Was that Veronica Mohr?" I asked brazenly.

"What?" He looked at me as if he just realized I was sitting in front of his desk. "I don't know. I thought I heard her voice. I couldn't hear that clearly, but we shouldn't take any chances."

"If it was Ronni Mohr, you were wise to have Miss Price call the police."

Eldon Marrs appeared defeated. He scanned the top of his desk as if the answer to his troubles were somewhere in the clutter. "Wisdom is in short supply here, Reverend. Chaos, however, seems to be running amok. I try to run a tight ship, but I feel there's a leak somewhere in the hull."

"You're only as good as your employees and associates, Mr. Marrs. Surely, you realize that."

"I realize that I can't be in a dozen places at the same time. I have to depend on my people. What's a man to do?" He looked at me apprehensively, then said, "If you're here about Miss Duval's contract—"

"I am."

"I haven't had time to produce it since the storm, Reverend. I need more time."

"Let's not kid ourselves, Mr. Marrs. There is no contract.

You're deceiving yourself to think Miss Price is going to pull it out of one of your cabinets even with more time. What you have here is an organization fraught with unethical, if not fraudulent tactics to deceive your clients."

"How dare you attack my integrity and accuse me of fraud."

"But I haven't seen anything to the contrary. Mismanagement is no excuse, should authorities be interested in what's transpiring here."

He paused. His jaw clenched as he thought. "I operate a sound organization, Reverend, and I provide a good product to my clients. You're as bad as your friend Portier. You're a religious zealot. Like Portier who looks for fraud, you look for sin and believe everyone but yourself is wallowing in it. Now, if you don't mind, I'm very busy."

Eldon Marrs walked from his desk to the door and opened it for me to leave. I took the cue and eased my way past his scowling face into the small lobby. A man—late twenties at best, tanned, handsome, and confident—stood in front of me, facing Melinda and blocking my way. He didn't seem to care that I tried to work my way around him. He stood his ground, more intent on impressing Melinda, who adjusted her stocking, exposing a sensuous sample of her thigh.

"Ah, DD, my man!" Marrs blurted to the man. "Come in! Come in! Always good to see you."

DD, as he was referred to, turned grudgingly away from Melinda's exposed leg to address Marrs but found me standing in his way instead. The provocative grin he had for Melinda vanished upon seeing me. His expression appeared even more disgusted at the sight of Eldon Marrs.

"Who is that?" I asked Melinda after the men entered Marrs's office and the door closed behind me. "A recording artist?"

She didn't answer, and based on the look in her eye, she

wasn't planning on answering.

Before I had a chance to step away, the door to Marrs's office opened again. Marrs peered out and said, "Miss Price, would you step in here, please? Bring your pad for some dictation."

Melinda grabbed her steno pad and a pen and walked to the door. "Good day, Reverend. We had the snags in the carpet repaired, by the way."

I pretended to take my leave, but returned when Marrs's door had closed. I had no intention of listening to the trio's conversation through the door. I had no interest in that. I did, however, have an interest in discovering what more she'd been typing while I'd conversed with Marrs in his office.

I tiptoed to her desk and opened a large drawer to see if folders hung within, but blank paper and typing supplies filled it. A smaller drawer looked promising, but when I opened it, I heard a thud as if something had shifted under the loose papers. I lifted the papers carefully, and underneath found a black Beretta pocket pistol containing an eight-round magazine. I didn't know much about pistols, but I knew enough to know this particular Jetfire didn't have a safety lever and was prone to misfire. It was ready at a moment's warning, however, which I suspected was why it was in her drawer in the first place. What job as a secretary was dangerous enough to require a pocket pistol was anybody's guess.

I spotted a wastebasket against the wall and easily identified the documents I wanted from inside it. I was particularly interested in the discarded carbon paper. They'd be just as revealing as the originals as long as Melinda didn't reuse the sheets more than once. I made sure enough paper remained in the bin to avoid Melinda's suspicion upon her return.

I rounded the corner of her desk and saw, down the hall ahead of me, a young receptionist speaking to an authoritative-looking man from the New Orleans Police Department. An officer stood by his side.

Robicheaux!

Just my luck, I thought. The only thing worse than getting caught by Melinda Price for absconding with the remnants of confidential documents was seeing Detective Robicheaux in the very office he told me not to be in just a couple of hours before. I had to think fast. The only place safe enough until the coast was clear was the men's restroom—located between me and where the detective stood down the hall. I walked carefully toward the restroom and ducked in, taking several deep breaths to quell my pounding heart.

I listened carefully at the door for his passing to Eldon Marrs's office, praying that he didn't need to use the facility before doing so. The clacking of the receptionist's heels led the way down the hall. She knocked on the executive's door, and I heard Eldon Marrs's voice. I couldn't hear what was said between Marrs and the man named DD, but they must've ended their conversation because I heard DD tell Marrs that he'd return later. More clacking of the receptionist's heels followed, along with the sound of a man's footsteps.

"I need to step in here," the man said, presumably to the receptionist.

I backed away but came face to face, once again, with the dapper musician named DD.

"Pardon me," he said as the door closed behind him. He tried to step around me, but I didn't budge.

"You're a singer, aren't you?" I asked.

The man appeared surprised by my inquiry.

"This is awkward, I know, but I have to ask. May I have your autograph? My granddaughter is enthralled with you." I pulled from my pocket a pen and a piece of paper that I'd taken from Melinda's trash bin and turned the paper over to expose the blank side.

"Really," he said, "I'm not . . . I just want to—"

"She's sixteen, sir," I pleaded. "I'll never have this opportunity again."

DD nodded reluctantly and took the piece of paper and my pen.

"To Donna, if you don't mind."

He placed the paper against the wall and scribbled Donna's name and his autograph. It appeared illegible from where I stood.

"You're so very kind," I said, "and I apologize for the inopportune timing."

I let DD go around me as I exited the restroom carefully, making sure the coast was clear. In the hallway just outside the door, I looked at what the musician had written on the paper: *To Donna, Dale Devoe (and the Dares).*

I couldn't help but gasp, turn around, and walk back into the restroom. Devoe stood at the urinal, oblivious to my reentry.

"She loves 'Sand Tan Catamaran,'" I said to him.

He turned, surprised again that I was standing there.

"My granddaughter Donna, that is."

He didn't answer.

"Sand tan—that's a color, isn't it?"

Devoe ignored me. He finished his business and walked to the basins to wash his hands.

"May I ask who writes your lyrics? Did you write that song yourself?"

He gave me a side glance, clearly wishing I'd go away.

"It's very good if you did," I said.

"No," he replied bluntly as if he hoped his reply would end our conversation. "I usually do write my own lyrics, but I bought

'Catamaran' from a young woman who was here in the studio."

"May I ask her name?"

"She's not well-known. You wouldn't know her," he said with finality. "Now, if you'll excuse me."

He exited the restroom ahead of me. As he passed, I wanted to tell him that I begged to differ. I believed I did know the name of the lyrics' author.

Chapter 22

I wasted no time, returning to Portier's cottage. Bentley greeted me at the door and turned to show me where the bologna was kept in the refrigerator.

"Don't let him fool you, Fountain," Portier said, removing his reading glasses and setting his newspaper aside. "I've given Bentley his treat. He's trying to connive you into another one." Bentley went to his master's side as if he knew what my friend had just said. Portier scratched behind his ears; amends were made. "What's that in your hands?" he asked me.

"Carbon paper I took from the wastebasket of Eldon Marrs's secretary. Come to the kitchen table with me. I want your opinion of them."

"Marrs should be more careful what they throw away," Portier replied as he followed me into the kitchen.

I set the carbon sheets on the table in front of the chair in which I thought he'd choose to sit and placed the mysterious puzzle of anagrams from Genny in front of my chair.

"Is Genny still asleep?" I asked.

Portier looked at the clock hanging on the wall. "Yes, out like a light. She should be getting up, however. I know she's upset, but at some point, she's got to face the events she's been through."

"Not now, though," I said. "I'd like a chance for us to look over these items first. Genny has a way of using her attention deficit as a screen to prevent me from getting to the bottom of her situation. I'd like our complete focus on these documents, if you don't mind."

Portier sat in the chair in which I knew he'd sit and picked up one of the carbon sheets. "What am I looking for?"

"Anything that can tell us what's in those recording contracts artists sign. Marrs's secretary says they don't do contracts with the artists. She implies that they're prepared and retained by Kip Harmon, but I don't believe her."

"How did you get them?"

"Miss Price was distracted and left her desk unattended."

"So she does type them, and you stole them." Portier frowned.

"You make opportunity sound so dishonest."

"What did they teach you in seminary anyway?" he asked judgmentally.

"*Romans*," I replied. "They taught us not to be overcome by evil, but to overcome evil with good. That's all I'm doing, trying to overcome evil."

"Did they also mention *Second Corinthians* to you—the part where even Satan disguises himself as an angel of light sometimes?"

I had no reply except to concede and ask him to give the carbon paper back. "I'll look over them myself if you're uncomfortable having them in your hands."

"Oh, give them here," he said. "I don't approve of your methods, Fountain, but I do know opportunity when it knocks. While I'm looking at these carbon copy contracts, what will you be doing?"

"These are those probable anagrams Genny had in her pocketbook. I'm trying to make sense of them, but they don't make any more sense to me now than they did the day she gave them to me."

"Perhaps you should ask the person who broke into her cottage."

"How am I supposed to do that?"

A snide expression spread across Portier's face. "Wait for Detective Robicheaux to finish his investigation."

"You know me better than that." I sat back in my chair to think. "Do you suppose these anagrams were the reason Genny was mugged, and her cottage was ransacked?"

Portier looked at me curiously. "Why do you say that?"

"Because the attacker was first interested in her purse. Not finding what he wanted, he then searched her cottage. That makes me wonder what was in Genny's purse that the attacker didn't find. The only item out of the ordinary at that time was this piece of paper of anagrams that Genny discovered she had and gave to me. That's why the attacker didn't find them in her purse or in her cottage."

He contemplated the idea briefly before saying, "That's plausible, except for one thing: How did the anagrams get into her purse in the first place?"

"I've been thinking about that also," I said. "The only reasonable explanation reverts back to a frustrating conversation Genny and I had with Cindy Mohr at a bistro in Uptown. She's a shrewd one, that Cindy. She turned a conversation that Genny and I coerced her into having into a scenario to her advantage, and we were foolish. We allowed Genny's purse to be unattended for several minutes. That gave Cindy plenty of time to stash the anagrams inside Genny's purse for safekeeping to retrieve later."

"Safekeeping?" Portier asked. "That's an odd word to describe the circumstances you just relayed."

"I know, Portier, but it's the best I can come up with. The Lord knows I've tried to think of everything."

"Then let me have another look," he said. Portier slid the page of anagrams toward himself to review. He studied the lines of letters and numbers carefully.

"What do you see?" I asked impatiently.

"Nothing yet," he said, unmoved by my prompting. "I can't decipher anything without a base of some kind. We need at least one name to unravel. That's all we need. I'm trying to find the anagram that fits Genevieve Duval."

"Ah, good idea. You could also see if Leon Adams or Dale Devoe appear."

"Better still," he said, sliding the paper back over to me and picking up a carbon sheet. "You look at the anagrams, now that you know what to look for. I'll try to decipher what was typed on these sheets."

I looked at the sheet of anagrams again, realizing quickly that none of the puzzles were long enough to be Genevieve Duval. They also weren't long enough for Genny Duval. *Ah! But G Duval.* There were letters for G Duval. I scanned the sheet for L Adams but found nothing. Perhaps Leon's involvement was too long ago. D Devoe, however, was located at the top of the page. "Now, if I only knew what the numbers meant," I said.

"You may have to wait until Genevieve wakes up," Portier replied. "I hope the numbers by her name mean something to her."

Muffled tapping upon a door caught my attention. I looked at Bentley, but he lay quietly beside us without alarm. "Did you hear something?" I asked Portier.

He lifted his head. "No. Was I supposed to?"

"Must've been nothing. Are you finding anything of interest in the carbon papers?"

Portier scratched his head and took a deep breath. "Yes, two of these sheets are what you suspected. They're recording contracts."

"So Miss Price lied to me when she said she didn't type contracts for Marrs Recording."

"She didn't lie," Portier said. "These contracts aren't between the artist and Eldon Marrs. They're between the artist and Christopher 'Kip' Harmon, but you already knew that."

"Yes, but didn't you find Marrs's name at all?"

My friend didn't have time to answer. More muffled rapping came from outside. This time Portier heard it too, and Bentley moved. I rose from my chair and looked out the kitchen window toward Genny's cottage but saw no one from my vantage that could explain the noise.

"But there's something more interesting about the contracts than who they're between," Portier said, uninterested in the noise. I walked toward the table. "Look at my fingers after handling the sheets, Fountain."

I looked but saw nothing on his fingers. I told him so.

"Exactly, but there should be. My fingers should have black carbon residue on them from touching the paper as I have."

"What does that mean?"

"It means this isn't carbon paper, Fountain. It's transfer paper."

I shook my head. "I still don't get it. What's the difference?"

"Little as far as how it's used, but a great deal in how it's made. Transfer paper is made with graphite. It's cleaner and presents a more professional look when the copy has been typed."

"That all sounds good to me. Clean, professional, and made of graphite. So what's the problem?"

"It's also erasable. Carbon is not."

I sat down to gather my bearings.

"Meaning, in case you're still not following me, Fountain, this Harmon fellow is using Miss Price to type two contracts at once—with the contract under the transfer paper being one that can be erased."

"That means the terms of the contract could be changed at his discretion," I said. "It also means that if Genny finds her copy of the contract, it may not even be the same version that Kip Harmon has in his possession."

Bentley stirred again beneath our feet.

"It's time for him to go out," Portier announced. "Here, Fountain, let me take him to the playground to romp a bit. He needs to do more than sleep all day."

"No, please, let me take him," I said. "Your discovery of the transfer paper has given me reason to pause. The exercise will do me good."

"Very well. I'll stay and see what else I can glean from the documents."

"Come 'ere, boy," I urged.

I leashed the lethargic Lab and stepped outside onto the stoop with him. The clouds were still heavy but more dispersed, giving a sense that the storm's remnants would pass completely in a couple of hours. My focus turned from the sky to the sidewalk where I saw the figure of a young woman walking away from Genny's cottage, her back toward me.

Gwen's presence caught me off guard. She was the last person I expected to see. My expression had to have been evident upon my face when she turned around. "Genny isn't home," I said firmly. "Is there something I can do for you?"

Gwen walked closer to me with a tinge of embarrassment. "No, Reverend, but thank you. I just wanted to see if she was in."

"Is there a message?"

"I gave her a folder of some of my song lyrics, and I . . . Well, I just wanted to know what she thought of them."

"Was that you I heard rapping on her door earlier?"

She nodded.

"Several times, in fact. You must really want to talk with her."

"Oh, I do. I think very highly of her opinion."

"I see," I said skeptically. "But how did you know where she lived?"

"I believe it was on that piece of paper you handed me the day Julie was killed."

I shook my head adamantly. "No, I only wrote my phone number and the club where she sang. Did you get her address from Marrs Recording? Were they the ones who told you?"

"What? Oh, no! It was . . . the club. Someone at Paradox told me."

I didn't believe her, but I had no reason to refute her statement out loud.

Gwen presented a bashful smile. "If you see her, Reverend, will you let her know I stopped by?"

"I'll let her know all right," I said sternly. When she turned to walk away, I called her name. She stopped but didn't turn around. "And when you talk to the person who sent you here, Gwen, have them give me a call."

Chapter 23

Genny was just coming out of the guest bedroom when I arrived back at the cottage from Cabrini Playground. Bentley waited patiently for me to unleash him before he made a beeline toward her staggering steps. His tail wagged fiercely, hoping for acknowledgment.

Genny waved him off. "Not now, Ben-buddy, not now. Besides . . . Oh, my, you stink. What did you let him roll in, Dickie?"

"He didn't roll. The playground is saturated with standing water from the storm. I think the mud collected every toxin known to man. I couldn't stand it myself, but he loved it."

Genny waved the air in front of her. "I can handle bologna breath better than this."

Bentley circled at hearing the word of his favorite treat.

Portier rose from his chair. "You just had to mention bologna, didn't you? Come 'ere, boy. Let's get you a treat, then out to the courtyard to air out."

Genny was glad to see Bentley scamper toward the kitchen. She plopped onto the settee and groaned, her blond curls drooping down the side of her face. She wore one of Portier's long, dark-blue dressing gowns that hung past her knees above furry slippers that didn't match. She didn't look like the Genny I knew without her rouge, mascara, earrings, and bangles.

"I didn't sleep well, Dickie," she said. "I didn't sleep well at all."

"Too much on your mind?"

"A bad dream. It wouldn't go away." She appeared as if she wanted to tell me the dream but didn't know how to put it into words. "I had surgery or something. Anyway, I was in the hospital. A nurse came in to help me go to the bathroom. I had to pee like a sailor. It was like I was swimming in the hospital bed, but there were these businessmen in dark suits and doctors in long white robes looking at the French doors leading out to a balcony."

"French doors? You must've had a very nice room."

"Yes, I did. It was like I was very wealthy, and they had me in this elegant private room."

"What were these men looking at?"

"The French doors. The doors were boarded with plywood."

"What for?"

Genny sat up to face me. "That's just it. There'd been a murder. A woman was killed in the very bed I was recovering in. She'd apparently racked up a great deal of gambling debt in Las Vegas and these goons broke in through the French doors and killed her. When I asked the men if I was in danger, they disappeared. I turned to the nurse, and she disappeared too. It was as if they couldn't help me and left. I was alone in bed unable to move. It was the most helpless feeling I'd ever experienced, anticipating being killed should the murderers come back."

"Hmm," Portier said, entering the room.

"Did you hear my story, Chuck?" Genny asked. "What do you mean 'hmm'?"

"Just what it implies," he said. "Very interesting."

"I don't think it's interesting at all."

"No, you wouldn't, given the uncanny similarity of the dream to your real life."

"Yes!" she exclaimed. "It was real life because when I woke up, I really did have to pee."

"You've missed my point, Genevieve."

She looked at me for an explanation.

"I think you know more about the danger you're in than you're letting on," I said. "You're evading the signs of danger you've experienced recently, but your subconscious refuses to be in denial."

"Then what am I to do?"

"It would help if you could tell us what these numbers mean beside your name on the page of anagrams."

Genny watched closely as Portier walked into the kitchen to retrieve the paper.

"We figured out this line of letters and numbers belongs to you, Genevieve," he said when he returned. "Do the numbers look familiar? Were they numbers that Mr. Harmon or Mr. Marrs discussed with you at one time about the revenue your song could bring in?"

She shook her head warily.

"I wonder, Portier," I said, having a thought pop into my head, "I wonder if those numbers represent what Genny's contract is worth to them or what sort of kickback they could expect—or did expect."

"Who's they?"

"Kip Harmon for one, expecting money from either Marrs or Genny herself. The Mohr sisters too, for that matter."

Portier thought for a moment. "That's the most plausible explanation I've heard so far. It would explain the urgency in wanting to get the paper back. It's evidence in the wrong hands."

"But I don't understand what advantage it was to give the paper to *me*," Genny said. "Why do I have it?"

"That's a good question," I said, "but let's think it through. Let's assume that Cindy is the person who slipped the paper into your pocketbook. She probably did it when we were talking at that sidewalk café in Uptown when you had to go to the restroom. If you remember, she'd been arguing with Kip Harmon and the man who slipped you that note. It was apparent she had something they wanted, but she wouldn't give it to them. Contrary to what she wanted us to believe, I believe she was frightened by them."

"They wanted that piece of paper."

"I believe so," I said. "I also believe it wasn't safe for her to have it on her person if they caught up with her."

"But why pass it on to me?"

"I suspect she believed you wouldn't realize it was in your purse, and it would be easy to take it back from you when the heat died down on Cindy."

"That's a big assumption she made."

"That's because she didn't count on you giving me the paper accidentally."

"But it couldn't have been her who mugged me, Dickie," Genny said thoughtfully. "It was definitely a man. It wasn't Cindy."

"We have no idea how many people she's in cahoots with, Genny. It could be anyone. At this point, it doesn't matter who did it. What matters is that Cindy wants it back."

There was a lull in our conversation when the phone rang on the stand near Portier's chair. "It's for you," Portier said, extending the receiver toward me. "A Miss Handerson."

I rose and took the receiver from him. "Yes? Reverend Fountain. That was fast, Gwen. I didn't expect to hear from you so soon."

"The person you asked about in front of Genny's cottage is interested in talking with you," she said.

"I asked you to have the person call me."

"They preferred I call you. Are you available to meet?"

"Who will I be meeting?"

Gwen hesitated. "You might not come if I told you."

"I doubt that," I replied. "It could be Kukla, Fran, or Ollie, and I'd still show up."

"Can you meet the person in thirty minutes at Paradox or The Marina?"

"No," I said definitively. "Someplace neutral, somewhere nice where my skin won't crawl. Say, Carousel Bar in the Hotel Monteleone."

"Thirty minutes?" Gwen asked.

"No later. When the carousel spins around once, the person won't find me any longer."

The phone clicked.

I replaced the receiver and looked at Portier and Genny who stared at me with wide eyes and ears pointed like antennae in my direction.

"Carousel?" Portier asked.

"Yes. Something wrong with that?"

"Not at all. In fact, let me come too. Buy me a Sazerac, and I'll spin quietly by your side. I won't listen to a word."

"No, I must go alone."

"Who is this person?" Genny asked.

"I don't know. I only have my suppositions. Guessing who it will be should keep you two entertained while I'm gone. Whoever guesses correctly when I return will be my guest at Carousel . . . next time."

~

I'll admit that I don't go to many lounges. It's not my thing as a rule, but I'd be remiss if I didn't say that Carousel Bar in the Hotel Monteleone was my favorite lounge in New Orleans. I purposely tried to arrive before the stated thirty minutes were up just so I could sit under the red-and-white canopy of the carousel and watch the people, but I underestimated my ability to walk from Ursulines Avenue to the hotel in mid-June's humidity, and I arrived just three minutes before the allotted time.

I passed the Swan Room in the hotel and peeked in out of curiosity. Although the room was alive with jazz and fashionable patrons, I saw no entertainers onstage that appeared to be famous—a trademark of the room. Too early, I guessed; either that, or I wouldn't know a famous entertainer if I bumped into him or her and knocked them down. I relied on my granddaughter Donna to keep up on such celebrities.

Besides, the Carousel beckoned me. Two dozen seats surrounded the rotating bar under a canopy with a lighted marquee overhead. Each seat had a panoramic view of the of the non-rotating sections of the lounge as the bar made a complete round every fifteen minutes. Men in pinstriped business suits with their matching fedoras upon their knees sat with women adorned in stylish pastel ensembles. They sipped Vieux Carrés and Pimm's Cups while laughing coyly and holding cigarettes to their side without smoking them. A smoky haze floated above the couples under dim overhead lights, creating an ashen ambiance and giving me second thoughts about meeting the mysterious person Gwen preferred not to identify.

I set my fedora upon the vacant seat next to me and ordered a Sazerac from a gentleman named Gordon behind the bar who appeared to be my age. He carried himself with an air of expertise and class. His salt-and-pepper mustache hid a professional smile as he placed a cocktail napkin in front of me. I gestured that a napkin could be placed in front of the stool beside me too. He made my drink as if he'd made thousands like them before and set it in front of me with a sense of ceremony.

I took the glass into my hand and took two sips. The first was rich and empowering. The second gave me the nerve to stay until my guest arrived.

I had a good idea who would walk into the lounge to meet me, but Gwen's statement that I wouldn't show if I knew in advance who the person was caused me apprehension. The only person I wouldn't care to see would've been Gwen herself.

I took a gulp.

Surely not. Please let it not be Gwen who appears.

I had nothing I wanted to say to Gwen even though I had plenty of questions. She was tied to Marrs Recording more closely than she let on, if she wrote the lyrics to "Sand Tan Catamaran" and Dale Devoe chose to record the song. Another thing: There wasn't any love lost between Dale Devoe and Eldon Marrs, from what I'd overheard at the studio. If Gwen worked with Devoe while he recorded "Catamaran," perhaps she knew something about their relationship that would be of some use.

By the fourth sip of my Sazerac, I hoped Gwen would be the one who'd appear in the entrance while I was still bold enough to obtain the answers that suddenly intrigued me.

I was disappointed, however. Seconds before completing my first full rotation on the carousel, a young woman in a white taffeta dress and a floppy-rimmed sun hat entered the smoky lounge and stopped when she saw my face.

The woman grimaced the same time I did.

I stood to indicate to her where I was seated and to greet her as a gentleman.

"Ah, your lady friend has arrived," Gordon said, noticing her entrance.

"She's not a friend," I corrected him, "nor a lady."

Cynthia Mohr sashayed around the carousel to my setting. She looked down at my fedora as if she couldn't believe I hadn't already removed it from the stool. I took it begrudgingly, sitting back down once she was situated comfortably.

"What would you like?" I asked.

"Out of here," she said, using the phrase I'd used on her at The Marina. Cindy looked at my drink. Her demeanor changed; she appeared impressed. "You have fine taste," she said. Cindy looked at Gordon and smiled. "Death in the Afternoon."

Gordon bowed and went to work on the cocktail. When he returned with the bubbly beverage, I toasted halfheartedly to our health. She smiled again and took a sip.

"Are you into Hemingway, Miss Mohr?" I asked.

"Mm, no, but I like his drinks."

"Absinthe and champagne, isn't it?"

She tipped her glass my way.

"Absinthe will drive you mad," I said.

"So they say, Reverend, but it's a misconception."

"With you, it's difficult to know the difference."

She laughed. "Then you know enough of me to understand."

"I know your kind. Poor mental health may have some role in the decisions of your sordid life, but I believe a sinful nature is more to blame."

Cindy's laugh sounded genuine this time. "How delightful you are, Reverend, to indulge me in intoxicating spirits as you accuse me of dancing with the devil. It's quite ingenious how you're able to justify your pompous behavior in such a clever way. Are your sermons just as clever?"

I ignored her. "Where's Ronni?" I asked instead.

"Is she who you hoped would come?"

"Not in particular, but I'm curious."

"I haven't seen her."

I frowned as if I didn't believe her. "She's in town," I said to call her bluff. "She was at Marrs's studio."

Cindy shrugged. "That doesn't mean I've seen her."

I glared at her, but she wasn't easily intimidated.

She sipped her drink and caught my stare before smiling again.

"Why did you agree to see me?" I asked.

Cindy tilted her head back and gazed at the carousel's intricate top before exaggerating a sigh. "I thought we could help each other."

"Help each other?" I asked, astounded. "In what way?"

"I have a problem, and . . . you want information."

"What problem do you have?" I suddenly remembered my last visit to Marrs Recording when I overheard Ronni talking to Melinda Price. "Is someone following you?"

Cindy looked at me. I think she was surprised that I guessed her problem so quickly. "Do you know who it is?"

I shook my head. "Ask the men guarding your home. Why haven't they been able to tell you?"

Cindy frowned. "There are no men guarding my house." Her response appeared genuine. "Where did you hear this?"

"I can't tell you."

She scoffed and sipped her cocktail. "Then your informant must've run into the men following us, mistaking them for my guards."

"Us?" I asked curiously. "Us who?"

Cindy realized her mistake but didn't try to hide it. "Ronni. Ronni's been followed too."

"But I thought you said you haven't seen her."

"I haven't. I haven't seen her since Julie's death, and I don't want to see her."

"Then how did you know she's being shadowed?"

"She called me and asked if I was the one having her tailed."

The comment amused me. "What did you say to that?"

"I hung up on her."

I pondered Cindy's answers momentarily before pushing my glass toward the edge of the bar for Gordon to pick up. "Finish your drink," I said.

"Why?"

"Because your lies are too farfetched to believe, Cindy. I don't know why you agreed to meet other than to manipulate a free drink out of me. I'm going to leave. I suggest you do the same."

She grasped my arm. "No, wait. We can help each other. I have information on Kip Harmon you need. That's why I had Gwen call you. I can tell you what you want to know about Genny's contract."

I relaxed a bit on my stool and eyed her with contempt. "I want to know what she's in debt for and how much."

"Okay, sure. I can tell you that too." Her voice sounded desperate. She grasped my arm tighter. The squeeze wasn't endearing but out of desperation and want.

"Then finish your drink," I said. "I'll buy you another as you talk."

She removed her hand and took her glass. "You'll have another with me?"

"Not on your life. I want my wits about me to discern from you what's the truth and what're lies."

"I'm not going to lie to you."

"How can I be sure?"

"Because I'm going to show you in person."

I hesitated. "What do you mean?"

"It would be easier to show you."

"I'm not going anywhere with you, Cindy."

"Please. You'll get the answers you want but not here. I can give you the actual documents and her account sheets. I can give you everything, but you have to come with me."

"At what price?"

She leaned toward me. "No price, just protection. I want protection."

I shook my head. "I can't do that, Cindy. I'm not a bodyguard, and I'm not a private detective. I have no way of knowing who's following you. My sleuthing is limited to Genny's interests."

"But you know Detective Robicheaux, don't you? Ask him what he knows about me."

I took a deep breath and exhaled slowly, realizing suddenly the real reason why Cindy was so interested in meeting with me. "Just as I thought," I said. "It's not protection you want. You want information. You want to know who the police suspect so that you can stay one step ahead of their game."

"Of course," she replied honestly. "I won't kid you. Their information *is* protection, dealing with the likes of Kip Harmon."

Her statement made sense, but I shook my head again. "I understand, but I'm not interested."

"Fine," she said as if there was nothing more to discuss.

"You did have a good idea, though, Cindy."

She set her glass down and looked at me as if she no longer cared.

"About going to the police, that is. I could go to Detective Robicheaux based upon what you've told me to have him investigate Kip Harmon."

"Tell the police what?" Cindy asked angrily. "That he's no good? You know as well as I do that the police can't go into a place of business and search for documents without probable cause."

"I didn't say Harmon had to be searched, but Robicheaux could ask questions."

"A lot of good that'll do. Robicheaux won't do that. That's what I'm trying to say. He needs proof before he goes on a wild goose chase."

"Then cut to the chase and tell me exactly what you are saying."

"We get the proof for him."

I pulled my drink back from the edge of the bar and drank what was left in the glass. "And how do we do that?" The warm sensation of the cocktail saturated my throat.

"We go to Harmon's place of business at night. No one's there at night."

"Oh, for crying out loud, Cindy! What makes you think I'd ever consider breaking into Harmon's building with you at night?"

"Because you want to help Genny, and you want to give evidence to the detective."

"Not this way. Not at the risk of getting arrested."

"Harmon would never press charges," she said. "Think about it. He wouldn't want the police nosing around his business. We'll be fine. Do you want to resolve Genny's situation or not?"

I took a deep breath and stared at the ice cubes melting rapidly in the ruddy remains at the bottom of my glass. I did want to help Genny. I feared for her. All I needed to resolve her issue was a copy of the contract Harmon held in his possession and a current accounting of what she owed him.

Cindy sensed I was about to relent. She reached for a clean cocktail napkin and asked me for a pen.

"You don't need to write down the address, if that's what you're planning to do," I said sullenly. "I know where Harmon works."

Chapter 24

I stepped out of the Hotel Monteleone and onto the sidewalk, no longer aware of the Quarter's oppressive humidity. I wasn't just reeling from the contemplation of committing a crime with a woman I despised, I was also angry, learning about the details of Cindy and Ronni Mohr being shadowed.

I strode to the garage where Portier stored his Studebaker.

Jeffrey was under the hood of a late-model Dodge Custom Royal Lancer. He poked his head around the hood, and when he saw me darting toward him, he stood and wiped perspiration from his face with a rag he pulled from a back pocket.

"The keys, please," I demanded.

He hesitated. "Mr. Charles called. He'll be needing the Hawk to go into the CBD. Something about his taxes."

I didn't care. "The keys," I repeated.

He studied the angst on my face, then nodded as if Portier's request for his own car was less important. He walked to a pegboard full of keys, took a set off the rack, and handed them to me.

"You going to be okay?" he asked. The look on Jeffrey's face indicated that he didn't think I would be.

I didn't answer. I climbed behind the wheel and slammed the door shut, then cranked the engine and left in a huff without giving Jeffrey instructions on how to explain the missing Hawk to Portier.

I don't remember the drive to Labreville. I honked at insolent drivers who dared to slow my way, but other than that, I scarcely remember the narrow streets of St. Roch. At the Labreville community, I saw several men standing around Miss Cora, who was handing out containers of fresh water. I walked past her without saying a word.

Miss Cora saw me, however, and apparently didn't like the expression on my face because she called my name. The ground was still soggy from the storm's deluge, and I heard her galoshes sucking mud from underfoot as she scrambled to catch up to me.

I turned around and stuck my index finger in the air for her to stop. "I want to do this alone," I said firmly.

Miss Cora appeared to sense it was Leon I wanted a word with. "Be careful, Reverend. He's out of sorts today."

"So am I."

"I won't have any trouble here, do you understand?"

"The truth is no trouble, Cora, unless you're hiding the truth as well."

She glared at me defiantly. "I have no idea what you're talking about."

"No, of course not," I said, not believing her for an instant. "So let me do this alone."

Leon Adams sat on a cement block, wiping his mouth after taking a swig from a tin can of what I presumed was water. He looked up as I approached, his expression indicating that my visit wasn't a surprise to him. He set the can on the ground and stuttered, "My m-mama used to have the same look on her face,

Rev. She called it her comin' to Jesus face."

"Then you must've lied to her as you've lied to me," I replied.

"No lie, Reverend. Just delayed the inevitable."

"Then tell me again how you got your face beat up and how you lost your penknife."

Leon shook his head. "Not much to tell."

"Then let me tell it for you. You didn't get beat up by any thugs hired to protect Cindy and Ronni Mohr at the house where they were living. You got beat up by your own friend, Dale Devoe, and his band of Dares, didn't you?"

"Couldn't have happened like that. D-Dale wouldn't have known where the M-Mohr sisters lived."

"Yes, he would've. He found out the same way you did—through a young woman by the name of Gwen Handerson."

Leon's face paled.

"Dale realized he'd been duped by Cindy and Ronni through Kip Harmon," I said. "Gwen Handerson would've done anything for you or Dale to have one of her song lyrics sung by someone being recorded by Eldon Marrs. She told you where the Mohrs lived. What happened? Did Dale arrive at the house before you?"

Leon gave me a look of contempt. "No, we arrived about the same time. I told him the M-Mohrs were mine. I wanted first crack at 'em. I only wanted to scare them, though, scare them into getting my m-money back from Harmon. D-Dale said no way, he wanted first crack. He was into m-more debt than I was with Kip."

"But he was hitting the charts around the country. He should've been making good money."

"He wasn't."

"Why not? Was it because 'Catamaran' was costing him more money than he was bringing in?"

Leon looked away. "You think you're so smart."

"Then I'm right."

"Nothin' right or wrong about it, just how it works. Harmon was paying DJs and radio stations b-big money to play the song to make 'Catamaran' look like it was hittin' it b-big. Harmon expected the money to come from Dale to pay them. Dale didn't have it."

"So he went after the Mohrs for getting him mixed up with Harmon in the first place."

Leon had trouble getting the words out, but he did so eventually. "Yeah, but the sisters weren't there like Gwen said they'd be. Gwen was supposed to be at the store makin' groceries and the Mohr sisters were supposed to be alone when Dale got to the house, but because he got into an argument with me near the house, Gwen got home before he could get in."

"So what happened?"

"I don't know," Leon said.

"Didn't Dale tell you?"

"Not really. I didn't want to know."

I stepped back and looked at Leon carefully to see if I thought he was telling the truth. "Did he kill Julie Moreno, thinking she was Ronni Mohr?"

Leon continued to stare at the ground. "I said I don't know."

I took another step back. I believed him that time. I believed he didn't want to know if Dale was a murderer. I also believed that Gwen Handerson wasn't only a desperate songwriter in search of a singer to bring life to her words. She was also a meaningful witness to a murder she claimed not to see. If that was the case, Gwen Handerson was also a horrible liar.

~

I dropped Portier's car off at the garage and told Jeffrey he could call Portier to inform him the car was available for his use. It was the least I could do, considering it was his car. I would've done it myself, but I wasn't ready to go back to the cottage. I had too many unanswered questions mulling through my mind to sit peacefully in the parlor while I listened to Genny lament her singing career.

I walked the several blocks to Marrs Recording Studio instead. To my surprise, Melinda Price was exiting the building.

"I'm going home now," she said before I had a chance to greet her.

"Have a pleasant evening," I responded.

She hesitated before taking another step. "You don't want to talk?"

"Yes, but not to you."

"Oh, I see. Well, I'm sorry, Mr. Marrs isn't in. He went for coffee, seeing it was late and I wasn't in the mood to make any more."

"Will he return soon?"

"What do you want?" she asked bluntly.

"Nothing from you, as I said. I simply want to know if he'll return soon."

She eyed me skeptically. "I don't know. Sometimes he returns, sometimes he sits at a table to unwind and talk with the locals. It just depends."

I tipped my fedora. "Thank you. That wasn't so hard now, was it?"

"If you're planning to upset him, Reverend, you should know he's had a very difficult day," she said as I turned to walk away. "Your detective friend wasn't very tactful with his questions."

"I would think Dale Devoe was a bigger thorn in his side. I saw Mr. Devoe as I was leaving. He didn't look at all content."

Melinda shrugged. "I wouldn't know about that. Now, if you don't mind."

I tipped my hat again and walked toward the coffee shop. It was a short walk down the street if Marrs went to the café I remembered from my visit to New Orleans a few months back. I didn't have coffee on my mind until I inhaled the rich aroma of the café's custom blend and warm French pastries.

A young man behind the counter handed me my coffee. I paid him and placed a nickel in the tip jar before sipping just enough to see if the coffee was going to scald the top layers of skin off my lips. When I looked up, I saw Marrs sitting at a table by the window. He was looking back at me but turned away the moment I spotted him.

"I trust you're doing well," I said as I approached.

A woman wearing a white apron and a server's cap walked by his table. He caught her attention before she whisked away.

"Ma'am, may I have this to go?" he asked impatiently, lifting his cup for her to take. He ignored my greeting. "If it's the contract you're here to talk about, Reverend, I'm afraid I haven't had a chance to look into it yet. My secretary is usually quite good about such things."

"Yes, she's a delight, isn't she? It doesn't matter anymore, really. You may ignore my request. I've found an alternative means of getting a copy."

He stood as the waitress arrived with a cup to go and fresh coffee inside. "I assume you're referring to the detective that visited me today."

"Not at all. Why? Did he ask about it?"

Marrs frowned. "No, but it's just a matter of time before you put the bug in his ear, I'm sure. Tell me, Reverend. I've asked this before: What compels men of your stature to do what you do? I've always assumed that such inquiries as yours stem from a personality defect from their adolescent years, much like the little-man syndrome. What do you think?"

I laughed. "I think you and Miss Price drink from the same water cooler."

"Please don't tell me you do it in the name of integrity."

"I don't plan to explain it to you at all. My inquiries have been legitimate. You entered into a recording contract with Genevieve Duval. That contract should be available for her to see, but you refuse to hand it over. Little-man syndrome or not, you have a fiduciary responsibility to provide a copy of that contract to Miss Duval."

Marrs walked toward the exit with his coffee in hand. I set my cup on the table to leave it behind.

"I do hope you're not following me to my office," he said.

We walked to the curb to cross Rampart. He stepped into the street before I called his name to have him turn around. I wasn't about to let him get away without a good scolding. "I will get to the bottom of what's going on at your studio whether you help me or not," I said. "Mark my words, I will . . . I'm going to—Oh! Marrs! My God, watch out!"

Out of the corner of my eye, I saw it coming. A large sedan darted without warning from a corner parking space and veered toward us. I grabbed Marrs's arm and swung him toward the café. We fell hard upon the pavement. Marrs's twisted body lay motionless for several seconds, while I struggled to keep from landing too heavily upon him.

A young couple ran to our rescue, helping both of us to our feet.

Marrs was visibly shaken, unable to grasp what had just happened. His right hand and arm had scraped against the pavement, causing an open wound. Blood penetrated through his right pant leg.

I looked down at myself. Blood stained the outside of my trousers as well, saturated around a two-inch rip in the fabric. Except for scrapes on my right elbow and both hands, I appeared to be fine. I was more concerned about Marrs, however, who took the brunt of our fall against the pavement. After assessing his injuries and determining them to be minor, I focused on what had happened.

I looked in both directions as if the avenue, now swollen with traffic, would reveal hidden clues as to the identity of the driver. Perhaps the driver knew he or she had missed us and was waiting for another opportunity. Perhaps the driver was content in knowing he or she had just frightened us and was eager to drive away.

"You okay?" I asked Marrs.

He didn't respond. He brushed dirt and pebbles from his clothing and surveyed the loss of a pocket ripped along the seam.

When I realized I wouldn't get an answer, I turned my attention to the young couple who saw the incident. They stood along the curb, shaking their heads as if unable to comprehend what they'd witnessed.

"Did you happen to see the driver or type of car?" I asked them.

"Oh, wow, it went so fast," the young man blurted out. "It was like a blur, you know. This car—a Mercury, I think—just came from that corner there and barreled across the intersection."

"A Mercury? Are you sure it wasn't a Buick, one of the large ones like a Roadmaster?"

"Oh, no, sir, no, sir. It was a Mercury all right. One of those two-toned Montclairs. A fifty-five I'd guess, by the looks of the chrome and taillights."

I shook the cobwebs out of my head. I hadn't come across anyone who drove a Mercury Montclair.

"Anyway, sir, it was like he was coming straight for you. All of a sudden he was there. Bam! Right there! Then he squealed his wheels. Did you hear him squeal his wheels, babe? And then he was down the street. Oh, wow, if you hadn't seen him coming, you two would've been goners. I'm tellin' you, both of you wouldn't be here talking to me right now. I can't believe it. Can you believe it, babe? Oh, wow, she can't believe it, either."

"Okay, okay, calm down now, okay?"

"Okay, yeah. I'm trying to, but it's like wow! You okay, babe? She's okay, man. Yeah, she's okay."

I put my hand on the young man's shoulder to compose him, but the adrenaline continued to pump through his body. His girlfriend stood in shock, nodding periodically when addressed, but otherwise unable to articulate what she'd seen.

"Oh, wow, we gotta call the cops," the man said his eyes wide with excitement. "I'm sure there's a phone in the café, 'cause we gotta call someone."

"No, we're fine," I said, continuing to pat his shoulder. "Just tell me something if you can. Was it a man driving?"

"Yes, sir, it was a man. I saw him."

"Did you get a license plate number?"

"What? Oh, no. It happened so fast. Did you get it, babe? Did you see the plate number? Sorry, sir. She didn't, either."

I allowed him to jabber a few more seconds before I realized I'd reached the extent of their knowledge. I thanked them and turned, realizing that Eldon Marrs no longer stood beside me.

The young man pointed his finger. "Hey, mister, he's going that way."

I thanked him again and hurried across the street.

"Get the hell away from me!" Marrs yelled as I approached from behind. He continued to walk, refusing to look at me. "I don't want to be anywhere near you or the kind of people you attract."

"You think the man who tried to mow us down was after *me*?"

"Who else do you think I'm talking about?" he answered, stopping to face me. "I've had nothing but trouble since you arrived. Before you, I had no trouble."

"None that you knew about or cared to know about anyway."

"That's how you get your jollies, isn't it, conjuring up crises, and making out like the police are going to raid my place at any moment so that you can weasel your way into my office."

"Why would I want to do that?"

"To try to get your friend out of her contract." Marrs turned and began to walk again. "Well, it's not going to happen," he yelled. "Miss Duval has a contract and it's going to stick."

"No!" I yelled. "No! You listen to me. Genny Duval has every intention of following through on her contractual obligations. The problems are yours, Marrs. You had problems even before Genny signed on with you. You were in so much denial that you didn't face them head on. You were too cowardly to ask the right questions about what was going on in your office."

"Go screw yourself."

"You know it's true. You have to know it's true. There isn't a rock large enough for you to crawl under for you not to know you're in charge of a corrupt organization."

Marrs stopped again. "I work my ass into the ground for these artists. If I didn't, nobody would. Nobody cares for their talent and what they have to say or offer. They need a voice like mine to help them along and to let them know they can be a star, and it will all be okay."

Eldon Marrs took a deep breath and looked down the street as he shook his head. "Well, it's not going to be okay, you asinine know-it-all," he added. "No one is going to listen to their songs. No one is going to call and invite them to be on *Ed*

Sullivan. There are pills that take away the pain in their joints after working at their two or three jobs, but there's nothing that takes away the pain in their hearts except what they write about in their songs."

"I'm not oblivious to their plight," I said. "What I'm talking about are the individuals who are taking advantage of their plight."

"Is that what you think I'm doing? Do you think I'm taking advantage of these artists?"

"No, I didn't say that, but I'm not sure about your office manager and the people she associates with. Ronni Mohr, for starters. What's she doing, having any business with you or your artists?"

"Ronni Mohr is no longer an issue."

"Are you naïve?" I asked. "I'm talking about kickbacks to people like her and Kip Harmon. Take a look at your artists' files—the real files, not the files Melinda Price lets you see. Take a look at the files belonging to Genny Duval, Leon Adams, and Dale Devoe, and after you do, tell me something isn't wrong with what they owe and who they owe it to."

Marrs looked at me with hate burning in his eyes. "There's nothing more to say, Reverend. Good evening."

He limped to the entrance of his office. I didn't follow. There was no reason to do so. He unlocked the entry door, but before stepping inside, Marrs turned abruptly to me and said, "Speaking of debt, Reverend, you owe me a cup of coffee. Somehow, I think I spilled mine."

Chapter 25

"You've stepped up your game, haven't you?" Portier asked when I walked through the door of his cottage. "And rather quickly too, I might add."

I had no idea what he was talking about, and I was in no mood to ask.

"You've gone from stealing transfer paper to stealing automobiles in a matter of hours," he added. "Well done, Fountain."

I had no excuse to give him for taking his car without permission. "I'm sorry about that. It was wrong of me, and I apologize. Were you able to get your situation cleared with the IRS?"

"Not yet. In an effort to correct their error, they double-billed me apparently, and now I owe twice the taxes."

"Goodness," I said. "What do you plan to do?"

"I plan to go back tomorrow and sit in the supervisor's office until they sort it out. I don't take incompetence lightly."

I started to walk to the kitchen to brew some chicory when Portier stopped me.

"Is there anything you want to discuss?" he asked.

"No, why should there be?"

"No reason; it's just that your clothes are torn, you've lost your fedora, blood is dripping from your trousers, your arms are scuffed, your face is haggard, and your expression is as if your dog just died."

"Yes, well, much is on my mind," I said irritably. "I wasn't paying attention to where I was walking, that's all. This town should place rubber mats over their sidewalks to make falls more comfortable."

"Do you need a doctor?"

"A doctor can't mend what's broken, I'm afraid. Would you like some coffee?"

"Not the kind you drink."

"I'll make regular then." I hesitated slightly. "May I borrow your car this evening?"

"For what purpose?"

"No purpose that I want to tell you about."

Portier mulled over the request. "Then I should say no for your own good, shouldn't I?"

"You should," I replied, "but that would force me to revert to my double life as an auto thief."

My friend didn't flinch at my honesty or my attempt at humor. "Then by all means call Jeffrey with my blessing, but I'm being sincere, Fountain. If you need to talk . . ."

I thanked him and limped my way to the kitchen.

~

Jeffrey pulled Portier's car in front of the cottage before he called it a day. I tipped him and took the keys without either one of us saying a word. Traffic was light from the Quarter down Claiborne Avenue, but the drive was slow going, mostly because the evening sun shone directly into my eyes just below the edge of the sun visor. I found my way, however, and pulled to a stop in front of Kip Harmon's place of business on a side street off Carrollton. The desolate commercial street of warehouses and trade buildings appeared exactly as I remembered, with one noticeable difference. The security guard who questioned Genny and I the last time we were on the premises was nowhere in sight.

Neither was Cindy.

Dusk quickly became night.

I glanced up and down the street to see if Cindy's shadow lurked in the darkness out of the light from the streetlamps. I saw nothing and contemplated whether I should wait for her. It didn't feel right being here as darkness grew, and the palms of my hands perspired.

Was there a back entrance?

Cindy didn't tell me to come to a back entrance, but it would make more sense. I walked down the alley to the back, crept to a windowsill, and looked in, but the room inside was dark. I couldn't make anything out. A steel door next to the window was securely locked. I looked for a car—any car—but none were parked near the building. I tried the back door one more time. It didn't budge.

I'd started to walk away when the steel door opened far enough for a female voice to call my name. I turned and walked cautiously toward the door. It opened wider, and a hand grabbed my arm and pulled me through the doorway into darkness.

"I don't have time for you," Cindy said.

"You didn't tell me where you'd be."

Cindy turned on a dim overhead light that illumined a small wooden desk strewn with papers. A lone coffee cup containing cold, stale coffee had cream coagulating on top.

"You don't listen," she said. "If you're not going to listen, I can't help you."

"I thought someone who worked here would be with us."

"I didn't say that."

"Then how did you get in?" I asked angrily. "Tell me again why this isn't breaking and entering."

She lifted a set of keys in front of my face. "Because I was given these. Does one break and enter with authorized keys?"

"First of all, I don't know how you got those keys. Second, I don't know the law well, but I suspect intent is a factor in determining whether the law is being broken."

"Well, I intend to shove these keys down your throat when I'm done if you don't keep quiet and follow instructions." She stared at me through the dull light with increasing impatience. "No gloves?"

"Why do I need gloves? I don't plan to leave fingerprints on anything I don't have a right to see."

"You're an idiot," she said. "Suit yourself, but I should warn you that I'm ignorance intolerant this evening. Do you understand?" Cindy turned toward an open doorway at the back of the room.

I grabbed her arm. "I mean it, Cindy," I said. "I'm not comfortable with this. I need to know exactly what we're going to do here. I came for two items and two items only: Genny's contract and her account statement."

"And that's what you'll get."

"Then why do I feel like a cat burglar?"

Cindy broke the grip from her arm and gave me a piercing glare. "This isn't going to work. You ask too many questions."

"No, I don't ask enough."

"You should leave."

"What?"

"I want you to go."

"Cindy, I came here on good faith based upon your word. You implied your word was good this time."

"My word *is* good, Reverend, but you need to keep your mouth shut. We're not here for your comfort. There's nothing comforting about either one of our situations. Do you understand?"

"Of course I do."

"Then understand this when I say I know where we're going and what we'll find. We can be in and out just like that, but not if you slow me down with your nerves and nonsense. So never mind how I got in here. Never mind where I got the keys. Just keep your eyes open and your mouth shut. You'll get what you came for. Otherwise, you'll get nothing."

I stood, bewildered, wanting to turn back but needing to follow.

"Come or go," she demanded. "You've already wasted valuable time—time we don't have."

Cindy turned without an answer and walked briskly toward the open doorway at the back of the room.

I took a deep breath and followed.

We entered a large room divided into smaller sections by metal shelving that held boxes marked with people's names and dates. A second, even larger room contained canisters of film strips and vinyl record albums. Several small offices lined the outer walls of the room, presumably for clerks in charge of maintaining the inventory. A closed door identified as *File Room* caught my eye immediately. I stopped to turn the knob for entry, but it was locked.

Cindy kept moving.

I trotted to catch up. "Why are we passing up the filing room?" I asked. "There could be valuable information in there."

"Do you want to lead the way? Please, feel free to lead the way."

"No, I was just—"

"Being helpful?" she asked snidely. "Yes, I know. Please, don't try to be. I know where I'm going and where we should go first. If we have time for one of your side field trips, we'll go, but right now I'm in a hurry."

"Where are we going?"

"We need to go upstairs."

We turned a corner, and I followed Cindy into a dark, narrow stairwell. A faint industrial smell I couldn't identify permeated the air. I grabbed the stair railing for support as I groped my way to a landing where we turned and went up more stairs. I could barely make out Cindy's silhouette ahead of me in the darkness, but I followed as closely as I could while making sure my feet hit each step squarely and securely.

We exited the stairwell onto a floor with dark, dull linoleum. Little light shone from the offices that lined both sides of the hall. Cindy walked a short distance before stopping in front of a closed door. She produced a key from a side pocket and tried to unlock the door, but she struggled to get the door open.

"What's wrong?" I asked.

She cursed but didn't answer. Instead, she moved swiftly to the next office. This time, the key she used fit perfectly. Cindy opened the door.

The office was small. No certificates of achievement or diplomas of education hung on the walls to indicate who the office belonged to, but the room was so dark that I doubted I could've read them even if they were there. The only things hanging were an unsigned watercolor of a generic French Quarter street across from the desk and a round white wall clock one could find in most filling stations. Behind the desk was a mirror that could've been purchased at a discount furniture or variety store. A small brass lamp sat on the corner of the desk as well as a half-full bottle of pop and a bronze obelisk for decoration. A larger, more contemporary lamp sat on an end table. Beside the desk was a trashcan full of discarded papers.

"I don't think we'll find much here," I said.

"Shut up," Cindy replied as she opened a drawer of the only filing cabinet in the room. "We'll find plenty. You look in here."

"Is this Harmon's office?"

"No, this is the Oval Office. Stop talking and start looking." Cindy left the cabinet and went to Harmon's desk.

I watched her out of the corner of my eye while I tried to look through the folders she said to go through. Cindy opened the top middle drawer of the desk but slammed it shut almost immediately, reaching simultaneously for a side drawer to rummage through its contents. She appeared frustrated and increasingly agitated.

I decided to concentrate on my task of reviewing papers within green hanging files. Nothing interested me, so I closed that drawer and opened a second one. This one looked more promising. The papers were letters to and from vendors, customer complaints, and legal notices. One letter caught my attention. I glanced toward Cindy to see that her focus was diverted elsewhere before I pulled the piece of paper completely out of the folder. I scanned it quickly. Cindy's name appeared several times throughout the document.

I replaced it and pulled out another letter with similar results.

"What do you have there?" Cindy asked me.

I stuffed the paper into the folder and closed the drawer.

"You were reading something. What was it?" she asked again.

"Nothing. I can barely see in this office, it's so dark. This is a wild goose chase, Cindy. You brought me here under false pretenses."

"You don't know what you're looking for. I'll finish the filing cabinet," she said. "You look in the end table. There's a drawer in it."

I scoffed and turned toward the end table, complaining that it was an unlikely place for someone to place contracts and account statements.

That's when everything went dark.

~

I awoke to silence. The room swirled around me without sound, darker than before. Acute pain from the back of my head and right shoulder made me gasp for breath. The bronze obelisk lay on the floor by my head.

I called Cindy's name, but she didn't answer. I tried to stand. My head spun wildly, and my stomach lurched. I got up on all fours and rocked until the sickness in the pit of my gut subsided.

How will I get out of here?

I mustered the strength to crawl on my hands and knees to the office doorway and into the hall. I remembered the stairwell was to the right, but I could get there faster if I walked. I leaned my back against the wall until I felt as if I could stand, then did so, using the wall as support. With short, unsteady steps, I made my way to the stairwell.

I can't walk down there. I'll topple for sure.

I sat on the top step and butt-scooted my way down the steps to the landing, then turned the corner and did the same until I reached the main floor. By the time I reached the bottom, I felt considerably weaker, dizzy again, and nauseous. I sat quietly and breathed deeply until the pangs of sickness subsided once again.

I had to reach the back exit to the alley. Cindy had tricked me into coming to Harmon's from the beginning, I realized—even set it up to appear as if I'd broken in and entered the building on my own accord. She had no intention of helping me find Genny's contract or her account statement.

Courage welled within me. I stood, determined to walk again, and shuffled through a doorway, but it looked unfamiliar. I continued to walk through my daze until I reached another doorway at the other end of the room. There, I stopped to rest. If I was right, the door to the alley would be straight ahead.

Stay the course! I tried to concentrate, but it was getting harder to do so. My steps slowed. My head spun. I grew weary. Sleepy. My stomach churned. I needed to rest—just for a moment. I remembered a desk and chair in the room when I came in. If I could get there, I knew I could . . . Umph! I tripped suddenly and fell to the floor. Everything went black once again.

Chapter 26

This time I awoke, bewildered and coughing, under a warm, wet washcloth draped over my eyes and the bridge of my nose. I was propped on a couch with soft down pillows under my back to support me in a half-sitting position on the cushions. I moved slightly, which made me cough again. It wasn't a deep cough but one that was raspy and dry. My mouth tasted of stale carpet. I heard nothing in the room and lifted my arm to remove the washcloth from my eyes to gain my bearings, but Portier's familiar voice warned me to leave it where it was.

"Where am I?" I asked.

"In your worst nightmare," he said. "Nothing is scarier than me being your nurse. Keep that cloth over your head."

"Where's Genny?"

"She went back to her cottage. She said it was about time."

I sighed deeply. "I feel so foolish. I tried to help her, but I couldn't. How did you find me?"

"Quiet. You shouldn't be talking, but I need you awake. You've taken a nasty bop on the back of the head. I called for a doctor. He said to keep you awake, but you'll be fine."

"But how did you find me, Portier, really?"

"You can thank Jeffrey for his quick thinking and that rusty old two-ton of his. I'm surprised you didn't spot him following you. He burns a quart of oil just starting the engine. It blew blue smoke all the way down Claiborne behind you."

"Were you with him?"

"You bet your sweet ass I was. You were in a terrible way yesterday afternoon when you came home, and you wouldn't tell me where you were going after you asked to borrow my car. You don't think I was going to let you go out by yourself in the state of mind you were in, do you? Your track record for evading trouble is abominable even when you're thinking clearly, let alone when you're in a funk.

"Jeffrey and I followed you to that side street off Carrollton. We knew you went into the back of that old block building. We saw a woman come out, but you didn't follow her. Jeffrey got out of the truck to investigate. Fortunately, the door was unlocked. He found you on the linoleum just inside the back door. You almost made it out into the alley, but almost wasn't good enough."

"I can explain myself," I said.

"I wish you wouldn't. I'd rather you remain quiet."

"But I'll fall asleep again."

"Then I'll have to slap you awake."

I sighed and tried not to laugh. "You'd like that, I know."

"Yes, very much, in fact."

I was about to explain what happened at Harmon's despite Portier's objections when several soft raps on his front door interrupted me.

"You'll not have any visitors," Portier warned.

"I'm not expecting any," I replied, "but it could be the police to question me."

"I don't believe the police rap softly as if they've made a loaf of gingerbread for you that they don't want to drop. Lie back down. I'll get rid of whoever it is."

Portier went to the door. "Yes?" he asked with a tone of indifference.

"I'm sorry to bother you," I heard a woman say, "but may I speak to a Reverend Fountain, please?"

"There isn't anyone here by that name," he said bluntly.

I rose quietly and tiptoed toward the door so that I could see her, but she couldn't see me.

"Oh, but there must be," she said with a note of desperation in her voice. "I was told that he would be at this address." The woman pulled a crumpled and dirty piece of notepaper from a side pocket of her purse. She pulled the folds open and validated the name and address.

"Yes, you're correct, but he isn't here at the moment," Portier said.

"I see." The woman sounded terribly disappointed. "May I leave a message?"

"Yes, I'll be happy to relay it to him."

"That would be very kind. I'm only in town for a short while. I must take care of some distressing business. I'm sure he can help me. If you would have him get in touch with me, I'd appreciate it. I need to speak with him immediately."

"Of course. What's your name and where can he reach you?"

"My last name is Moreno."

I poked my head from my hiding place and eyed the young woman with apprehension. "Moreno?" I asked her.

"Yes," she responded, surprised that my face suddenly appeared. "Julie Moreno."

"Please come in, Miss Moreno," Portier said. "The man whose mouth is gaping is Richard Fountain, the person you want to see. I'm sorry I had to be deceptive, but he took quite a bump to the back of his head last night. I was trying to make sure he rested without interruption, but you're a special exception. Won't you have a seat? May I offer you something to drink?"

She refused politely, keeping her gaze upon me as if her visit really was genuine, and she had to speak with me urgently. She smiled graciously and sat with perfect posture, yet there was a tenacious spirit in her presence, one that commanded respect and interest. She was fashionably dressed, but modest in style and color. She wore a hint of cosmetics that accentuated her eyes—deep, dark brown, and compelling. She appeared nothing like her former roommates, the Mohr sisters and Gwen Handerson.

"It's kind of you to see me, Reverend," she said.

"Not at all, but I must say your presence has startled me. You're supposed to be dead. How are you still alive?"

My inquiry seemed to amuse her. "The question shouldn't be Why am I still alive; it should be Why should I be dead?"

I stammered for words. "Well, because, Miss Moreno, we all thought you were. If you're not dead, then who was found murdered in your bed?"

She shook her head. "I don't know."

I frowned, unsure whether or not to believe her.

"Forgive me," she continued. "No doubt my presence is startling. I'll admit that Ronni and I had a terrible row the night I was supposed to have been killed, but I left the house before the argument could escalate and then left town soon after."

"To return to St. Louis?"

Julie shook her head. "I've lived in St. Louis before, that's true, but I'm originally from Des Moines. I figured the Mohrs would try to look for me in St. Louis. That's why I couldn't go there."

"Ah! But how did you know to come to Mr. Portier's cottage?"

Julie handed me the crumpled letter that was still in her

hand. "This is the name and address Gwennie had waiting for me."

I read the note. It was just my name, Portier's address, and his phone number. "Waiting for you how?"

"Under a flowerpot in the side garden. Gwennie and I often left notes for each other under that flowerpot when we didn't want Cindy or Ronni to know what we wanted to share. You see, it was extremely difficult living with the Mohrs. They were constantly at odds with each other and did everything in their power to draw us in to choose a side."

"Cindy would have us believe they were close sisters," I said.

"Maybe with her other sister Sheila, but certainly not with Ronni. She misled you if that's what she wanted you to believe."

"I did know she had another sister," I said, "but it didn't mean anything to me at the time."

"Sheila lives in St. Louis but visits Cindy and Ronni in New Orleans often. I'm surprised she's not here now to lend support to them."

"But how did you know there'd be a note with my name on it under the flowerpot?"

"Ronni and I had a big row, as I just said. Perhaps you heard about it. I left, and Gwennie was the only person who I confided in as to where I could be contacted. I hadn't heard from her until a couple of days ago when she sent me a telegram. Here, I'll show it to you." She reached inside her pocketbook and pulled out another piece of crumpled paper.

I read the telegram quickly. "But this is gibberish," I said. "It doesn't make sense."

"It does if you knew Gwennie's code. She often wrote song lyrics that were beautifully crafted but made no sense at all. That's because the lyrics, like this telegram, are written acrostically, Reverend. Read the telegram again but with only the first letters of each word, and you'll see very clearly it reads: *Stay Dead!* It was a warning for me to stay in Des Moines."

"Obviously you didn't follow her directions," I said.

"How could I? If people thought I'd been murdered, I feared Gwennie was in grave danger herself."

I took a deep breath and thought for a moment. "You speak of Gwen in the past tense, Miss Moreno."

Julie looked down at her hands folded nervously in her lap. "Yes, that's why I'm here. I fear something terrible has happened to Gwennie. Have you seen her lately?"

"I saw her yesterday." My answer didn't seem to give Miss Moreno much comfort. "What is it?" I asked.

"Nothing. I don't know, but I fear something has happened to her since then. She's nowhere where we'd often go to get away, but she indicated that you may have some information that can help me."

"About what?"

"For one thing, knowing why I'm supposed to be dead. That would help. Maybe Gwennie isn't dead, either."

I shook my head. "I was hoping you could tell me that. I certainly don't know. Have you been to the police?"

"Not yet, but I'm planning to go there after I talk with you."

I thought carefully. "I'm sure the most important question they're going to ask you is If you're not dead then who was found murdered in your bed?"

"I'm sure they will, but I told you the truth. I don't know. It's all so upsetting."

"Then tell me what happened that night. Are you sure you wouldn't like a refreshment? Coffee, perhaps?"

"On second thought, yes, that would be nice," she replied.

Portier frowned. He'd been very reserved, listening to Julie's story. Now he appeared perturbed that I'd mention coffee at this moment, knowing I'd expect him to prepare it and potentially miss more of what she had to say.

"Do you take cream or sugar?" I asked.

"Only cream, thank you," she said as Portier rose from his seat.

I smiled graciously at him as he continued to look at me with contempt. "I'd like cream as well," I said.

When he left, I urged Miss Moreno to continue. "You were saying about that night."

"Yes, Reverend, that night I had a terrible row with Ronni. She insisted we had to move. I could take no more. It's been difficult, coming to New Orleans to make a living, but I've been making some strides. I wasn't ready to move out, but I'd scraped enough funds together to do so. Ronni's instability and poor decisions threatened to erase all that I'd gained, so I began packing my things."

"That corroborates what Gwen told me. She also said that when the argument got stronger between you two, she went to bed. She heard doors opening and closing, cars starting and driving away. Is that true?"

"Oh, I wouldn't know about that."

"What do you mean?"

"I didn't argue with Ronni long enough to know."

I sat back in my seat and scratched my head. "You mean you left the house?"

"Oh, yes, indeed."

"This is where your and Gwen's stories differ, I'm afraid."

"I'm sorry, but I'm telling you the truth. I left the house immediately when our argument began to heat up. Ronni can be unreasonable, and I wanted no more of it."

"I see. Well, I have no reason to doubt you. Quite frankly, I found Gwen's version of the events difficult to fathom. So you left as you say. That was it?"

Portier stood in the kitchen doorway to listen. I could hear the percolator popping. The aroma of Community Coffee soon followed.

"Not entirely," Julie said. "I left without my grip, planning to return later when Ronni had cooled off. I saw the most extraordinary thing, however. Cindy was sitting in her car, peering out her window. Her focus was on a group of men a couple of houses down the street. It appeared that a group of four or five men had some differences with a shabbily dressed fellow. They argued and had a scuffle."

I looked at Portier for his reaction. "Leon Adams and Dale Devoe," I said. "I'd bet my money on it."

"The scruffy man was knocked to the ground," she added. "The other men left him lying on the sidewalk. I couldn't see their features very well because it was dark, but I saw what happened."

"And Cindy was just sitting in her car, looking at them?"

"Yes. She asked where I was going. I said, 'Out.' I was more interested in what she was doing. She said she was waiting for someone she works with."

"Do you know who?"

Julie shook her head. "She often goes out with this coworker named Juanita, I think, who works with Kip Harmon, a talent agent in town or whatever he is. I use the term coworker loosely, Reverend. They're more like cohorts."

"But it sounds as if you don't believe she was waiting for this Juanita at all."

"No, I believe she was more interested in the men, but if you're asking about another body and who the body could be, this woman she works with makes sense."

"Why do you say that?"

"Because if Ronni wanted it to look as if I was dead when I

really wasn't, she needed another body in place of mine. Juanita is just as shady as Cindy and Ronni, and her physical features are very similar to mine. I suggest the police find out if a woman named Juanita is missing."

"Let me ask something, Julie. Cindy would have me believe that Ronni needed to move because of creditors. What's your take on that?"

Portier returned to the kitchen and came out with three coffees and a creamer on a tray. We fixed our coffees to our liking as Julie thought carefully about how to respond to my question.

"Creditors," she said as if they were a thorn in her side. "Yes, there were creditors, but Ronni wasn't the type of woman to be afraid of a few bill collectors. Neither was Cindy. Me? I was careful to pay my bills in full and on time, but Ronni couldn't care less about it. No, she wouldn't be intimidated by a few phone calls or house visits from creditors."

"Then why did she really want to move?"

Julie set her cup on its saucer and pondered her words as if they were difficult to speak out loud. "Something more sinister, I'm afraid," she said. "That's why I stayed out of sight for so long until I knew I couldn't stay out of sight any longer."

"I don't understand," I said, hoping she'd say more.

"I don't understand it, either; not at all," she replied, "but there was always an uneasy feeling in the house. I attributed it to the unethical business they were involved with at Harmon's. Gwennie's message to me to stay dead, however, and her note under the flowerpot with your name and contact information in case I got into trouble . . . Well, I don't know myself anymore, but I know it isn't good."

"The answer lies within Gwen," I said.

Julie nodded timidly and picked up her cup from the table. Her hand shook as she sipped her coffee and fought back her tears.

"Okay," I said to prevent a deluge from her eyes. I set my coffee cup aside. "Then here's what you should do. You should go straight to the police. Better yet, I'll call Detective Robicheaux from here to have one of his officers come get you. After you speak with the detective—you'll find him very personable, by the way—you should leave New Orleans if he agrees and return to Des Moines immediately. Do you understand? Your life could be in jeopardy here in New Orleans, Miss Moreno, and I don't believe it's safe. Then, while you're in Des Moines, you continue to keep a low profile until the police are able to sort this mystery out."

Julie nodded her understanding.

"Do you think you can do all of that for me?" I asked.

"Certainly," she said. "Among other things, the most important is that I keep low." She leaned back in her seat and chuckled under her breath. "I can do that, Reverend. After all, keeping low is what dead people do best."

Chapter 27

Portier and I sat in his back courtyard, sipping lemonade. He seemed content, reading the paper and sucking on ice cubes as Bentley lay underfoot. My glass had hardly been touched, however, and I was sure the nervous tapping of my foot under the canopied table irritated my friend to no end.

"It's only been three or four hours," Portier said nonchalantly, without lifting his head from the paper. "I don't know why you're so anxious."

"I expected a call from the detective by now," I replied.

"Forgive him, Fountain, but a dead girl just appeared in his office. He may have a few questions about that."

I sighed heavily. "I hope he isn't too cross."

That comment drew Portier's head above the pages. "About what?"

"About how this case is going. I'm certain he was hoping it would be open and shut. On top of that, it got me to thinking. I wonder if he's made heads or tails out of that man who wanted to claim Julie's body in the first place. You know, the one who claimed to be her brother."

"I'm sure I couldn't tell you, but I must say your case has

made my income tax issues seem insignificant. I do wish, however, you could come to New Orleans sometime and mind your own business. Between you and Genevieve, I'm running out of washcloths and Merthiolate."

Bentley's ears perked up and his head rose even before we heard the heavy knocking on the front door through the open screen to the kitchen. Portier didn't bother to rise. We both were certain the visitor, whoever it was, was for me.

Sure enough, it was.

Detective Robicheaux and an officer stood on the sidewalk when I opened the door. Robicheaux tipped his hat and introduced Officer Malois. I invited them into the parlor where Bentley greeted them with a gusto tantamount to meeting two hot-dog vendors.

"He's friendly, Detective," I assured him.

"I can see." He attempted to pat the Lab but changed his mind, instead shielding himself by lifting a brown folder he'd brought with him.

"And smells of a radioactive waste dump," I added. "My apologies on that, but the tomato juice Mr. Portier bathed him in hasn't quite done the trick yet."

Portier grabbed the collar around Bentley's neck and led him back into the courtyard.

"Not to worry," Robicheaux said. "We've interviewed mangier creatures than him before. We have a few questions, if you have a moment."

"Certainly. Not sure how I can help, but I'm willing to do so."

"I had a most interesting visitor this morning thanks to your recommendation that Miss Moreno come to see me."

"I thought your morning could use a lift."

The detective described in detail the conversation he and Julie had together. In turn, I verified that what she told him was what she relayed to me as well.

"What do you make of it?" he asked.

"Well, Detective, I believe she has a more credible story than Gwen Handerson, if you want my honest opinion. It seems more likely that Miss Moreno left the house when she says she did and saw Cindy Mohr in her car, looking at some men arguing not far away. If you remember, Gwen's recollection of the murder includes her cowering under covers and falling asleep. Perhaps she can be reinterviewed to see if she wants to change her story."

"We've tried to track down Miss Handerson without any luck. Do you know where she could be?"

"I doubt she'd be there even if I had any suggestions."

"Why is that?"

"She's either hiding or dead."

Robicheaux frowned. "Yes. That's what Miss Moreno believes also."

"Any luck determining who the dead woman is now that we know she isn't Miss Moreno?" I asked.

He hesitated before saying, "No, that's why we're eager to interview Miss Handerson. But there was another interesting development, Reverend. The man called again to claim the body, insisting it is Julie Moreno. He even came into the station this morning as I was interviewing Miss Moreno. He's still waiting in the station." Robicheaux turned to his officer and asked, "Or should I say he's being held?"

Officer Malois nodded his head at the latter.

Robicheaux took a black-and-white photograph from his folder and extended it to me. "Ever see this man?"

I looked carefully. "Why, yes, Detective. I don't know his name, but he handed Genny Duval an ominous note one day while she was singing at Paradox. He wore a brown-checkered suit, and I later discovered he drives a forest-green Buick

Roadmaster."

Portier walked back into the room. I showed the photograph to him.

"His name is Alan Bendford," Robicheaux said.

"Is he the person wanting to claim the dead girl's body?" I asked.

"Yes. We have him in our criminal files in Orleans Parish. He's a racketeer, been arrested numerous times for assault and trespassing. We believe he's a strong suspect in the murder of a DJ in Biloxi, Mississippi."

"Ah! I've heard about that. Do you recognize the photograph, Portier?"

"No, and I'm glad I don't. So if you know who the man is, Detective, why are you asking us?"

"Because this Al Bendford apparently works for a Christopher 'Kip' Harmon. I believe you know Mr. Harmon, Reverend."

"Know *of* him," I corrected. "Mr. Harmon is the agent Genny Duval signed a contract with to have her song 'Honey, Be By Me' recorded and played on the airwaves through Eldon Marrs."

My answer didn't seem to satisfy the detective. He took a couple of deep breaths and waited for more information from me, but I had none to provide. I thought I'd done well by giving him a description of the suit Bendford wore and the model of car he drove.

Robicheaux looked at his officer.

"We received an anonymous tip from a young woman about a possible break-in at Mr. Harmon's place of business last night," Officer Malois said in a deep, bland voice.

"What does that have to do with me?"

"She mentioned your name."

I appeared shocked and dismayed—or at least I hoped I did. "Why would I do that? What would I possibly have to gain by breaking and entering into Harmon's place of business?"

"That's what we'd like to know."

"Have you talked with Mr. Harmon?" I asked, my voice starting to quiver.

"Yes," Malois responded in his same monotone. "He says there wasn't a break-in. He surveyed his place, and we had a look around. There didn't appear to be anything missing or evidence of a disturbance, so my men left."

"Well, there you go," I said, half-relieved.

"Yes, but you can see why we had to ask," Robicheaux said. He looked me over as if he continued to assess whether I was telling the truth.

"Of course. My name was mentioned. You had to follow up. Any idea of who the young woman was who called in the tip?"

Malois shook his head. "She didn't talk long enough for us to find out."

"Then it can only mean one thing," I said confidently. "I must be getting close to the perpetrators who're trying to defraud Miss Duval."

Robicheaux raised his index finger to protest. "I must warn you not to go there, Reverend. I wasn't convinced at first that this case was nothing more than a bad business investment on Miss Duval's part. I'm convinced now that it's something more ominous than that. We have an investigation in full swing. I recommend there be no more 'getting close to perpetrators,' as you put it."

I decided it was best that I not respond.

Robicheaux continued to assess me, however. "May I ask what happened to you, by the way?"

I pretended to not know what he was talking about.

"The scrapes, the bandage, the bruising, and the stench of Merthiolate coming from you. I noticed you escorted us into the room with a slight limp."

"Ah, yes!" Portier exclaimed on my behalf. "You might as well tell him, Fountain. I took the training wheels off your bicycle this morning. It didn't go at all well." He laughed, but he was the only one who did. "That's not true, Detective, but the real story is just as bad. He took a nasty fall on one of our sidewalks during his morning stroll. You know the condition of our walks in the Quarter: broken, cracked, and riddled with potholes. As a public servant of this city, I'm sure you'll bring this problem to city hall's attention."

Robicheaux frowned. "Yes, I'll jump right on it, seeing as I have nothing else to do. So is this the truth, Reverend?"

"That I fell? Most certainly, Detective. I can say that with honesty."

"Mm," he said. He looked at Officer Malois for his take.

Malois just shrugged.

Chapter 28

The officers left Portier's cottage, and I dashed for the telephone.

"Who are you calling?" Portier asked.

"*Candid Camera*," I said. "I'm fairly certain our lives would make a good episode." I ignored my friend and dialed the number to Miss Cora's phone. She didn't answer. I tried again. This time, an elderly man answered the phone. "Is this Miss Cora's residence?" I asked.

"It is," he said, "but she's not here right now."

"Who am I speaking with?"

"Her friend Mort," he said with hesitation. "Who are you?"

"We've met before. My name is Reverend Fountain from Labreville."

"I remember you. Fancy Studebaker you came in, didn't you?"

"I did, so you do remember. When do you expect Miss Cora back?"

"I can't tell ya. Don't know. I've been workin' in her flower garden. She's got carpetweed and bullhorns growin' out of the wazoo, she has. She went and took some men from that community to the free clinic in Broadmoor. No tellin' when those folks'll be able to get to 'em to treat 'em. No tellin' when she'll be back."

"I understand," I said, needing no further explanation. "You say she went to the free clinic? Do you know who she took? Was a man by the name of Leon Adams with her?"

"Leon Adams, you say? No, sir, I don't know if she even told me."

"I understand. Thank you. Will you tell her I called? It's very important. She'll get the message?"

"Yeah, I'll tell her," he said, his voice fading. "Don't know when she'll be back."

I told him again that I understood. I remembered ol' Mort when I first saw Miss Cora some months back. He was a hearty old gentleman, but years of hard work and toil were taking their toll on his weathered frame and mind. I expected he'd be repeating my instructions often, doubting himself as he thought about them. I ended the call gracefully before turning to my friend.

"We'll see how far that gets me," I said.

"I heard you ask about Leon Adams. Why do you even want to talk with him?"

"To verify what Miss Moreno said to us about the men she and Cindy saw arguing on the street. Something doesn't sit right about that with me."

Portier's eyes narrowed. "Do you think she's lying? She seemed very genuine to me."

"No, I don't think she's lying at all," I said. "Leon, however, I'm not so sure."

I looked about the room. "Did Genny take those papers home with her, the ones of Gwen Handerson's lyrics, the anagrams, and the transfer copies?"

"No, those things represent trouble to Genny. Trouble

follows her automatically. She doesn't have to grab it purposefully and take it with her."

"Then I'll be back. I assume she'll still be home. I want to talk with her."

Portier waved me out of the door.

Genny welcomed me into her cottage as if she'd been quarantined for weeks with polio. "Am I glad to see you!" she exclaimed.

"Why? Has something happened?" I asked.

"No, that's just it. Nothing's happened. I'm bored to tears. If it weren't for the occasional skip in my step, I'd go mad."

I chuckled. "What's put the occasional skip in your step? Have friends come around to cheer you up?"

"Somewhat, yes," she said coyly.

"Ah, then not friends plural but friend singular."

She giggled loudly and twirled in the middle of the room. "Yes, and I have you to thank for that, Dickie!"

"Oh, no," I said. "I don't care who this person is, but I do care that my name is attached to any sort of matchmaking, especially when I had no idea I did it."

"Relax," she replied, still giggling. "I knew him long before his name came up again." She saw the papers in my hand. "Haven't you given up on those yet?" She landed on her last twirl and turned for the kitchen.

"Not yet. Why? Have you?" I asked, following her.

"I want them to go away."

"So do I, but things don't generally go away on their own. They fester and get worse unattended."

"Denial is easier."

"And deadlier," I reminded her. "Do you mind making us some coffee? We'll sit and chat some more."

Genny walked to the counter and pulled out the coffee tin,

then pulled the percolator toward her to fill its canister with water. "I think whoever wanted those anagrams, Dickie, has lost interest in them."

"Why do you say that? Have there been no further attempts to get them from you?"

"None at all."

"Well then, they've lost their appeal for some reason. Maybe because there's been increased interest by the police."

"What's caused the police's interest?"

"Julie's return, for one."

"Yes, Chuck told me about Julie after the detective left. He brought me up to date on a lot of events, including that bop on your head."

"But did he tell you that a man went to the morgue this morning to claim Julie Moreno's body?"

Genny turned to me abruptly. "No," she said astonished.

"They have an idea who he is. Detective Robicheaux said his name is Alan Bendford. Ever hear of him?" When Genny shook her head, I said, "I doubt Bendford's detainment at the police station has gone unnoticed by his colleagues. I bet whoever put him up to the task is wishing they'd not done so. They won't be after you or any of these papers. They'll want to keep their distance for a couple of days to prevent further suspicion. Besides, I think Cindy got what she wanted when we entered Harmon's place of business, making many things moot now, including the anagrams."

"What did she take?"

"Documents that Harmon held to keep her under his control. I saw them briefly. They documented her involvement in his schemes so that she'd never go to the police to rat him out or to testify against him, should the cause arise. She used these anagrams as leverage against him, but it didn't work. She made a mistake by giving them to you and not being able to get them back. But that doesn't mean the papers aren't still important to *us*."

"What do you mean?"

I opened the folder to Gwen's lyrics and looked at them. After several minutes of sifting through various lines, particularly the odd ones that didn't make sense on the surface, I closed the folder and accepted a coffee cup and saucer Genny had in her hand filled with creamy rich coffee.

"What are you smirking at?" she asked as she sat in the chair next to me at the table.

"Oh, was I smirking?"

"Like a Cheshire cat."

I laughed. "Well, I was thinking that these lyrics tie everything together quite nicely. Gwen is very clever in a stupid sort of way."

"I'm afraid you've lost me."

"What I'm trying to say, Genny, is that people can be very ingenious about the crimes they commit. It doesn't always have to be conspicuous for it to be unlawful. I guess that's why white-collar crime is so hard to fathom as a crime to some people, me included. This has been a very ingenious crime. Murder can be the same way." I could see Genny growing impatient as I took a sip of my coffee. "Why, I remember a couple in my congregation back in Spiceland a few years ago."

"Tell me their names or I'll lose track of the story, Dickie. You tend to drag these things out."

"McKinney was their name. Nice couple, upper sixties, hard workers, modest surroundings, but Mrs. McKinney became extremely weary of her husband. She'd grown tired of their relationship, I guess you could say."

"What did she do?"

"It was Christmastime. We had a very nice Advent season

that year, I remember. Poinsettias were abundant and beautiful in the sanctuary. Snow blanketed our little churchyard. Candles glowed with timeless ambiance at our evening services. I think the beauty of the season that year made Mrs. McKinney's actions all the more heinous, but it also provided the perfect scenario for her crime."

"Did she kill him?"

"Oh, he's dead all right."

Genny leaned closer. "How?"

I leaned toward her. "Nutmeg."

Her eyes nearly popped out of her head. She asked if she heard correctly.

"Oh, indeed. Nutmeg is quite toxic in large quantities," I said. "What Mrs. McKinney didn't understand was how much nutmeg it actually took to render a human useless. She tried to overdose her husband with nutmeg throughout the Advent season by dosing it in his milk punch before bed."

"Did it work?"

"Of course not. Mr. McKinney soon realized what she was trying to do."

"What did he do?"

"Not nearly enough apparently. He died Christmas Eve."

Genny sat back in her chair. "But I thought you said—"

"I said he died, but I didn't say he died by nutmeg. The nutmeg didn't work. She turned to rat poison. Much more effective."

"I'm a little confused."

"My point is this, Genny. The crime Mrs. McKinney perpetrated began long before she used rat poison on her husband that Christmas Eve. It started with the nutmeg."

"Serving nutmeg to a person is hardly a crime."

"That's true, but her intent was criminal even if she couldn't be prosecuted for it. That's what we're looking at in this case. The killing of that poor girl in Julie's bed—whoever she is—began long before it happened. We haven't looked at the events before anyone realized they were important."

"But it's impossible to look at clues before they become important or significant."

"And that's what the perpetrators counted on. People have been telling and giving us clues all along the way. You have one in this folder of hideously written song lyrics that Gwen asked you to review. We may not have had the benefit of foresight, Genny, but we do have an excellent opportunity to use our hindsight."

Chapter 29

"What do you want me to do?" Genny asked, leaning forward once again. "I'll do anything to put this whole mess behind me, but I must admit, I'm a bit of a numbskull when it comes to solving crimes."

"What I'm going to ask you to do is as easy as throwing a piece of bologna at Bentley. They'll snatch it, swallow it, and never know they ate it."

"What bait do you plan to use?" she asked.

"Money."

Genny laughed. "Well, then, the joke is on you. Money is the one thing I don't have."

"That's true, but you didn't have money before your recording contract, and they still signed you on. Tell them you're desperate for another contract. They're sharks, Genny. They'll smell your blood and circle for an attack."

"Them?"

"I'm sorry, I should've been more specific. First it will be her, then it will be them."

"Attack isn't a motivating word for me." Genny smiled and winked, indicating that she was with me on my plan.

"Good. Do you have Ronni's number?" I asked.

"Yes, but she hasn't answered it for some time. If she's on the run—"

"She's not on the run," I said. "She's in New Orleans doing business as usual. I heard her speaking at Marrs Recording Studio with Melinda Price."

"But how do I get her to answer?"

"Does no one ever answer her phone?"

"Cindy does on occasion, but what she usually says is laced with expletives and innuendos of what I can do with my message."

"Ah, dear Cindy," I said, smiling, reflecting on earlier conversations with her. "Better yet then, I think you should try Melinda Price."

~

I spent thirty minutes with Genny, coaching her on what to say to Melinda to arrange a meeting with Ronni. There wasn't much coaching needed. Genny was a born actress, intuitive about how she should portray her distressing situation to get results out of Marrs's apparent right-hand woman—or I should say Harmon's right-hand woman.

"Do you have another extension so that I can listen in?" I asked her.

"No, this is it."

"Then we'll have to do this at Portier's," I said dejectedly. "I'd like to listen to how Melinda responds, but . . . hmm, I don't want Portier eavesdropping either."

"Don't you think he'll approve?" She looked at my face after asking the question. "Never mind."

"Exactly, but I just remembered, Bentley needs his romp in the playground. That will give us plenty of time to make the call. It won't be a long conversation. You can use the phone in his parlor, and I'll listen in on the extension in his den."

I went next door, finding Portier trimming dead twigs from his satsuma tree in the courtyard. I made a point to mention how antsy Bentley appeared and how long it had been since he last performed his duties.

"You're in the habit of monitoring his bowels, Fountain?"

"No, but don't you think he has a bit of cabin fever, being stuck in the cottage all day?"

We looked at the lethargic pup, lying listlessly on the paving stones in the shade under the canopied table.

"Not in particular," he responded. "He looks more like he needs a good shot of Geritol and a kick in the ass."

I hated to admit it, but ol' Bentley did look like a kick in the rear would do him better than a romp in the playground.

"You're probably right, though, Fountain. It's rather warm today, but we can't wait for a cold spell before we go to the playground. Come on, boy. Up you go."

Bentley lifted his head upon hearing the word *boy* but did nothing further. In fact, his head returned to the paving stones immediately.

"No, you don't. Let's go."

This time the obedient Lab sprang to life and followed his master to the parlor where I heard Portier giving him instructions on what he could roll in and what he could not at the playground. The 'could not' list was longer than the 'could' list.

I walked into the parlor after the front door closed. "They're gone," I said to Genny on the telephone. "Better come quick."

Genny scurried to the cottage on cue. She'd gotten dressed

up for the occasion with new rouge, mascara, bangles, and a shiny tiara to hold her curls in place.

"She can't see you," I said, confused at why she'd dress in stage costume.

"You should know by now that every performance is a dress rehearsal, Dickie. Besides, I look fabulous, don't I?"

"You do," I said, walking into the den. "Now, I need you to sound fabulous too."

I picked up the receiver to the other extension as Genny was dialing. Melinda answered the phone promptly, but the greeting was curt and unapologetic. Commotion in the background at the recording studio made listening difficult.

"I'm on the phone," Melinda said to someone in the studio making the ruckus. "I'm sorry, ma'am. You were saying?"

"It's me, Melinda. Genny Duval."

"What do you want? You can tell we're extremely busy today. Can it wait?"

"I'd rather it not," Genny said in her most pathetic voice.

"What's the matter, dear?"

"I could use another recording deal, Melinda. It's been a while since 'Honey, Be By Me.' I'm desperate for another chance."

"Mr. Marrs is busy today. We have a tight schedule."

"What about you, Melinda?" Genny began to whimper. "Do you have time to meet with me?"

"No, that's impossible," Melinda said. "I'll be working late with Mr. Marrs. I told you, Genny. We're very busy."

"Well, then . . . what about Ronni? She helped arrange the first deal. She could talk to Kip. Maybe Kip could talk to Mr. Marrs."

There was silence on the other end of the line.

"You haven't paid everything due on the first contract yet,"

Melinda said bluntly.

"Oh, but I plan to. You see, Mr. Chuck said he'd help finance it."

"Mr. Portier?"

"Yes, that's right. He liked what he heard. He was in Atlanta, and he said the song was extremely popular there. People were requesting it constantly. I know he'd finance another recording."

Genny's last comment seemed to make a difference. Melinda's sigh turned into a "hmm." "When can you meet?" she asked.

"Tonight, if possible. I sing tomorrow night. Do you think you can arrange it?"

"Where?"

"I don't care. I can get us a quiet table at Paradox."

"She knows people at Paradox."

"Then how about Fabuleux, that gumbo shop around the corner? It's got a few secluded tables in the back."

There was more hesitation. "Is this for real, Genny?" she asked. "You know Kip's friends don't like to be tricked. If Ronni shows up, you better be there."

"I'll be there."

"Alone?"

"Yes," Genny said softly.

"Two hundred dollars."

"What?"

The tone of Melinda's voice lowered. She spoke slowly. "You're to hand Ronni two hundred dollars as soon as you arrive. It'll help her hear what you have to say better. What's the matter? Doesn't Mr. Portier have two hundred dollars to give you?"

Genny stammered. "Yes, he has it."

"Seven o'clock then." Melinda hung up.

~

"I'm sorry, Dickie, I didn't know she was going to ask for money," Genny said as I locked the door to Portier's cottage.

I gave her an admonishing look. "We're not giving Ronni two cents, let alone two hundred dollars. First of all, she's taken enough. Second of all, that's not why we're meeting her. We're not after another recording contract, and I don't want you stargazed by what she has to say."

A light mist floated around us as we stepped from the stoop.

"What time is it?" Genny asked.

"Six thirty. We have plenty of time to get there."

"I didn't know it was going to rain," she said. "Perhaps I should wear something else."

I glanced at what she wore—an outlandish short-sleeved frock with southwestern designs, burnt-orange earrings, and a necklace of turquoise stones. Her hair was curled and held in place by a pick made of peacock feathers.

"Like what?" I asked. "You look like you."

"You have no style, Dickie. A woman of class doesn't wear a dress like this when it rains."

"It's only misting. People won't give you a second look."

I was wrong, of course. People looked twice at us all the way to Fabuleux. I'm sure they wondered where the fiesta was.

The mist appeared to hamper traffic, especially at intersections. We darted between vehicles to cross streets and dodged people stopped in the middle of the sidewalk under the shelter of iron balconies.

"Are we still on time?" she asked.

I glanced at my watch. "We're fine."

"How are you feeling about this?"

I looked at her to see if her question had a double meaning. "Fine. Aren't you?"

"My stomach is tingling with butterflies," she confessed.

"Mine is burning with contempt. Ronni hasn't said a word to us yet, and I'm already seething about what I think she'll say."

"She's very brave, showing up tonight."

I looked at Genny again. I was convinced bravery had little to do with Ronni agreeing to meet us.

"I mean, being wanted for murder and all," Genny explained.

"I don't believe she's wanted anymore. The police would still like to talk with her, but I'm fairly certain that Mr. Bendford's appearance at the morgue to claim Julie Moreno's body and his ties to that murder in Biloxi changed the police's focus from Ronni to Bendford."

The cool mist shrouded the Fabuleux entrance. As I opened the door for Genny to enter, three people exited ahead of her. The first two individuals laughed jovially at a one-liner one of the women made to the other. The third person, a striking man in a stylish overcoat, followed close behind the women. All three passed without acknowledgment or courtesy as I held the door. The man was particularly careful to avoid direct eye contact.

"I know that man," Genny said, pointing her finger in the direction he turned to walk.

I thought carefully and realized I knew him too. "That was Dale Devoe, wasn't it?"

"Yes. I wonder if he was here to see Ronni as well."

"That's too great a coincidence, if he was," I said. "Stay here. Don't talk to Ronni without me, but don't follow me either. I want to see where Devoe goes."

I released my hold on the door and strode after Devoe, careful not to trip in holes in the sidewalk covered by puddles of rainwater. I rounded the street corner just in time to see him climb into the driver's seat of his car—a modern two-toned Mercury Montclair.

I stopped, needing to see nothing else. My heart pounded at the thought that Dale Devoe was the driver of the car that nearly ran down Eldon Marrs and me on North Rampart Street. I wasted no more time shadowing him and returned quickly to Fabuleux where Genny stood inside the doorway just as I requested.

The restaurant was dimly lit, but I could see two young men and a woman at separate tables. Two older women sat away from them, laughing overtly, oblivious to our entry. An elderly gentleman was immersed in the evening newspaper nearby, and a woman in a dark-blue outfit sat in a corner booth with her back facing us.

Genny pointed toward her. Unlike the Ronni I'd heard in the hallway at Marrs Recording Studio, talking to Melinda in an animated tone about being followed, this Ronni seemed to be sitting quietly—rather subdued and passive.

A waitress approached Ronni's table before us and asked Ronni if she'd like something more to drink.

She didn't answer.

"We'll be joining her," Genny said to the young waitress. "We'll have something to drink, also, but we'd like to talk before we order food."

The waitress appeared breathless. Her eyes, wide with astonishment, focused on Ronni's unnatural position in the booth. She stepped back and shook her head. "Something's wrong with your friend."

I nudged Genny to one side so I could take a look. Ronni's head was slumped forward, her face covered by thick, brown hair that cascaded across her cheek. I brushed her hair away just enough to see her face. Blood trickled from a small nick in her neck.

"Call the manager," I instructed the waitress. "Quickly, but quietly, please."

The waitress did as she was told, maneuvering calmly past patrons to the manager's office in the back of the restaurant.

"Is she dead?" Genny asked.

I nodded. Haphazard thoughts rambled in my head.

Genny stepped to my side for a closer look. She gasped, and I wrapped my arm around her shoulder for comfort and support. "I'm okay," she said, "but this woman . . ."

I waited for Genny to say more but she just shook her head. "But this woman what?" I asked.

"She looks like Ronni, but she's not."

I swung Genny around to face me. "What are you saying?"

"Look at her," she said. "It isn't Ronni, but we've seen her before."

I looked more closely at the woman slumped in the booth beside me. I had never seen Ronni Mohr in person, only heard her voice in the hallway at Marrs Recording, so I wouldn't know her face if I saw it, but just as Genny said, I had seen this woman before, peering at us through the open window of her taxi. She was the woman Genny had mistaken for Ronni at the airport.

Who might this woman be? I wondered. "Stay here," I said.

Alarm reflected from Genny's eyes. "Where are you going? No, don't leave me here!"

"You need to help the manager and the police when they arrive. Tell them what you know."

"I don't know anything about this woman!"

"You will before the night is over, trust me," I said. "We both will. It's all starting to make sense to me now, but you have to stay here. It's too dangerous for you elsewhere. Do me a favor. Urge the police to go to Marrs Recording Studio . . .

before there's yet another murder."

~

I ran from Fabuleux to evade the manager, his probing questions, and his attempt to call the police in my presence. If what I thought was true, and if Dale Devoe had killed the woman at Fabuleux, believing she was Ronni Mohr, then Melinda Price's life was in danger.

Perspiration and mist slid down the side of my face as I darted as fast as I could across the Quarter to North Rampart Street where Marrs Studio was located. I reached the property only to be dismayed at seeing Devoe's Montclair on the side of the building.

A chill ran down the back of my neck.

The car looked empty, which meant Devoe had either made his way into the office or was surveying the outside of the building for a way to get in. No lights showed in the windows on the second floor. The main floor also appeared dark, except for the lobby and offices along the front of the building where Eldon Marrs had his office and Melinda Price had her reception area. My gaze darted from one side of the building to the other. No shadows lurched from the corners, and no one lurked in the shrubbery.

Dread consumed me as I thought of what might be happening inside and how helpless I was in the face of it.

I decided to walk along the sidewalk to obtain a different vantage of Devoe's Montclair parked alongside the building. Although it was still misting, I noticed his driver's side car window was rolled down completely. Something else wasn't right. The steering wheel appeared contorted and unnatural.

I tried to get a better look. A man bent behind the wheel, watching me as I observed the car. I stood paralyzed with fear. I thought of turning and running, but an image of being shot in the back compelled me to stand my ground. Dale Devoe was not going to see me run. After all that I'd faced and endured for Genny's sake, I wasn't about to run away now. I stood and waited for the shooter to point a loaded weapon, but nothing happened. The figure didn't rise from behind the wheel to confront me.

I inched closer to the car. My legs felt like sandbags as I put one foot in front of the other. Fear pounded in my chest. My head spun. When I finally reached the driver's side of the vehicle, I peered through the open window and gasped.

Dale Devoe was dead, shot at least once in his side at chest level.

Chapter 30

I looked at the seat beside him and into the back seat, but both were empty. The outside of the late-model Mercury was unscathed except for droplets of rainwater that fell through the open window, saturating his overcoat.

I left Devoe slumped over the steering wheel, made my way to the studio's entrance, and rapped loudly upon the glass door. When no one appeared immediately, I used the palm of my hand to pound even harder on the frame.

Eldon Marrs came to the door, his face drawn and ashen in the dim light of the streetlamps on the sidewalk. The lobby was quiet and lit faintly by a floor lamp in the corner of the room. He looked solemnly at me, then said, "Go away."

"You know I can't do that," I replied. "You have a problem in the parking lot."

Marrs stared at me blankly as if he knew about Devoe's body but didn't want to admit it.

"Have you called the police?"

He shook his head.

"You must."

He opened the door wide enough for me to enter. "Be my

guest telling *her* that," he said.

I passed through the doorway and stepped cautiously down the hall toward Marrs's office. Melinda's desk was unoccupied. Her typewriter and ten-key adding machine were under plastic cover as if she'd closed shop to call it a night.

"Are we the only ones here?" I asked Marrs.

He didn't answer. Instead, he extended his hand to show me the way to his office.

Melinda Price sat crosswise in one of the chairs in front of Marrs's desk so that she could face me when I entered. Her right arm rested upon the surface of his desk, a sleek Beretta Jetfire held loosely in her palm.

Melinda didn't greet me, and I dared not say a word.

She, too, looked drawn and ashen. Lines of worry and faded mascara and foundation marred her usually impeccable appearance.

"We had some trouble this evening, Reverend," Marrs said, crossing the room to sit behind his desk. "Please, have a seat so that we can tell you about it."

I sat uncomfortably on the edge of a chair away from Melinda's menacing glare.

"Mr. Devoe has been an unsatisfied customer of late," Marrs said. "Melinda was just telling me about it. I had no idea how bothersome our relationship had been. Isn't that right?"

Melinda's stoic expression didn't waver.

"Anyway," he said, "Mr. Devoe came into the office. He made some accusations of fraud and deceit to Melinda that were unfounded. The argument escalated. He threatened her life."

"How?" I asked.

"He had a hypodermic needle in his hand," Marrs replied. "You'll see it on the floor beside you."

I looked down. A syringe as would be used in any physician's office or clinic was just where Marrs said it would be.

"It was self-defense," Melinda said.

"From his car?" I asked, astounded at her claim. "You'll excuse me for questioning your ordeal, but you'll be hard-pressed to convince the police of imminent danger if you followed him to his car and shot him point blank."

The two looked at me as if they'd already figured that out.

"That's where you come in, Reverend," Marrs said.

"How so?"

"We'd like your corroboration that he came into the building, threatened Miss Price for being a part of an unfounded plot to extort him of recording revenue and threatened to inject a deadly poison into her body. I think when the police have the syringe tested at the laboratory, they'll find such a poison inside. Before he had a chance to act, I knocked the syringe from his hand in a short scuffle, and Miss Price shot him for fear of my safety."

"That doesn't explain why he's sitting in his car."

Eldon Marrs and Melinda Price looked at each other.

"That's where your ministerial influence to convince the police of our story will be of great advantage to us," Marrs replied.

I stood and walked to where they indicated Devoe had fallen.

"But there's no blood on the carpet," I said in a further attempt to expose where the police would find a hole in their story. "Even as convincing as I can be, I can't produce blood on cue. And besides, after all you've done to Genny Duval, what makes you think I'd ever consider such a dastardly lie?"

"I may be able to convince Mr. Harmon to release Genny Duval from some of her contractual obligations," Melinda said. "Besides, I believe you owe me. You have no idea the extent of bloodshed you're responsible for shedding. I should kill you right now for the harm and suffering you've caused. You've been intent on destroying the lives of our clients by interfering in their happiness and self-worth with their recordings."

I took two steps forward. I couldn't believe what I'd just heard from her. I looked at Marrs and asked if he believed that what she said was true.

Before he could respond, Melinda waved the gun and blurted, "Of course, it's true, Eldon. He's destroying what we have!"

Marrs lowered his head and looked woefully toward the floor from behind his desk. "And what do we have, Melinda?" he asked.

She stood and glared at him. "You don't know?"

Marrs shook his head. "No, I don't think I do. I don't think I ever did."

"We have a partnership!" she proclaimed. "You and I."

The recording executive appeared stunned. "Partnership? Is that what you thought this was? I was the one at the top, creating new talent for voices who didn't have an opportunity to be heard. *You* were my secretary. I hired you years ago as my employee."

"Oh, come on, Eldon. You've got to be kidding me. You mean to tell me that you believe these voices you recorded had talent and that their records were being heard on the airwaves around the region because the public thought they were good? You mean you can sit there and tell me straight to my face that you knew nothing at all about what was going on?" Melinda laughed heartily as ire flared in her eyes. "I always thought it was too easy."

"What was?" I asked, stepping forward some more.

"This!" she screamed as if she couldn't fathom why I hadn't figured it out. "This whole ruse Kip and I created with the Mohr sisters right here in this office, and you never said a word, Eldon. I seriously thought you knew but turned a blind eye to what was going on because you wanted the revenue as much as we did. What you didn't know wasn't going to hurt you, was it, Eldon? What you didn't ask didn't happen. Oh, I laugh now. I laugh to think of your pretentiousness that you created the success in this studio all by yourself. You honestly believed you had the gift to turn poor melodies and lyrics sung by voices with sour notes into hit songs."

"Let me say something, Melinda," Marrs said on his behalf.

"No, let me tell *you*," she spouted. "I kept you going. Kip Harmon kept you going. The Mohrs, Alvin Bendford—all of us—kept you going. It was *our* gifts that sustained you, not your petty two cents here and there. The only gift you offered, Eldon, was complacency. For that, I should be thankful."

Eldon Marrs rose from his chair, looking at his secretary with an intense expression of grief and anguish.

I used the moment to take two more undetected steps toward them.

Melinda's shoulders dipped and tears began to well in her eyes. She set the gun on the table and sat down. Regret and remorse shrouded the room. "Oh, what's the use?" she said. "It was all a ruse. Their voices, their contracts, the money—it was all a ruse."

"Melinda, we're not going to satisfy the police with one more."

She looked at him as if she didn't know to what he referred. "One more what?"

I wasn't sure what he was talking about either, until I remembered Dale Devoe's body outside in his Montclair. I took a small step forward.

Melinda nodded as if she also remembered Devoe's body and turned away to focus on the syringe on the floor.

Marrs reached across the table for the Beretta.

She turned back and shook her head, pulling the pistol out

of his reach. "Not yet. I'm not ready." She shivered and tears streamed down her face.

Marrs leaned farther over the desk toward her.

"No, I swear," she said calmly, standing once again. She lifted the gun as if she'd shoot if he came closer. "I'll kill you just like I killed Devoe in his car. He wanted me to give him back everything he said we stole from him." Her gaze shifted as if she'd had a sudden thought. "He wanted everything back, the same way Reverend Fountain wants it back." She pointed the gun at me. "You want it all too, don't you, Reverend?"

"You're wrong, Melinda," Marrs said. "Reverend Fountain wants nothing but to make us accountable."

"Accountable?" she asked. "Did I actually hear the word *accountable* coming from your mouth, Eldon? The mysterious man behind the recording curtain suddenly sees the need to be accountable?"

Melinda's glare at Marrs was so intense that she didn't see me lunge from her side and knock her hand so the gun fell to the floor. I pushed her aside and grabbed the pistol quickly, waving it back and forth to keep both Melinda Price and Eldon Marrs at bay.

She tried to lunge back at me, but I thwarted her advance. "Please, Melinda," I said. "Don't make this harder than it already is. Please."

Melinda stopped. She nodded. Her shivering stopped, and she sat passively. Peace shrouded her as she smiled for the first time. There was an eerie, tranquil, divine sense of solace in her simper. Melinda took a deep breath and exhaled slowly. "Okay, Reverend, so what now?" she asked. "Are you going to call the police? Obviously, my gunshot didn't call anyone on Rampart into action or the police would've been here by now. Don't you think?"

Marrs reached for the receiver on his phone. "I'll call," he said.

"No," I said. "They'll be here soon enough. I want something in return first. Three phone calls. You're going to make them, Melinda."

She brushed back strands of her hair and looked at Marrs. He pushed the telephone to a point where she could reach it.

"You're going to call Cindy Mohr, and you're going to tell her that I want to meet with her. No compromising. She has to do it."

"She's a stubborn woman, Reverend. You should know that by now."

"I do, but you're going to give her the news that her sister is dead, and that she's next if she doesn't comply."

Melinda's eyes widened.

"No questions, Melinda. Just do it," I said. "Carousel, Hotel Monteleone."

She sniffed twice to clear her nose then picked up the receiver and made the call. Cindy Mohr didn't ask many questions apparently. The call was brief. Melinda didn't allow questions or rebuttals.

"Next, I want you to call my driver, Jeffrey," I said. "I've walked and run about as much as I can this evening. I want him to take me."

"The third call?" she asked.

"Detective Robicheaux. I want him here immediately, with backup. I also want two plainclothes officers at Carousel. He knows Cindy Mohr. The men are to sit on both sides of Cindy at the carousel, saving a seat for me in between."

I stopped giving orders long enough for her to make the calls. When she finished, I extended the grip of the Beretta to Eldon Marrs in good faith. "You know you're dead if she gets ahold of this gun, don't you?"

He nodded.

"And don't do anything foolish against me before I leave," I added. "You heard the calls she made. My driver will be here any minute. The police will be here soon after. You'd be more of an imbecile than Melinda implied you were if you do anything foolish like kill me before they get here."

He took the gun and confirmed that he understood everything. "I'm surprised, though," he added. "The gun could have misfired when you knocked it out of her hand and it hit the floor. These Berettas tend to do that, you know. You could've been killed."

I shrugged and looked at him as if it didn't make any difference. "The night's not over," I said.

Chapter 31

Jeffrey dropped me off at the entrance of Hotel Monteleone in his old two-ton. It sounded as though it was going to backfire as the bellman opened the door for me to exit. I entered the hotel without incident, however, ignoring the lively crowd in the Swan Room to enter Carousel.

Cindy Mohr sat at the rotating bar under the red-and-white canopy and marquee lights. She had tears in her eyes—tears she didn't try to hide. I stepped onto the carousel and sat on the empty stool beside her.

She nursed a Death in the Afternoon and smoked a Tareyton. "Care for one of Hemingway's drinks?" she asked.

I looked for Gordon, the bartender who usually waited on me when I came to Carousel, but he was nowhere to be seen. I shook my head.

"Cigarette?" She pushed her pack and lighter my way.

I ignored them.

"Suit yourself," she said. A tear fell down the side of her face. She didn't attempt to wipe it away. "Aren't you going to offer condolences?"

Offering condolences wasn't something I did lightly. Doing

so meant that I commiserated with her as if I felt her pain, understood her grief, and wanted the best for her under the circumstances. I felt none of that for her. Still, I felt an obligation to say something.

"I *am* sorry, Cindy. I'm sincere when I say I never wanted it to end like this."

Cindy smiled. "Certainly not for Ronni," she said.

"Especially not for Ronni. I don't care what you think of me or why you think I wanted to find Ronni for Genny's sake. I wanted to get to the bottom of Genny's contract obligations, I won't lie, but I also wanted to make sure Ronni was unharmed."

Cindy looked at me with indifference.

"I didn't get what I wanted, did I?" I asked.

She puffed on her Tareyton but snuffed the butt out abruptly in a nearby ashtray. "No, you didn't," she said coolly.

We sat quietly, staring each other down with contempt.

"Poor Ronni," she said eventually. "I'm going to miss her very much. I loved her, no matter what you think."

"Ronni?"

"Yes, Ronni. Why do you shake your head?"

I hoped my expression indicated that I didn't believe her. "Don't you mean Sheila?"

Cindy turned pale.

"Don't play me for stupid," I said. "Those tears aren't for Ronni. They're for your other sister Sheila. Sheila's the one who died tonight. Dale Devoe killed her in Fabuleux."

Cindy inhaled deeply and tried to speak, but she had nothing to say that could refute what I already knew to be true. She picked up her drink and sipped absinthe and champagne instead.

"I know Sheila is the sister you were close to, Cindy," I said. "You had no use for Ronni. I don't know why, but you had contempt for her. She's the one you killed and tried to pretend the body belonged to Julie Moreno."

"And how did I manage to do that?"

"You made Ronni's body look like Julie. You even changed her to have her wear Julie's clothes, and you had Alvin Bendford claim her body at the morgue as Julie's. You had Sheila fly down from St. Louis so that she could take the place of Ronni until you devised a plan and gathered enough money for your escape. You didn't count on Dale Devoe seeking revenge for the payola ruse you pulled on him. You didn't know he was angry enough to kill because of it, using a syringe with a drug that could cause death almost instantly. You didn't count on him taking Sheila's life tonight, thinking she was Ronni, did you?"

Cindy sat complacently as I talked. She drew a breath and held it, but that was the only reaction I received.

"You'll be happy to know Dale Devoe is dead," I said.

Cindy's eyebrows rose.

"Melinda Price shot him in his car in cold blood. I guess you can thank Melinda for saving your life. I figure Dale went to the studio to kill Melinda before he came after you. Somehow, she saw and got to him first. She'll contend that he got into the studio to confront her, and his death was self-defense, but I know that can't be true based upon what I saw, standing next to his body. She saw the syringe he had after she shot him and staged the scene inside the studio."

I watched Cindy closely. She remained calm and sipped occasionally.

"The bottom line for you is that Dale Devoe is dead," I said. "I thought you'd want to know that. It might bring some satisfaction to the end of your miserable day. Alvin Bendford is behind bars too. I suspect Melinda is on her way to jail right now. It's just you and Kip Harmon to carry on the racket. You're the only ones left. Oh, and maybe Gwen Handerson, but I doubt it. Is she still alive, by any chance?"

Cindy reached for her Tareytons.

"I'd like to know, Cindy. Is Gwen still alive or did you take care of her too? I wouldn't be surprised if you got rid of her because she was a loose cannon."

"Gwen," Cindy said with disgust. "Her and those damn song lyrics. She tried to undermine us by having singers at Marrs use her lyrics so that she could get a cut on their contracts."

"If it weren't for her lyrics, I may not have found out for certain about you," I said. I reached into my jacket and pulled out one set of lyrics that stood out above the rest for me. "'Our Mother in Yellow,' by Gwen Handerson," I said. "Interesting title. Very significant, wouldn't you say?"

"I wouldn't know."

"Wouldn't you say you treated Gwen, Ronni, and Julie like their mother while you all were in New Orleans?"

"I had to," she said defiantly. "Ronni and Gwen were like children. They were immature. Ronni had no idea what she was doing, working for Harmon. She was sloppy. She made mistakes. Kip told me she had to go."

"You mean from the business?"

Cindy scoffed. "Yeah, right. That's what he meant. You're a moron, Rev. No, when a guy like Kip Harmon says someone has to go, he means they have to *go*. Gone. Dead gone."

I sat in disbelief. "You'd kill your own sister simply because he said to?"

"Don't be naïve. I was more than glad to do it. Ronni was cutting into the profits, threatening to expose all by her stupid mistakes. It was either her or me. Kip would've had Bendford kill me just as easily as he would've Ronni."

"But you're the one who killed her, not Bendford."

She curled her lip and took a puff. "Are you sure you wouldn't like a cigarette? You look like you could use one."

I ignored her. "That's why Gwen used the color yellow to describe you," I said.

Cindy shook her head. "Yellow is the color of light. The sun is yellow. It's bright and optimistic."

"It also stands for a coward," I replied quickly. "Someone whose ego is too large to see past their selfishness and greed to the point that they'll betray those under their care who stand in their way. That was you. She was describing you to a tee in these lyrics."

"There's no proof in that."

"No? Read the lyrics," I said.

Cindy picked up the piece of paper and read out loud. "*Cadence sang beautifully in tune with a vision of you near the lake, donning a soft yellow bonnet of the sun.* Gibberish. Chaos in words, Reverend. They mean nothing."

"Read it again as Gwen meant for them to be read," I said firmly. "She wrote those lyrics acrostically:

Cadence, sang beautifully
In tune with a vision of you
Near the lake,
Donning a soft
Yellow bonnet of the sun.

"The first letter in each line spells out CINDY. It's very clear. It was a message to us that you were Ronni's killer."

The lyrics didn't seem to faze her.

"Why do I care that you're telling me this, Reverend?" she asked. "Here we sit together—alone in a bar with dozens of other people. You speak words that'll vanish into the smoky air when we leave. This is nonsense."

"Is it?"

I leaned back slightly on my stool. The plainclothes officer on my left turned to the right as the plainclothes officer on Cindy's right turned to his left.

Cindy sighed deeply.

I stood and placed enough cash on the counter to pay for all of the drinks consumed. "Goodbye, Cindy. You may consider this meeting the official end to my investigation into Genny's contract and my futile attempt to speak with your sister Ronni. You may not get everything you think you deserve in this life, but I promise you that you'll get everything you deserve—especially if I have anything to say about it."

I stepped off the rotating portion of the bar and turned to leave.

"Reverend Fountain," she called. "Step back on."

I don't know why I did, but I stepped back quickly to regain my place at the carousel.

"You leave too soon," she said. "Don't you want to know why? All good investigators end their story by asking the villain why they did what they did. It makes for the perfect ending."

"You've told me enough," I said.

"But I haven't told you everything. All good investigators want to know everything."

I gave her a genuine look of disgust. "Not me," I said. "I have no desire to know something that abhors me so much."

She smiled broadly. "Please sit," she requested softly. "Listen to me, please. The story of my life isn't good, and you won't like what I have to say, but if you're going to judge me as you will then you should at least hear my whole story and the reasons why."

"You mistake discernment for judgment, Cindy."

She patted the stool. I sat down reluctantly.

Cindy consumed the remainder of her drink. She held the empty glass in front of her for the bartender to see and smacked her lips. “Do you think I have time for one more before I have to go?”

“If what you have to say is of interest to these gentlemen beside you, I believe they’ll concede.”

“You’ll have one with me?”

I softened the skeptical look on my face and nodded. “Yes, I’ll have one with you. Make it a Dark and Stormy.”

Cindy laughed at the symbolism. She winked coyly and said, “My treat.”

Chapter 32

I sulked quietly for two days, unable to grasp the turn of events that had occurred. I didn't want to find Ronni Mohr murdered by Dale Devoe because I really did want to talk with her. Discovering that she wasn't Ronni but her sister Sheila at least helped me put the final pieces of Genny's mystery into place. Doing so was quite a shock. Finding Dale Devoe murdered by Melinda Price shocked me even more. But it was the news that Melinda tried to take her own life after I left her in Eldon Marrs's care that shocked me the worst.

I'd been so careless. I blame myself for what happened. I should've foreseen, or at least remembered, the hypodermic syringe that lay on the floor on Marrs's office, the one Dale Devoe supposedly threatened Melinda with. I could've removed it easily out of harm's way before Melinda lunged for it in desperation, stabbing herself and slipping into a deep coma. Her action saddened me in a way I never thought possible. I was disappointed in what she, Ronni, and Dale did two nights ago, but I never wanted harm to happen to any of them.

Portier was at the Internal Revenue Service office again, but Bentley sat beside me. As most good dogs do, the Lab sensed something was wrong and commiserated with me.

"I'm sorry, old boy. I'm not very good company, am I?" I asked.

He sat up, inched toward me, and rested his head upon my lap, allowing his big, sad eyes to soak in my sorrow—almost as if he hoped it lessened my pain. I patted his head and told him what a good boy he was.

The phone rang beside me. I debated whether I had the strength—or the nerve—to answer it, but I'm glad I did.

"Reverend Fountain?" the voice asked. "Detective Robicheaux, New Orleans Homicide."

The sound of his voice gave me hope, but I didn't know why. "Good day, Detective. More questions for me?"

"No, no," he said. "I have information this time."

"You're a hard man to read. I can't tell if it's good news or bad news, sir."

"A little of both. I'm sorry to say Melinda Price passed away about two hours ago. I thought you'd want to know."

My heart sank, but I was able to thank him.

"The good news, however, is that Gwen Handerson was located at her grandfather's farm in northcentral Missouri, near the Iowa border."

"That is good news," I said, "although I must admit I'm a bit surprised by it."

"You and me both. Nice girl, but too naïve for her own good, I'd say. At least she had the presence of mind to go someplace remote, away from New Orleans or St. Louis."

"About the only presence of mind she had, Detective. Although some of those song lyrics detailed more of a sound thought process than what she was able to articulate in person. Did you read any of them?"

"Once we were able to get past their baffling absurdity, they were quite revealing," Robicheaux said. "How are you getting along, by the way? The DA will need you at trial."

"He'll have me. I'm glad it's months away. I still haven't recuperated."

Someone suddenly pounded on Portier's front door so loud that it shook the house.

"What was that?" the detective asked. "I hear something over the line."

"Someone's using their foot on the door," I said.

"I'll send an officer," he said.

"No need, detective. Portier's dog recognizes the foot, apparently. He's wagging his tail profusely."

I ended the call to answer the door. The intruder was Genny, and the reason for Genny's use of her foot became clear once the door was opened. She held a warm, covered dish in her hands and didn't want to release her grip to knock on the door. Genny grinned with glee upon seeing me in the open doorway.

"I'm glad you're alive," she said. "I tried to call, but the line was busy."

"There's nothing alarming about that."

"There is if you're calling an ambulance. I worry about you, Dickie. You need to get out and about. It's not good for you to sit here like you did yesterday and think about what happened."

"Haven't you thought about it? After all, I left you with Sheila's dead body at Fabuleux."

"Yes, and I was mad as a hatter about it, too, but I got over it . . . and you should too."

Genny was right, despite my mood. "I've been a dull boy," I admitted. "I do need to get out. It'll be a good time to take you and Portier to Carousel, as I promised days ago."

"Carousel's a special place, but it's too soon, don't you think? Let's go to Leroux instead. Look! I brought you something to cheer you up."

Genny stuck the covered dish under my nose.

"Looks nice."

"No, silly, open the top. You can't see that it's nice by gawking at the lid."

I uncovered the dish. The rich aroma of chicken stock, celery, onion, and spices permeated my nose, providing a warm recollection of home back in Indiana.

"It's ribley soup," she said proudly. "I told Chuck I wanted to make you something special to cheer you up. He said you could use some nourishment more than cheering."

"He picked a fine choice."

"That's because he said you two were fond of it as kids when he lived up there during part of his childhood. I had no idea what it was."

"You've never heard of ribley soup?"

"Not a clue," she replied. "If it doesn't lurk in swamp water, I know nothing about it. Chuck told me how to make it. I hope it's good. Some of the ribleys are quite large. My fingers got tired of twisting the dough. A couple of them look more like dumplings, but I do want you to eat something, Dickie, despite what they look like."

I eased into a chair, and she went into the kitchen to put the dish on the counter. When she returned, I asked her for a hug to express my appreciation. She smelled of chypre and Jorgen's lotion.

"A new scent, Genny?"

She beamed and flipped her curls. "Don't I smell pretty? I bought a bottle of Fille d'Eve. It was just released at Maison-Blanche, and I thought I deserved a bottle now that my troubles are behind me."

I frowned. "Was it expensive?"

"Like nobody's business," she said.

"You're not a rich woman, Genny, even though it may feel like it. The end of your contract with Kip Harmon didn't make you rich, it just kept you from getting poorer—or should I say it kept Jeffrey from getting poorer. He was working off your debt by slaving under the hood of Harmon's DeSoto."

"I know. Jeffrey's a sweet boy, isn't he? I suppose the bottle of Fille d'Eve belongs to him."

"I wouldn't give it to him. It'll clash with the Pennzoil smell in the garage."

She laughed. "You know, I can go with you and Chuck tonight for dinner, but I can't stay long."

"Why? Do you have a date with a mystery admirer?"

She flipped her curls again and giggled. "No, I have to sing at Paradox. Oh, Dickie, I wouldn't know how to act on a date. I haven't been on a real date for oodles of ages. I think men are intimidated by a woman of my class and caliber, don't you think? It's either that or my curls slap them silly when I flip my head."

I agreed to both reasons.

~

I didn't know if it was Genny's lively visit or the hearty richness of the ribley soup that I ate with fresh French bread, but my spirits had picked up by late afternoon when Portier came trudging into the cottage after another afternoon at the offices of the Internal Revenue Service.

"Don't ask until I've had a drink," he said as I opened my mouth.

"Better yet, Portier, how about a good dinner then drinks at Carousel?"

"Carousel? Isn't it . . .?"

"No, it's not too soon," I said before he could say it. "In fact, it's just what I need."

Portier agreed. It didn't take us long to freshen up and exit the cottage. Genny met us outside, dressed brightly in stage costume. I'd forgotten that she had to sing at Paradox after our dinner. Portier didn't lose his jovial spirit even though it took several glances before he could get used to the shade of her eye shadow and the number of bangles on her wrists.

We decided to go to Leroux first. Dinner was pleasant but uneventful. We didn't discuss the other evening until Genny's curiosity got the best of her. She was desperate to know what Cindy Mohr had had to say for herself.

"Not much that I hadn't heard during my ministry from people who are remorseful not for what they did but for getting caught," I said. "Her excuses for her behavior were all a show for the officers who sat next to her. They heard every word. You're a great performer onstage, Genny, but I'm afraid Cindy's performance topped you many times over that night. She laid it on thick. At least she was able to finish her pack of Tareytons before they took her away."

Portier grinned as he set his coffee cup on a saucer.

"What's so funny?" I asked.

"Nothing. I just find it ironic that a man of your stature should dole out so little compassion and mercy to the imprisoned."

"That's just it, Portier. Cindy didn't ask for compassion or mercy. She didn't believe she'd done anything wrong that required compassion or mercy. I listened to her drudging story, however."

"And the police officers?"

"They listened to half of it before one of them stood up and said, 'We're through here. Time to go.'"

"At least you didn't cut her off like I'm going to have to do with you," Genny replied. "Gotta get to the club. Thank you for dinner, gentlemen. Will I see you later at Paradox?"

I said she would. Portier declined.

Genny kissed me. "I promise to sing 'Honey, Be By Me' and dedicate it to you." She blew us a kiss then turned to leave. Her bangles jingled loudly across Leroux's dining room floor.

I paid the bill. Portier and I walked out of the restaurant and stood momentarily on the sidewalk. The Quarter's lights shone brightly. Muffled jazz could be heard in the distance. The tinny sound of a muted cornet cut through the warm June air.

Portier inhaled deeply and remarked what a wonderful evening it was.

"Do you care for a nightcap?" I asked.

He obliged, and we walked to Hotel Monteleone. The Carousel appeared to be only three-quarters to capacity; the evening was still young. Portier and I found two places on the carousel away from other patrons.

Gordon set two cocktail napkins in front of us. He recognized me immediately.

"Didn't see you the other night," I said to him.

"I had a night off. Missed an interesting evening, I hear."

I shrugged. "If you're talking about the young woman—"

Gordon raised his hand to stop me. "Tell me what you'd like to drink. That's all I need to know, and this first one'll be on me," he said.

We ordered. Gordon made the drinks promptly and set them in front of us. Portier and I cheered and sat for several minutes not saying a word. We ordered another round and nearly had them emptied before we said anything about Genny's situation.

"Still believe that white-collar crime doesn't have a victim, Fountain?" Portier asked subtly.

"I never believed there wasn't, Portier. I just didn't understand it. I don't believe a lot of folks understand such crimes and who they affect. I understand the issue a lot better now. I'm glad it's over for now."

"Are you planning to head back north or spend more time in New Orleans, helping Miss Cora at Labreville?"

I hesitated before saying that I was staying in town a little while longer. I didn't admit that I wasn't going to be volunteering at Labreville anytime soon. It was too soon to run into Leon Adams, considering we hadn't been hitting it off in recent conversations. I evaded further conversation by asking, "Are you ready to go?"

Portier indicated that he was.

I raised my hand to Gordon for the bill.

Portier noticed my reluctance in answering his last question. "What's the matter? There's something still bothering you."

"I don't know what it is," I said. "There's a piece of the puzzle still missing that I haven't figured out. I feel I should stay away from Labreville for a while, but I don't know exactly why."

"What does the puzzle have to do with Labreville?"

"It doesn't," I said. "It's more about someone who lives at Labreville."

"Leon Adams?"

I nodded. "How and why he got beat up the night Ronni was murdered bothers me."

My friend put his hand on my shoulder. "If you ask me, it sounds as if you've got the final piece of the puzzle in your hand. You just don't want to fit it into place."

"What are you saying?"

"I'm saying that I know you well enough to know that you

don't leave stones unturned. I believe you do know how and why Leon got beat up. You just don't want to face the truth."

Portier's answer saddened me because he was right.

"Want to talk it through?" he asked.

I shook my head. "No, we better go so that I can listen to Genny sing a couple of tunes and get back to the cottage at a decent hour." Gordon set the tab in front of me and waited as I took my billfold out of my overcoat pocket. "I'll deal with him soon enough," I said to close the conversation.

"Are you talking about Leon Adams?" Gordon asked, picking up the cash I laid on the counter.

I raised my eyebrows, surprised that he knew to whom I referred. "I didn't say a name, Gordon."

"You didn't have to. The guys behind the bar here were talking about him when I came in. It was a hunch that you were talking about him too."

"What were they saying?"

"We all know Leon here. He used to sing in the Swan Room when everyone thought he was going to hit it big. He was here the other night when you were talking with that young woman."

I shook the cobwebs out of my head. "Leon Adams was here?"

"That's what they said. Sat in the non-rotating part of the bar. The guys said they couldn't help but notice him. He sat alone at that table over there, drinking highballs, and staring into the back of the head of that woman you were with as you passed in front of him on the carousel."

"It was fairly crowded that night, if I remember. Why would they even notice him?"

"We have a fine reputation, so we keep tabs on anything that doesn't look right. Apparently, Leon Adams didn't look right."

Portier and I climbed off our stools so that Gordon could

wipe our portion of the bar for the next customer. I looked at Gordon with disbelief.

"Take it for what it's worth," Gordon said, noticing my reticence, "but their exact words were, 'if looks could kill . . .'"

Chapter 33

"I think I'll go with you," Portier said as we grabbed our fedoras to leave the lounge.

I stopped and shook my head. "I'm going to Paradox, you know. Why the change of heart?"

"Don't you want me to tag along?"

"Not in particular. Your partying skills are a bit rusty."

"Says the minister."

"I've been known to sneak two desserts at the women's circle luncheons," I retorted.

We stepped onto the sidewalk outside of the Monteleone. "Such the risk taker," he said. "That's why you need me along. You're a wild man."

I glanced to see the expression on his face. "Gordon's conversation bothered you, didn't it? That's why you want to come."

Portier didn't acknowledge the reason; he simply said, "I'd just feel better if you weren't alone."

The air was close as we walked to Paradox. A breeze barely blew from the Mississippi through the narrow streets of the Quarter. Perspiration formed over my brow. Even still, my fedora remained squarely upon my head. It was brand new, and I was quite proud of it, having lost my other one the day Dale Devoe tried to run Eldon Marrs and me off Rampart Street.

Paradox was in full swing. Revelers twirled in the smoky haze by the stage where Genny sang a lively rendition of Perry Como's "Hot Diggity (Dog Ziggity Boom)." Her fans embellished every *Boom!* in the lyrics. I pointed to an empty table on one side of the room. Portier agreed, mentioning the benefit of the table being against a wall so that our backs could be protected.

"We're here to have fun just like everyone else. How dangerous can diggities and ziggities be?" I argued.

"It's the booms I'm concerned about."

I lifted my index finger in the air. "Ah! Good point."

"Gentlemen," a waitress said as she approached the table. "I was informed by the star performer onstage that your drinks are on the house. What can I get for you?"

"Gimlet," Portier said without ponder, "and if the man next to me orders a ginger ale, you're to turn it into a highball. From the well is fine. His taste is unsophisticated. He won't know the difference."

I disagreed. "Canadian Club," I said to her before she left. I then turned to my friend. "Tell me something, if you will, Portier. You were conspicuously absent during most of Genny's ordeal. Was there a reason?"

"I spent most of it in the revenue office, if you remember."

"So you say."

"I'll have you know, Fountain, they had my taxes mixed up with a gentleman by the name of Charles Porter, not Portier, of Orleans, Indiana, not New Orleans, Louisiana. Is there an Orleans in Indiana or were they making that up just to appease me?"

"It's real," I said, "named after the Battle of New Orleans, but it's just a burg."

"Burg or not, they managed to mix me up with this man. He's a cutter by trade. What's that?"

"He cuts limestone. Orleans is rich in oolitic limestone. You're evading my question."

"So I am, with good reason."

"And what reason is that?" I asked.

"Genny must learn how to fight her own battles. She has a victim mentality and didn't want me to know about her financial problems because she was too embarrassed to admit she was in trouble and too woeful to ask for help. I had to stay away for her own benefit."

"But you told me once when I wanted to step away that I should stay close to the situation."

"That was you. She takes kindlier to your advice."

"I should've known that would be your strategy," I said as the waitress returned with our drinks. "So you purposely stayed out of her business."

"And good thing I did," he said, lifting his glass. "Turned out to be more of a bloody mess than I anticipated. Thanks for taking the brunt of it. Cheers, good man."

I responded with a halfhearted cheer in return.

Portier pointed to the front. A man jumped onstage and took the mic from Genny's hand. "Do you know that man? He has the appearance of someone you'd know."

I looked and grimaced. Leon Adams stood next to Genny, smiling broadly. He had done little to groom himself for the occasion. His hair was unkempt, his suitcoat was ratty, his beard was untrimmed and growing down his neck. His eyes, however, glimmered under the spotlights as he sang to Genny Johnny Mathis's "Wonderful! Wonderful!" without a stammer.

"Oh, no," I said under my breath.

"What is it?" Portier asked.

I set my glass squarely on the table with such a clamor that part of the drink spilled over the top. "I can't believe it."

Portier laughed. "Genny's secret admirer. You didn't know?"

I curled my upper lip. "You should've ordered me a double."

In Leon's defense, he did sing beautifully. I'd heard of people who stuttered but had a flawless singing voice. I was overcome to hear such a voice in person. I listened intently to the rich harmony when Genny joined in. Both were natural entertainers. Had their recording deals gone as they'd dreamed, I was confident both of them would've been stars.

Leon and Genny continued to sing passionately, a song Leon had written and recorded at Marrs's studio. As the couple reached the song's climax, I realized their chemistry wasn't simply their ability to woo an audience for entertainment or applause. Their underlying dynamic was something deeper, subtler, secretive . . . forbidden.

When the last note finished with Genny embraced in Leon's arms, Genny blew him a kiss. Leon stepped off stage to thunderous applause. He waved to the crowd. Out of the corner of his eye, he caught me staring at him, the only person in the room withholding any admiration. He hesitated a moment before relenting to walk through the maze of cheering fans to reach me.

My curled lip didn't escape his attention. "Evenin', Rev. Got a b-bad drink there? You don't look happy."

"You're kidding, right?" I asked. "You and Genny?"

"I like her."

"I didn't even know you knew her."

"We all know each other in this town," he replied.

I leaned toward him. "I'll not have it, Leon," I said firmly. "You and Genny."

Leon smirked. "I didn't know you had any say in that. B-Besides, what have I done to you that makes you feel you must p-protect her from me?"

"You gave me half-truths about your whereabouts, for one. You're this close to being an accessory to murder, for another." I held my index finger and thumb an inch apart in front of his face to show how close I meant.

Leon continued to look at me with contempt. "You're full of it, you know that?" he asked.

"Yes, strangely enough I've been told that before."

"Then buzz off, why don't you?"

"Not if you want us to pay for your drinks," I said. "You'll sit there and listen to what I have to say."

Our waitress arrived and smiled at Leon for his pleasure. He contemplated whether ordering a free drink was worth the earful of scorn I was about to unleash upon him.

"Rye whiskey, is it?" Portier asked. "I've heard through sources that rye whiskey is your escape of choice—ever since your recording contract went bad, that is."

A look of confusion and surprise spread across Leon's face.

Portier turned to me to explain. "Jeffrey knows this clown, Fountain. I knew all about him through Jeffrey because Jeffrey cares about Genny too. I didn't spend *all* of my time in the revenue office. I did some digging around myself." He turned to the waitress. "Our friend here will have a Seagram, ma'am."

She left to get his drink, but the prospect of a free belt didn't seem to appease Leon's sour demeanor. "I still don't get why you're so pissed," he said, his stuttering more pronounced.

"You used Miss Cora to get a ride to the free clinic," I replied bluntly. "You didn't go for a checkup. You went to steal hypodermic syringes from the clinic, maybe even a drug that you knew would be lethal."

"Syringes and drugs are never left unattended at clinics, Reverend."

"Aren't they? Please, we both know better. They're a sound clinic and provide great care, but the facility isn't equipped for adequate controls when someone like you is bent on stealing from them."

"Someone like *me*?"

"They trust you at the clinic, Leon. You used to be one of them. I remembered from a conversation with Miss Cora that in addition to being a singer, you gave your time and effort unselfishly as a volunteer to that clinic. You knew all about them. You knew their procedures, their strengths and weaknesses, even their controls over medications and supplies . . . or the lack thereof."

Leon tried to disguise his alarm at my accusation by wiping his mouth with the top of his hand. The waitress brought him his Seagram. He swallowed it in one gulp before she had a chance to leave.

"One more," he said.

Portier nodded to her that another drink was okay.

"You can't p-prove anything," Leon said blandly. "There isn't one ounce of p-proof that'll back your theory."

"Maybe not, but the police have the syringe Dale Devoe used to kill Sheila Mohr. It's probably the same syringe he wanted to use on Melinda Price. The proof doesn't have to come from me. I'm sure the detectives are capable of finding all they need to tie the syringe to the clinic and back to you."

"You have it wrong," he said. "I was justified, stealing those syringes, taking the drug, and giving them to Devoe. Harmon and the Mohrs were all crooks. They cheated Dale and me out of everything we had. I have nothing because of them, Reverend. Look at me. I'm nobody. They took everything I worked for and left me with nothing but debt and despair."

"But there are ways other than murder to deal with such matters."

"They didn't work. Not for me. I didn't have the money to hire a lawyer to sue their ass and to take them for everything they had."

"Is that why Devoe and his men beat you up? Because you wanted to kill the Mohr sisters yourself?"

Leon wiped his mouth with the back of his hand again and snarled under his breath. "I was supposed to give the syringes to Dale. That was the plan."

"But what? You changed your mind? You had a change of heart?"

Leon grinned. "No, Rev, no change of heart, more like nothing left to lose. I decided I didn't want to hand over the syringes to Dale. I wanted to scare the Mohrs myself. Dale was too strong, though, and all his guys were there. They jumped me, roughed me up, and took my knife and the syringes."

"Why didn't you go to the police?"

Leon laughed. "The police," he spouted. "Don't you think Kip Harmon was in cahoots with the p-police so that they'd overlook what he was doing? He didn't just p-pay DJs and radio stations to have our songs played. He bribed the police and attorneys to look the other way. He could afford to do so. So Dale and I did the only thing we could do. We took justice into our own hands."

"It's not justice, Leon. It's called revenge. Your destruction of life and property wasn't done out of justification. You can rationalize the destruction any way you want, but in the end, the real motive for your violence is evident."

Ire burned in Leon's eyes. He spoke defiantly without stuttering a word. "I'm living for right now, Reverend. If you're gonna preach to me about a Higher Power—which is probably what you're leading up to do—you can save your breath. I'll think about such a power when the time comes. Right now, my bones ache for shelter and my belly pangs for food. Whatever your Higher Power has to say to me can be said while he's putting a roof over my head and handing me a cheeseburger."

"I'm not going to talk to you about heaven, if that's what you're thinking, Leon. I'm talking about everlasting life. There's a difference."

"One like yours?" he asked, smirking.

"Don't laugh. My life may not be filled with DeSoto Fireflites and lucrative recording contracts like you dream about, but it's still rich and full. This tit for tat killing and destruction you choose to follow isn't justice, and it isn't abundant. It's definitely not everlasting."

Leon continued to glare into my eyes. "Be it as it may, Reverend, it's the life I've chosen," he said with finality.

"Then suit yourself, but don't expect revenge to change the world or to soothe your wounds. And stay away from Genny."

Leon started to retaliate, but Genny finished a song and requested him back onstage. He rose from the table and smiled broadly at me. "I'm going to sing again with her, but I have a song for you too. It's a seafaring song I wrote years ago for occasions such as this. Want to hear it?"

"No."

"It's just a little ditty about kissing my ass. Won't take long."

"Come on, Leon!" Genny called again.

"You'd better go."

Leon faced her.

"What shall we sing?" she asked with anticipation from the stage.

Leon gave me a side glance before calling back to her out

loud. "How about 'Let's Misbehave'?"

Genny laughed with glee. "You're on, baby doll! Get your sweet britches up here!"

Chapter 34

Portier invited Genny to his cottage the next morning for breakfast. He fried andouille, and I made tomato gravy and buttermilk biscuits while Genny sipped strong, black coffee. She was still elated by her performance with Leon Adams the night before and moved by the raucous reaction from the crowd. I ignored her the best I could as she relived the highlights of the songs they sang and the laughs they shared in front of their fans. Portier ignored her too.

She must have sensed our reticence to join in her enthusiasm. She lowered her voice an octave and sat complacently at the kitchen table. "Oh, boys," she replied humbly, "you needn't worry about me."

"I'm sorry, Genevieve," Portier said, "but you must be mistaking hunger for worry."

"Don't give me that. You two haven't said two words all morning. I know you're concerned about me. Leon said you and he had a tiff, Dickie."

"No tiff," I replied. "Just a difference of opinion about justification, revenge, and everlasting life. Nothing heavy."

"I have no intention of being in a relationship with Leon

Adams. He's a fabulous singer, and our voices meld together in wondrous harmony, but our lives . . . well, our lives—"

"You don't need to explain, Genny," I replied. "I know you have better judgment than to spend your life with him."

Portier was conspicuously quiet.

Genny waited patiently for a response from him. "Chuck?" she asked.

Portier turned to let the sausages cook on their own in the skillet. He walked to her and took her coffee cup to set it on the table. He lifted her hand and kissed it gently. "Genny, dear, you don't need my approval about anything you do in your life. You've always had it and always will. I love everything about you unconditionally . . . except maybe that perfume you're wearing. What is it?"

"Fille d'Eve," she said proudly. "Don't you like it?"

"Why, yes, I love the smell of old libraries," he said, returning to the skillet. "Just not on women."

Genny jumped from her chair and hugged him from behind.

"What's this for?" he asked surprised.

"I love you, you old candy ass, and your insults too. Deep down, I suppose it means you care. You really do care about me. We should do something special today, the three of us. Shall we?"

I gave her an apologetic look. "I'm sorry. I'd love to, Genny, but I can't. Not this morning, anyway. This afternoon perhaps. I promised someone something, and I need to make good on that promise."

~

A sign posted on the glass door of Marrs Recording Studio indicated the studio would be closed until further notice. I knocked rapidly on the door, hoping someone was in. The cup of hot coffee I bought at the café nearby burned my fingers.

The receptionist Marrs employed to monitor the entrance came to the door. I recognized her as the young woman who'd intercepted Sheila Mohr the day Sheila complained to Melinda about being followed. The receptionist came to the door and unlocked it reluctantly, opening it just enough for us to converse. She didn't look at all happy to see me.

I managed a smile and asked if Mr. Marrs was in.

"You're that pastor from up north, aren't you?" she asked.

"Richard Fountain, yes."

"He may not want to see you."

"I understand, but would you mind asking for me?"

She hesitated. "No, I don't mind asking, but he's taken quite a shock, you know."

"Yes, I know. What happened was difficult, and it's awkward that I'm here, but I'd appreciate it if I could see him."

The receptionist started to open the door wider but stopped. "No, I'm not sure you do know," she said. "It's not just the loss of Melinda, you see. It's his life he's lost too. You do realize that."

"Yes, I fully understand."

"And the Feds were here yesterday too."

"The Feds? I had no idea."

"Yes, they came yesterday afternoon. Mr. Marrs was still recovering at home from that night. They came to his house and took all the papers they could find that might connect him to the crime Harmon masterminded. They came to the studio at the same time to take everything they could from our offices. They took practically everything, including equipment."

"I'm sorry, I didn't know. They probably want to open an

investigation."

"It was a raid," she said emphatically. "Mr. Marrs could have survived an investigation. He would've cooperated with them fully, but a raid was too much for him."

"Is he not here?" I asked.

"Oh, he's here. I told you he was here. He's in his office, writing letters to the artists he's currently working with; that is, if he can remember who they all were. He has to work from memory. They took his ledger books, including names and addresses."

"I'm so sorry to hear about this, Miss. I really am."

"Please don't express your sorrow to him. He isn't ready to hear how sorry you are, nor do I think he ever will be. I'm going to let you in, but don't tell him you're sorry."

I nodded, and she led me down the hall to Eldon Marrs's office. The walk felt cold and dark. A stale odor lingered in the air, sickening my stomach as I thought of the torrent of events that had tarnished the reputation his office once held.

The young woman stopped just inside Marrs's doorway. "Mr. Marrs, you have a visitor," she announced respectfully.

Marrs didn't look up. He continued to write until the paragraph he was constructing was completed. When he finally lifted his eyes from the paper, I saw what the toll three nights of not sleeping had had on the recording executive. His face was drawn, his eyes bloodshot and lifeless. Rosacea sprouted from his nose and across his cheeks in such a way that I thought he could have a stroke at any minute.

The receptionist stepped away and returned to her station without saying anything further.

"I brought you something," I said.

Upon hearing my voice, Marrs set his pen on the letters and looked at me as if he could think of nothing in this world that he'd want to accept from me.

I approached him slowly to set the hot cup of coffee on his desk beside his pen. He looked at the cup without batting an eye.

"You said I owed you a cup of coffee from the other day, if you remember," I said.

Marrs smiled. "If I remember?" he asked. "What in tarnation makes you think I could ever forget anything that's happened to me over the past several days, Reverend? I'll remember every damn moment for the rest of my life."

I didn't have an answer. I turned to go.

"Why are you leaving?"

"I don't know," I said. "I guess because I shouldn't have come in the first place. I don't know why I did come, now that I think about it."

"To see what's happening at the studio, perhaps? Look around, Reverend. As you can see, not much is happening at all. There isn't much to happen with. They've taken everything that makes up my livelihood. You do know Federal agents came and took everything yesterday afternoon?"

"No, I didn't know that."

"Well, they did. You do know what a raid is, don't you?"

I nodded.

"It doesn't matter if you knew or not," Marrs said. "The Feds are going to do what the Feds are going to do. It doesn't matter what you or I say or do to rectify the matter because it just doesn't matter anymore."

I stood quietly, watching him suffer internally.

"I should be going," I said.

"I don't blame you, Reverend," Marrs retorted. "I don't blame you at all for what happened. You may think that I do based upon what I've said to you in the past, but I don't. I realize what was happening to me was going to end badly whether you came along or not. You had nothing to do with my professional demise. I want you to know that, but I also want you to know something else." Marrs thought carefully before he continued. "I don't deserve to go to prison, if that's what will happen."

"No one can say that it will. You have character witnesses who can vouch for you. They will say you weren't directly involved in the racket."

"Because of ignorance?"

"You weren't ignorant," I replied. "You were complacent but not ignorant. Complacency led to this horrible ruse. Even you seemed to be horrified at what happened under your watch."

"Oh, I am, Reverend. I'm mortified, totally mortified. Don't think for a moment that I'm not."

"But you have an uphill battle. The Feds don't take kindly to professional complacency any more than they do intentional fraud, especially when innocent people have been robbed of their life savings."

"It isn't complacency to believe in your staff."

"No, but your disengagement in the administration of your business contributed to it."

"But I did do good, Reverend. I gave my artists a voice."

"Yes, you did, sir. Many were blessed by your skills. You gave your artists self-esteem and a sense that they were contributing to the culture of this community, but like many executives, you trusted your administrative functions too highly to others."

"We have to trust in someone. The job of leadership is too big now."

"But in the end, it's still your life that's at stake. It's *your* business, not Harmon's or Melinda's. You must be the one to preserve the good in what you do to ensure there are better times to come."

Marrs sighed and paused for several seconds. "I was raised in

Illinois, Reverend."

I didn't know what that had to do with anything, but I said kindly, "Then we were neighbors once. I'm from Indiana."

"Then you probably remember as a boy, having to memorize quotes and other words of wisdom from Abraham Lincoln."

Yes, I remembered.

"Of all the quotes I memorized in my younger years, there was one that stood out for me above all the others," Marrs said. "I never knew why it had such significance in my life until today. Perhaps I was destined to remember it all of these years just for this day alone."

"What quote is it?"

Marrs crossed his arms in front of him, leaned back in his chair, and closed his eyes as if doing so helped him recite the words exactly as he'd memorized them. "'Die when I may, I want it said of me by those who knew me best, that I always plucked a thistle and planted a flower where I thought a flower would grow.'"

"That's a great quote," I said.

"Oh, it's a marvelous quote. It's a quote every living human being should strive to live by every day. I really believe I tried to do so, believe it as you may. There wasn't a day I entered this studio that I didn't think about leaving my artists in a better place than when I arrived. That's why it pains me to no end that people may say that quote about my life but will have to add a footnote when they finish because of what had happened."

"Don't say that," I said. "It may not be like that. Every profession is in the same boat with you. Every profession has its Rubicon. What good is it to discover wrong but do nothing to make it right?"

"This isn't a time when any one of us can be complacent, is it, Reverend? Everyone wants to be heard. They need to be heard. Every voice."

Eldon Marrs looked at me as he spoke with a determination and passion that I'd not heard in him before.

"I can see their faces," he said, his voice quivering.

"Whose faces?" I asked.

"Everyone who has walked through the doors of this studio, Reverend. I can still see the blank expressions of the men who came back from Europe after the war and now from Korea. They don't know how to release their pain except through song.

"There are the Coloreds in Tremé and the Ninth Ward. They have a spirit that people outside of those areas need to hear.

"There are mothers who sing to their children at night after toiling with them all day. They sing about a life that's being taken for granted.

"And, of course, there's the men who work long hours for just pennies a day and sing on the street corners to feed their families. They all have songs, Reverend. I've listened to them. I gave them an opportunity to be heard."

I stepped closer and sat on a chair near to him. "I know you did, but there are people out there like Kip Harmon, Alvin Bendford, Melinda Pierce, and Cynthia Mohr ready to take advantage of their plight. These people use all the right words to get them to sign papers and to record songs. It's not to help them. It's to keep them under their control so that they're always indebted to them. That's why someone like you needs to be more than just a good listener and a good person. You must also be a good steward as well. That's the only way you can protect them; that's the only way any of us can protect them."

"Is that why you were so persistent with me?"

I nodded. "Genny was vulnerable. She made a poor business decision, but over time it angered me that she was being taken advantage of. I appreciate that you gave her a voice, don't get me wrong, but I get angry at those who try to take her voice away and those who look in the opposite direction."

Eldon Marrs sat back and studied me. I didn't know what he was thinking, whether he thought I was full of malarkey or if my words made sense. After a few seconds, however, he nodded and asked, "So what's next for you now?"

I chuckled. I thought his asking about my future when his was hanging tenuously on a limb was an awkward way to change the subject. I gave him a genuine answer, however. "It wasn't that long ago that I gave my granddaughter a lecture on making a difference in the world," I said. "I need to make good on that lecture."

"Do you have something in mind?"

"Yes. There's a homeless community that could use extra shelter and food. I'll be heading that way to do some work."

Marrs smiled. "Good . . . and thank you."

"For what?" I asked.

"I needed to hear what you were going to do. I needed to hear that life goes on. I'm lamenting my life right now. It appears to be over, but you've just pointed out to me that there's still work to do."

"Yes," I said. "Life must go on while there are voices yet to be heard."

A note to my readers

I wish I could say there was a profound purpose for writing Payola. I also wish I could say it included a deep-seated message to create a paradigm shift in human behavior that would change the world. That's not the case, however. Payola didn't rise from the depths of yawning reflection. In fact, its beginning came from a very unlikely source.

Wayne Farrell is 85 years young from Woodstock, Georgia. He bought and read my first book, *Why Birds Fall*, and shared it with other residents at the assisted-living facility where he resided. We began corresponding regularly via email. Wayne was curious to learn how I developed the plots to my mysteries and how I was able to entwine the personalities of each of the characters into the stories' events. Over time, our emails increased.

When *Masquerade of Truth* was released, the vivacious Genevieve "Genny" Duval captured his intrigue. He was quite certain there was more behind her entertaining spirit that I wasn't sharing—a dark side if you will.

I had to agree with him. Characters like Genny Duval are three-dimensional. Her fun-loving persona exuded mischief as well as good times. It didn't take long for me to scratch out an outline with a caper that only Genny could get herself into. Of course, it had to be worthy of Wayne's critical analysis. So I tweaked and edited. I included real-life history from the late 1950s entertainment world and often worked through the early morning hours to have it ready for professional editing. Before long I had it. There it was. Payola! And I knew upon completion that Wayne's 85 years of human insight and experience was right all along. Genny's mischief kept the Reverend Fountain hopping the moment he stepped from the train in New Orleans.

That's because Genny was good at denial—like most of us. We are good at convincing ourselves that our situations aren't as bad as they feel or appear. There may be plenty of red flags. There may be ominous signs to the contrary, but it's as if we can't help ourselves. We sidestep intervention until problems get out of hand. That's not only true in our personal lives, but true in business. Corporations ignore red flags with as much proficiency as individuals. They fail to properly manage, react timely, and accept responsibility and accountability. It's easier to ignore than to correct until it becomes too late.

This book is dedicated to Wayne Farrell and his inquisitive imagination. Without his intuition and prompting, Payola may have never materialized, and I would've been guilty of not seeing the possibility of another great mystery that was not only fun to write but a joy to know who I was writing it for. Perhaps there was a profound purpose to Payola after all.

Thank you, Wayne, and to all my fans at Merrill Gardens Senior Living in Woodstock, Georgia.

If you enjoyed this book, I'd be very grateful if you'd write a review and publish it at your point of purchase. Your review, even a brief one, will help other readers decide if they'll enjoy my work.

If you'd like to be notified of new release from myself and other AIA Publishing authors, please sign up to the AIA Publishing email list. You'll find the sign-up button on the right-hand side under the photo at www.aiapublishing.com. Of course, your information will never be shared, and the publisher won't inundate you with emails, just let you know of new releases.

And please be sure to visit my personal website at www.garykreigh.com.

Gary Lee Edward Kreigh
New Orleans, Louisiana
October 4, 2021